Darkness in Vélez-Málaga

Paul S. Bradley

Paul S. Bradley is a pen name.

© 2020 Paul Bradley of Nerja, Spain.

The moral right of Paul Bradley to be identified as the author of this work has been asserted in accordance with the Copyright, Design and Patents Act, 1988. All rights reserved.

No part of this publication may be reproduced or transmitted in any form or by any means, electronic or mechanical, including photocopy, recording, or any information storage and retrieval system, without permission in writing from the publisher.

This is a work of fiction. Any resemblance of characters to actual persons, living or dead, is purely coincidental.

Editor: Gary Smailes; www.bubblecow.com

Cover Illustration: Jill Carrott; www.virtue.es

Rear cover: Convento Santa Clara, Vélez-Málaga circa 1935; courtesy of Archivo Temboury.

Layout: Paul Bradley; Nerja, Spain.

Darkness in Vélez-Málaga is the third volume of the Andalusian Mystery Series.

Publisher: Paul Bradley, Nerja, Spain.

First Edition: March 2020.

Contact: info@paulbradley.eu

www.paulbradley.eu

ISBN13: 9788409201051

The Andalusian Mystery Series

Andalucía is wrapped in sunlight, packed with history, and shrouded in legend. Her stunning landscapes, rich cuisine, friendly people, and a vibrant lifestyle provide an idyllic setting for four mysteries linked by shared darkness. Whilst each book can be read on its own, the author strongly recommends reading them in numerical order.

1- *Darkness in Málaga.*
2- *Darkness in Ronda.*
3- *Darkness in Vélez-Málaga*
4- *Darkness in Granada*

Dedication

For my family

Acknowledgments

My heartfelt thanks to Gabriel Soll, Jill Carrott, Elizabeth Francis, Fran Poelman, Mark Shurey, Judy O'Hara, Barbara O'Hara, Renate Bradley, Francisco Torres, and editor Gary Smailes. The mistakes continue to be all mine.

Paul S. Bradley

1

The allure of enthralling entertainment at Málaga's prestigious temple to the arts was proving irresistible. The bustling tapas bars surrounding Plaza de La Merced were beginning to empty as the migration toward the grand Cervantes Theater gained momentum. Spain's premier Flamenco dancer, Salome Mendosa, was due on stage for her third of four weekday performances in the provincial capital.

From all over the province, dedicated fans were flocking to the richly decorated eclectic styled theater, inaugurated in 1870. The light was fading fast on a balmy December evening. A half-moon was peeking over the rooftop antennas.

An elegantly dressed, tall athletic man in his early forties with shaggy blond hair and steel-blue eyes was seated on a terrace table at Restaurant Cortijo de Pepe overlooking the tree lined plaza. He raised his eyes at the attractive, younger woman opposite. She nodded.

He gestured the waiter to bring the bill, stood,

extracted his wallet from his blue serge blazer pocket, counted out two ten euro notes and placed them under the serviette holder. She tightened her wrap around bare shoulders then flicked her long raven hair, so it hung free outside of the pink material. He pulled out her chair, helped her to her feet and they joined the throng of theater goers.

"Where do we pick up our tickets?" said Phillip Armitage as they walked along with the good-natured crowd.

"We have to knock on the stage door," said Amanda Salisbury.

There was a flurry of activity at the stage door. It was constantly open as an endless stream of messengers dropped off floral tributes. A uniformed doorman checked each arrival for security risks, then passed it inside to a harassed apprentice for distribution to the tetchy performers as they went through their warmup rituals.

"Tickets for Salisbury?" said Amanda.

The doorman dug deep into his multi-tasking capabilities, scratched his ear, and reached for a bunch of envelopes on a shelf inside the door. He checked them through, stopped at the last but one, and handed it over as another bouquet was thrust into his other hand by a breathless, lycra clad cyclist carrying a large square box strapped to his back.

They joined the queue at the front door. When their tickets had been scanned, a young, uniformed girl stepped forward, smiled and said "Follow me, please." She led them up a busy staircase to the first floor and into a long curving corridor. At the far end, she opened the last door and waved them into a luxurious private box. "Enjoy the show," she said and left them to it.

"Wow," said Phillip as they entered the enclosed space and saw the stage almost within touching distance. "I didn't expect this."

"Me neither," said Amanda slipping off her wrap and hanging it over the back of a plush blue chair.

"When was the last time you saw Salome dance?" said Phillip leaning on the balcony to survey the noisy crowd jostling for their seats in the auditorium below.

"Not live since we were in the same year together at university in Madrid," said Amanda settling into her seat. "Then only at the occasional juerga."

"Juerga?" said Phillip taking off his jacket. It hung on it the back of his chair and sat down next to her. "Not heard that word before."

"It means an impromptu gathering of Flamenco artists, usually gypsy dancers, singers, and musicians. They just turn up at their regular bar and do their thing. No rehearsal, no program, just spontaneous heartfelt performances fueled by copious draughts of their favorite beverage. Then they split the pot at the end of the evening. Many have lived off that for decades."

"Not many places like that anymore," said Phillip.

"One of the downsides of gentrification," said Amanda tossing her glossy hair. "It might scrub up a neighborhood, but it has forced the less well-off gypsies too far from the town center. Which is a shame because I prefer their pure, raw Flamenco. It makes my hair stand on end. Somehow, when it's choreographed, it loses something."

"Did Salome study Flamenco at Uni?"

"No. She wanted something to fall back on if she couldn't make it dancing, so took a master's degree in Business Administration and Management. She's actually her own manager."

"We should write a Flamenco article for our Spanish guide my love and explain its nuances to our subscribers."

"Good idea," said Amanda smiling as she glanced down at her engagement ring; an oval sapphire surrounded by a modest nest of diamonds which sparkled in the box lighting. She reached out, grasped his hand, and gazed lovingly into his eyes. "Perhaps Salome could help us?"

"That would be fantastic, but would she?" he said admiring her elfin looks and sexy curves barely covered in a low cut sleeveless black dress. "After all she's a megastar nowadays." He reached out and stroked her cheek, then looked toward the stage as the announcer pleaded for mobile phones to be turned off.

Amanda squeezed his hand. "Let's ask her at the restaurant later."

As the lights began to dim, the magnificent Bernardo Ferrandiz ceiling painting gradually faded into the gloom until darkness prevailed and the audience chatter abated; interspersed by an occasional cough. For a moment, total silence engulfed the theater.

A single guitar chord shattered the stillness. A spotlight faded up to reveal a statuesque woman in her mid-thirties poised stock still in center stage. She wore a vivid blood-red, figure-hugging Flamenco dress with a long-ruffled train and matching dancing shoes.

Salome Mendosa leaned forward slightly from the waist, weight favoring her left leg, arms raised above her head forming a heart shape as the still unseen guitarist continued strumming the introduction. Her long, black, glossy hair was gathered into a ponytail and a red rose pinned behind her left ear. She glanced at the audience through dark brown eyes set in a striking face with well-defined cheekbones. She smiled before setting her jaw in a serious mask of concentration.

"Ladies and Gentlemen," resumed the announcer. "The Cervantes Theater presents the Salome Mendoza Flamenco Spectacular."

The guitarist upped his tempo and volume. The fluid rhythm of the traditional Spanish instrument echoed around the theater as dexterous fingers with long fingernails reinforced with super glue; flew over the frets and strings.

The guitarist paused. Salome breathed in deeply, her pert breasts rising under her sleeveless gown. She raised a thigh, stamped her heels three times, bent one knee, pointed her foot at the floor and tapped it once with her toe. The raised wooden floor built on top of the theater stage amplified the raucous sound, highlighting the difference between the robust stomp of a heel and the more delicate tap of the toe. The music restarted.

The rear of the stage gradually brightened to reveal a kitchen table surrounded by four high back wooden chairs. Standing behind the seating were three women, all with roses behind their right ear, hands ready to clap. These were the performers of *Jaleo - jaleadores*. Jaleo means racket or noise, but in this application describes the loud clapping that forms a key element of discerning Flamenco. One will clap the beat, another the offbeat, the third will weave in and around the others.

Seated at two of the chairs were the talented but overweight male guitarist and a well-rounded, middle-aged, mousy haired female singer. Next to the end chair was a percussionist; a somewhat grand description for a slender young man sitting on top of a wooden box tapping its front. He provided the base tone and rhythm. The men were dressed in black pants and frilly white shirts, the ladies in full length sky-blue Spanish dresses.

Amanda glanced at the program which described the first item of the ninety-minute show as a *soleá*; a highly expressive individual dance.

The singer, whose rasping but powerful voice reminded Phillip of the late Joe Cocker, began to wail her way through a sad poem of unrequited love. The jaleadores took turns to call out; *olé* or *así se canta*, that's the way to sing, or *así se baila*, that's the way to dance. Salome began to twirl, moving her arms, wrists, and hands then stamping in beautifully coordinated elegant movements. The harmonious combination of guitar, clapping, foot-stamping and box tapping generated a thunderous noise that bounced around the far corners of the theater and reached out to the inner musicians of the audience as they tapped feet or fingers more or less in time.

While the music created the ambiance, it was Salome that captured everyone's hearts. Her accentuated hip and body movement drew the eye to her curvaceous femininity. Her waving hands and arms emphasized her hips, waist, breasts, and swan-like neck while her sparkling eyes engaged the spectators with smoldering, intense glances.

Phillip was mesmerized by the speed of Salome's foot stamping. Her heels and toes thundered against the floorboards which at times created a sound that reminded him of the drum rolls on parade during his military days. Then she spun out of the stamping into a series of elegant pirouettes where she lifted her skirt, exposing bare athletic legs. She swept the ruffled train of her dress up in the air with one leg, while spinning around on the other. Amanda wished that she could move so gracefully.

This was Flamenco surpassing its finest, blood stirring, erotic and captivating.

After Salome finished the soleá to tumultuous applause, she performed a mixed bag of traditional dances including a *buleria;* a fast-moving dance that originated in Jerez de la Frontera considered the home of Flamenco. The music is octosyllabic with the three, sometimes four verses varying in mood from deep pain and sadness to abject joy and pleasure. The jaleadores expressed each emotion with their body language, facial expressions, and cries of agony or delight.

Then followed a selection of modern Flamenco that fused elements from other dance forms such as ballet and tap. The audience gasped as in a complete break from convention, the musicians and jaleadores stood and walked forward to surround Salome under the same spotlight as she danced. The percussionist left his ungainly box behind and joined in the Jaleo. Normally, musicians remained at the back leaving the dancers to take center stage.

After the number finished to a deafening roar of 'ole' from the audience, the musicians returned to their seats at the table where they were joined by another singer and guitarist.

Salome stood center stage with arms by her sides, head bowed, waiting, and breathing hard.

A spotlight focused on the curtain at the left side of the stage where a tall, handsome man with long dark hair and a superb physique was waiting in the wings. He was dressed in tight black pants, a frilly white shirt and carried two pairs of *castañuelas* or *palillos* also known as castanets or clackers. The musicians began their introduction, the man skipped over to join Salome and handed her one set of the traditional percussion instrument.

They faced the audience, bowed, turned toward each other, raised their arms, and clicked their castanets simultaneously. Then the pair weaved around each other turning, arms undulating, foot-stamping and castanets clacking in a fast-moving fandango. But this display was far more than just a dance. Their hip movements and admiring glances toward each other as they moved around the stage were subtle, but no one could miss the raw sexual chemistry that exuded between them even though they never actually touched.

The evening's entertainment progressed to its climax with another final spine-tingling fandango. The performers joined hands, came to the front of the stage, and bowed to a well-deserved standing ovation. An encore was inevitable.

At last, it was over. As the performers moved once more to the front of the stage for a final bow, Salome looked up at Amanda who smiled, expecting something similar in return from her closest friend, but all she could see was a fleeting look of abject despair.

2

"Why do you think Salome looked so worried?" said Amanda tightening her pink wrap around her shoulders as they jostled out of the main entrance to the theater and headed left toward the restaurant in Plaza de La Merced.

"At the end you mean?" said Phillip.

"Yes. When she saw me, she switched momentarily from a happy dancer to a miserable person in a blink of an eye."

"Did she say why she wanted to see you?"

"She wanted to meet you and talk about her role at our wedding in Gibraltar next spring."

"It was generous of her to send the complimentary tickets. That box must have cost a fortune."

"She can afford it, but she was given them for free for her family to use."

"Then why give them to us?"

"She doesn't have any."

"Unusual for a Spanish lass. There are normally

hundreds of them."

"She was adopted as a baby by an elderly couple. They died when we were at uni. I went to both funerals."

"How sad," said Phillip as they walked along at a snail's pace hemmed in by the dispersing theater crowd onto Calle Ramos Martin. Phillip nodded at the now-familiar Comisaría, the Police Station where they both occasionally worked as translators for Detective Inspector Leon Prado. "Perhaps seeing you reminded her of their deaths."

"Unlikely, it was a long time ago. It must be something else," said Amanda following the line of his gesture. "It's been ages since we've seen Leon."

"Not since the Ronda case," said Phillip as they turned onto the cobblestones of Calle Gomez Pallete, passing a gastro market on one side of the street and apartment blocks on the other. "Perhaps, we foreigners are behaving ourselves for a change but I'm sure he'll call when he wants something. Does Salome know anything of her natural family? Surely those dancing talents must have come from somewhere?"

"All her adoptive mother told her was that when the time was right, she would find out and she shouldn't worry about it."

"That must have been difficult to deal with?"

"She was in therapy for a while and seems to have come to terms with it."

"Is she having a relationship with the male dancer? They looked extremely comfortable and familiar with each other."

"Unlikely, he's gay."

"What about a boyfriend?"

"She prefers men but never settled in one place long

enough to have anything more than brief affairs."

"Like you were then?"

"Until you came along. You don't have a secret brother somewhere for her, do you?"

"Ha, no, there's just me and my sister Glenda. We could share though, except."

"Greedy bastard," said Amanda punching his arm lightly and grinning. "Except what?"

"She's not my type. Too leggy and muscular, face too boney. You know I prefer my lady's petite, elfin and soft, just like you."

"Creep."

"You'd prefer no compliments?"

"I'm not used to it, that's all."

"Should I stop?"

"Don't you dare."

She squeezed his arm as they passed Pablo Picasso's birthplace and arrived at Restaurant La Plaza; a high-class establishment with a renowned British Chef and accustomed to catering to celebrities, especially during the annual Málaga Film Festival.

The terrace was packed. A waiter opened the high wooden door and they went inside.

"Have you a reservation, Sir," said the distinguished Maître D, a tall man in his early fifties with silver hair.

"For three in the name of Mendosa," said Phillip.

"This way, please."

They followed the man over the terracotta tiled floor through the busy restaurant to one remaining isolated table at the rear where they could talk without being overheard.

"May I offer you a drink while you wait for the Señora?" said the Maître D.

"Cava, for me please," said Amanda

"Oloroso for me and agua sin gas," said Phillip.

The Maître D helped Amanda with her chair, and they sat down facing each other.

"How long will she be?" said Phillip.

"About ten minutes," said Amanda. "She hired a local car with a driver, who will drop her off."

Another waiter served their drinks and handed them a menu each to study while they waited.

Phillip was pondering over the braised ox cheek or the Moroccan lamb when the Maître D led Salome over to the table. Salome had changed into tight black pants and a red silk blouse. She slipped out of her black leather bolero style jacket, handed it to the Maître D, placed her bag by the chair on the floor and turned to face Amanda. They both stood to greet Salome. Phillip watched as the two old friends hugged and exchanged cheek kisses. Salome's mood had changed since the final bow at the theater, now her expression was pure joy at seeing Amanda again. Salome turned to Phillip who held out his hand politely. Salome ignored it and hugged him. He hugged her back.

"You are a lucky man," said Salome in perfect English with a slight American drawl. "This gorgeous girl has broken many a heart, but I can see that you are just right for her."

"I have to agree," said Phillip, "But how did you identify that in such a short time."

"Ha," said Salome. "What are you, five years older?"

"Eight," said Phillip.

"Really. You don't look it," said Salome.

"Perhaps I've chosen the wrong girl?" said Phillip.

"Nope, you've made the perfect selection," said Salome. "She's always preferred her men more seasoned, but you have that rare combination that includes all her other preferred qualities."

"What has she been telling you?" said Phillip mocking concern.

"I could say, tall, athletic, blond shaggy hair, blue eyes, and chiseled looks," said Salome. "But what Amanda could never resist is a calm, kindly demeanor and you're comfortable with smart beautiful women. Most of her exes couldn't hack that she was more successful."

Salome turned to Amanda and grasped her hand. "You better look after him or I might just take him for myself."

"Ha," said Amanda. "Actually, Phillip did offer to share."

"Now that is food for thought," said Salome grinning while pulling out her chair. "Shall we sit and talk about it?"

Phillip stepped forward and helped push her towards the table.

"And such a gentleman, thank you, Phillip," said Salome smiling at him. "Have you guys ordered already?"

"No," said Amanda as she and Phillip sat down. "We waited for you."

"Then let's order Cava and drink a toast to your forthcoming nuptials," said Salome turning to attract the waiter. "Then you can tell me what it is that you want me to do at the ceremony and after that," she paused, and her expression changed to one of despair. "I will tell you my news."

The waiter served the Cava.

They raised their glasses.

"To the happiness of my dearest friend and her

husband to be," said Salome as they chinked glasses. "May you have lots of sex and babies." Amanda blushed as they sipped their Cava. "Seriously though," said Salome replacing her glass on the table and picking up a menu. "Do you intend to have children?"

"We do," said Amanda. "And, if it's a girl, we'll call her Salome."

"How does Phillip feel about that, having met me?"

"Phillip feels just fine," he said smiling at Amanda. "And the sooner the better before my little swimmers need artificial respiration."

"Then may I suggest the oysters," said Salome grinning. She paused, the sadness returning to her eyes. "They say more mature fathers make better parents. I don't know if Amanda told you Phillip, but I was adopted as a baby by an elderly couple. They were already in their fifties and were wonderful. I miss them terribly."

Salome covered her eyes with her hands and breathed deeply while she collected herself. "Sorry to sour your happy moment with my pathetic emotions," she said looking up. "But would you mind if I tell you my news right now. It's just that I've been bottling it up for a while and once I've dumped it on you, will feel better equipped to talk about the wedding."

The waiter chose that moment to take their orders.

They opted for mains and desserts. Phillip went for the lamb; the ladies chose the sea bream.

"I've received a disturbing letter," said Salome as the waiter tapped their order into his machine and headed to the next table. "From an *Abogado*, lawyer in Vélez-Málaga."

"Is someone suing you?" said Phillip.

"On the contrary. They've invited me to collect my

inheritance from my birth family."

"Wow," said Amanda. "Didn't your mum say that something like this might happen and that you shouldn't worry about it?"

"I knew you would remember," said Salome with tears in her eyes. She reached for her bag under the table and burrowed for a while before extracting a packet of tissues.

"Is that why you looked so sad on stage?" said Amanda.

"You saw that. Shit, I thought I'd hidden it better."

"It was extremely brief, I doubt anybody else noticed," said Amanda.

"That's a relief. Truth is, I've been a bit weepy since the letter arrived. It's forced me to reappraise what I'm doing."

"You have a wonderful life," said Amanda.

"On a career front, yes, but emotionally I'm a complete mess. Now my natural family is also deceased, it means I'm completely alone in this world. Other than you guys, and a couple of other dear friends, I have no one to love or to love me, and that scares me."

Salome reached out and gripped a hand from each and squeezed hard. "Listen, I'm just not up to lawyers on my own tomorrow. Are you free to come with me?"

"When?" said Phillip.

"In the morning at eleven," said Salome. "I could pick you up around nine-thirty."

"I'm so sorry but I'm committed," said Phillip.

"Don't worry my dear friend, I will come," said Amanda.

"Thanks," said Salome, eyes watering again but looking relieved as the waiter served the food. "Now what do you want me to do at your wedding and why Gibraltar?"

"We don't need you to do anything," said Amanda trying a forkful of the fish and nodding her approval. "Just be there and witness the event. It's a simple civil ceremony in the old Gibraltar library and the paperwork there is so much easier for us foreigners than marrying in Spain. Especially as I'm American and he's British. It's why John Lennon and Yoko Ono married there."

"Posh frocks or jeans?"

"Nothing over the top," said Amanda. "But what about your schedule? Surely you won't have time to help me choose my dress?"

Salome looked down, gathered her thoughts, and said. "Actually, that's my next bit of news. I have one more show here in Málaga, then I'm off for a week. Hopefully, that will be enough time to sort out this inheritance thing before I'm due in Barcelona. After that, I'm done until Antonio Banderas opens his new Soho Theater here in Málaga next December where I'm making a special appearance in his Chorus Line production. What that means is, I'll have plenty of time to assist in your dress selection."

"Fantastic," said Amanda looking concerned. "But what are you going to do with yourself?"

Salome wrung her hands and looked at her old friend. "I don't know. What I am sure of, is that I've had enough of trailing around living out of a suitcase. I want to settle in one place. Teach maybe. Frankly, while I'm so busy, I really can't think too clearly about the future, only what's happening tomorrow."

"Perhaps," said Phillip relishing his lamb. "This birth family thing might open some doors, or give you some ideas?"

"Let's hope so," said Salome. "Because the uncertainty is depressing me."

"Then perhaps wedding dress shopping is just the therapy you need," said Amanda.

"I hadn't thought of it like that," said Salome brightening. "Sorry. I'm being selfish. Enough of my problems. Tell me, what kind of look are you thinking of?"

As the girls lost themselves in the technicalities of clothes and accessories, Phillip watched them both eating and talking avidly. What have I done to deserve this? He wondered. My beautiful fiancée and her gorgeous friend. It would be devastating to lose either of them.

"Are we boring you, darling?" said Amanda looking concerned about him as the waiter cleared the plates.

"Not at all," said Phillip. "Whatever you guys decide to wear, you'll both look stunning. I'm wondering if I'll be able to control myself on the day."

"You don't need to on my account," said Salome smiling and licking her lips as the waiter returned with the desserts. They had all chosen the Crème Brule with Amaretto accompanied by warmed summer fruits.

Silence prevailed between them as they savored the delicious flavors.

"Did you agree on a dress?" said Phillip after finishing his last mouthful and wiping his lips with a serviette.

"Good Lord, no," said Amanda.

"Lot's more debate to go," said Salome.

"Well you know what I have in my wardrobe," said Phillip. "Just tell me what you want me to wear. The pink floral suit or the bright orange blazer."

Salome's expression was epic.

"He's joking," said Amanda.

"Whew," said Salome.

"Darling, you wear whatever you want," said Amanda placing her well licked spoon on the empty plate. "Just be there."

"Now you're joking," said Phillip reaching for his wallet. "Where else would I be? I'll get this."

"It's my treat," said Salome signaling for the check. "Consider it a thank you for sharing your precious day plans with me."

Salome paid with her card. Phillip helped her on with her jacket then Amanda her wrap and they left.

Outside, they exchanged cheek kisses and farewells.

Amanda and Phillip stood, arms around each other and watched Salome speaking into her phone as she strode to the corner of Plaza de la Merced to meet her driver. Two minutes later, she climbed into the back of the hire car and drove off. When she disappeared, Amanda turned to Phillip. "Are you OK my love, only you looked a little preoccupied back there. Not scaring you off, am I?"

Phillip picked her up and swung her around nearly bumping into an elderly couple. They apologized profusely but the couple laughed with them enjoying their playfulness.

"I used to be able to do that," said the old man.

"You used to be able to a lot of things," said the old lady cackling.

"Only good for changing light bulbs and putting out the trash nowadays."

"Oh, I don't know," said the old lady. "You can still light my candle."

"Not as often as I'd like."

"Don't want you having a heart attack."

They all laughed and parted company.

"Ain't love grand?" said Phillip. "We'll be just like that in our dotage."

"Weren't they lovely, but I'll be wanting to play with your wick zillions more than her."

"I'll do my very best."

"Promise that you'll tell me if you're not happy with anything."

"Yes, dear."

"Never say those two words to me ever again."

"Yes…"

"No…not ever," Amanda said punching him hard on the upper arm. "We're an equal partnership and I never want my man to think of me as 'the missus' or 'her indoors' as we grow older. Otherwise, before you know it, you'll be in the potting shed looking at porn, which would be devastating when you can have the real thing whenever you want."

"We don't have a potting shed."

"You know what I mean. I don't want us to fade away into being just friends that tolerate sharing decades together but each doing their own thing. I'm blessed to have you as part of my life. For the first time, I feel like a complete woman and I want to stay like that. Thank you, darling."

Phillip stooped to kiss her on the lips. "That's one of the many things I love about you, Amanda. You tell it straight and I know exactly where I stand."

"Then we're in accord, which is a relief because I have something else to tell you that could change your mind."

Phillip stopped in the middle of the street put his arms around her shoulders and gazed directly into her eye's eyebrows raised, desperately concerned about what she was going to say.

"Well, er… you know we agreed that," she said. "That we would wait until after the wedding before we began our earnest quest to have children?

"Uh-huh," he said.

"What you implied in the restaurant about your little swimmers made me think?"

"Er… Uh-huh."

"Darling, I've changed my mind. I don't want to waste any more of our lives waiting. I want you to make me pregnant right now."

"The policeman over there might have something to say about that."

"Not here silly. Let's dash home as fast as we can."

3

Detective Inspector Leon Prado, leaned back in his tilting chair, plonked his shiny black leather shoes on his spacious desk and gazed out of the Málaga Central Comisaría window where gray clouds dulled the ubiquitous Andalusian azure. He appeared to be deep in thought but was distracted by the black lacy underwear, and an assortment of skimpy feminine laundry drying on the rear balcony on the top floor of the apartment block opposite. He wondered if his recent reconciliation with his wife Inma might benefit from such frivolity.

"Forget about it, Prado," he said to himself. "The excitement would kill you."

Prado was a well-built, mid-height man in his early fifties with thick silver hair and a round friendly face, dressed smartly in a grey suit, white shirt, and pink tie. His trademark Panama hat perched on the edge of his desk; jacket draped over the back of the chair.

As the most senior Detective in the Cuerpo de

Policia Nacional, he was responsible for the rapidly growing number of crimes involving foreigners throughout Andalucía. While he mostly teleworked from his car or home in Ronda, today he had to attend his office in Comisaría Central, Málaga. The boss had summoned him for a workload review.

He turned to face the desk and regarded the two thick files that had been troubling him. Darkness in Málaga was printed on the front cover of the top file. He picked it up and flicked through, mulling over the details. He repeated the process with the other file titled, 'Darkness in Ronda'. He rubbed his left earlobe, and with a pensive expression sorted his disparate thoughts into some sort of order.

The door burst open.

"Ah, Leon," said Jefe Superior, Provincia de Málaga: Francisco González Ruiz closing the door behind him. "Working hard as usual?"

"My first boss," said Prado staying exactly as he was. "Taught me that detective work is ninety-nine percent perspiration and the remainder pure inspiration. This is my inspiration seeking mode."

"Nice that you have time for such luxuries," said el jefe.

González was a short, slight man, in his early forties, with thin black hair swept straight back from his forehead. Chiseled features, a Roman nose, and cold obsidian eyes lent him a hard, imposing disposition. He wore his full, dark blue uniform, a colorful array of medal ribbons sewn onto his left breast.

He nodded at the files in Prado's hands. "I've read your reports on those two cases. As far as I'm concerned, we have both perpetrators locked up in Alhaurin Prison awaiting a trial date, with no chance of bail, and have more than enough evidence for lengthy convictions for both."

"I agree, sir."

"Then why are you wasting police time seeking inspiration? We have a number of other incidents that need your urgent attention."

"Because there's a major outstanding issue that needs resolving, before moving on."

"And that is?"

"One of the things I've observed doing this job is that foreigners have a different mindset from us Spanish. No better or worse, simply different. It means we need to appraise and evaluate their cases wearing their hats, not ours which is where Phillip and Amanda are so useful to me.

"I'll remind you that these two darkness files involve two bi-lingual foreigners. Malcolm Crown, a recently released pedophile from the UK, came to Spain to set up a sexual slavery and people trafficking ring. Patrick O'Reilly, of dual Irish/Spanish citizenship, operated an illegal gambling website specializing in bullfighting. If these were two unconnected individuals, I'd be happy to let justice take its course. But I'm positive that they are not. There are too many coincidences. Both forty-seven and attended the same school, at the same time. They shared a dark web hosting company, plus lawyers and banks in Spain and Gibraltar. They both operated completely off the grid, and had no assets in their names, or anywhere else that we can establish. Yet, both businesses must have needed thousands of euros for set up costs. Where did they obtain this money from?"

"So, you're looking for what connects them and who their investors might be?"

"Correct. It could be a single mastermind or a group of wealthy individuals. If any Spaniards are involved, we need to find and stop them."

El jefe stared hard at Prado, who didn't flinch.

"Have Crown and O'Reilly added to their statements?"

"No, sir."

"Has the monitoring of conversations in their cell yielded anything fruitful?"

"No, they continue to pretend not to know each other, yet should Crown be threatened by other prisoners, O'Reilly defends him brutally."

"Do you think Crown and O'Reilly's silence is an act of loyalty to this alleged mastermind, or is fear holding them back?"

"Could be either."

"Have you made any progress in tracing this mastermind?"

"No, sir, but we do have a roll of old film we found hidden in the garage roof of Crown's late parent's Cortijo. I'm still waiting on the prints being developed."

"Where is the film now?"

"It was stuck together. I sent it to a specialist laboratory in the United States. The prints are due back imminently."

"And you're hoping they may lead you somewhere."

"Unless the banks in Gibraltar suddenly become our best friends and send us account records, yes."

"Unlikely," said el jefe scratching his chin. He glared briefly at Prado, stood, and headed for the door, paused, turned back to Prado, and added. "Good work Leon, carry on."

4

The clouds were just thinning when a sleek, white Seat Alhambra SUV pulled up outside Amanda's apartment building opposite the impressive Moorish entrance of Málaga's central market, Mercado Central Atarazanas.

"I've been wondering," said Salome, as Amanda slid onto the rear black leather seats. "If the letter concerning my birth family came from a lawyer in Vélez-Málaga, does that imply my ancestors also originated there?"

"Good morning dear friend. How are you today?" said Amanda strapping herself in as Salome's female driver threaded into the stream of traffic.

"Erm… fine thanks. Good morning," said Salome nodding to the front seat. "That's Barbara by the way."

"Hola Barbara," said Amanda, "Soy Amanda."

"Encantada," said Barbara, early fifties with a round alluring face and short dark hair. She glanced quickly in the rearview mirror at Amanda and smiled, her brown eyes twinkling.

"Sorry for my manners," said Salome. "But I've been awake most of the night worrying about our meeting."

Amanda reached over and gripped Salome's hand.

"Forgive me, I should have been more sensitive, but try not to speculate about what may or may not transpire. We'll be arriving at the lawyers in about an hour. Then we'll find out for sure."

"You're right, but you can't blame me for wondering about it. It could be a life-changing day for me. Listen, I forgot to ask last night but didn't you say that you and Phillip work together; don't you find that a bit much, all that time in each other's company?"

"I much prefer it to my previous lifestyle. Working long hours every day, mostly on my own wasn't much fun, plus I never had any time for relationships."

"Tell me about it. The price of being a successful woman."

"But now I have the best of both worlds. A man who isn't threatened by my achievements, and treats me as an equal but more importantly is as keen to start a family as I am. Being together most of the time allows us to switch off and enjoy a siesta whenever we want."

"Dirty girl," said Salome giggling.

"No complaints. Especially last night."

"I wondered why you looked particularly serene this morning. Listen, have you done any articles about Vélez-Málaga?" said Salome as Barbara turned onto the Guadalmedina riverside road that led up to the coastal motorway. The traffic was unusually light, and the palm trees swayed gently in the chilly breeze as they passed the Rosaleda, Málaga's Football Stadium, on the opposite bank.

"Actually, we finished one recently. When you have

a moment, look on our Spanish guide at nuestra-españa.com. I had a lot of fun doing it too. The people from the tourist office who showed me around were really friendly."

"Then just hit me with the main points for now."

"Vélez, as most locals shorten it to, has a current population of just over eighty thousand. It's the principal town of La Axarquía, the region to the east of Málaga. To me, it's one of the most underrated and unknown historical gems in Andalusia. Several famous people are associated with Vélez. Cervantes lived in the town as a tax collector in 1594 and mentions it favorably in *Don Quixote*. It was the birthplace of twentieth-century philosopher María Zambrano Alarcón and painter Evaristo Guerra Zamora. Flamenco artists Juan Breva and José Beltran were born there and there's still a thriving gypsy community in the town center actively participating in a buoyant Flamenco scene. It's a hilltop town with pretty narrow streets, bustling squares with a thriving municipal market, yet it's way off the tourist radar; there's hardly a foreigner in sight."

"I'm starting to like it already. How old is it?"

"Vélez was originally located at the mouth of the estuary. Historians suspect it was a port built by the Phoenicians to ship out the tin they mined in the hills up near what is now Lake Viñuela, a massive reservoir. However, after an earthquake in the mid-fourth century, tidal waves destroyed the town and rather than rebuild it they moved inland to somewhere safer where eventually the fortress was built. Almost every new building project uncovers yet more archeology, yet little is being done to preserve or show them off."

"Perhaps the council can't afford it?"

"Logically it should do. Vélez has been the main distribution center for the abundant fruit and vegetables produced around the area for decades yet they prefer to squander money on a luxury streetcar system linking the town with its coastal sister, Torre del Mar. It had to close due to lack of use, but there's talk about opening it up again."

"An ambitious project for such a small town," said Salome.

"I have nothing against big ideas, but they need to be realistic and in keeping with the needs of the community. Most people use the bus because it's substantially cheaper and more regular. They would have been better off spending their money on refurbishing some of their amazing ancient monuments. It would attract more visitors and put Vélez firmly on the tourist map. Then they could afford a streetcar system."

"Which monument would you refurbish first?"

"My favorite is Convento Las Claras."

"Didn't know you were bothered about old churches?"

"I'm still as atheist as ever but this one is special."

"Tell me."

"It was originally built under the invocation of Nuestra Señora de Gracia in 1555 in La Villa neighborhood and donated by the Catholic monarchs. However, due to its small size and poor condition, a new and much larger Baroque church with convent and cloisters was constructed on Calle Felix Lomas during the mid-sixteenth century and renamed Convento Las Claras de Vélez-Málaga. It was severely damaged in the massive earthquake in December 1884 and then reformed into its current layout.

"Gradually, the number of nuns dropped to a level where it became too much to maintain for so few. A new and much smaller convent was built for the remaining nuns outside of town on the road to Arenas in 2008. Since they moved out, it's been empty and basically left to rot. There have been conversations about redeveloping what is a prime town center location into a Parador hotel, but the local architect who took it on hasn't been able to raise enough interest. The whole thing is now in the hands of an uncaring bank and in desperate need of repair before it collapses.

"Salome, all it needs is a crowdfunding exercise plus a grant from the European Union to bring it back to its former glory. I'm convinced that the townspeople would contribute, they love the place to bits and flock there when the bank deems to open it for the occasional festival. They could use it to attract tourists interested in history. The old sisters' cells could even be used for accommodation."

"Good idea. Maybe I'll look at it, but for now, it's not on my list of priorities."

"Sorry, I've been banging on. It's just," said Amanda shaking her head. "Beautiful old buildings deserve our respect. Our ancestors put so much in to creating them."

"I remember your passion about these things," said Salome patting Amanda's arm. "You're right of course. Do we turn off here?"

"Wow, Torre del Mar already. That was quick. We're way too early for the appointment."

"Blame Barbara, she thinks she's Lewis Hamilton. Can we stop for something to calm my nerves?"

"There's a café near the lawyer's office," said

Barbara.

Barbara followed the Satnav instructions from the motorway up into Vélez old quarter, dropped them outside Café San Francisco and drove off to park. Salome wrapped herself into a full-length black felt coat with fake fur collar and hid her face behind a massive pair of sunglasses. They walked into the busy glass-fronted café. Salome took a seat while Amanda approached the bar.

"Yes?" said a surly waiter in a white shirt and black pants.

"Dos *carajillos*," said Amanda and went to join Salome at a window table overlooking Plaza San Francisco.

The waiter delivered their coffee. The buzz of conversation and the noise of the machine-made conversation difficult so they leaned forward as sipped their drinks, savoring the caffeine kick boosted by the shot of brandy.

"I enjoyed meeting Phillip," said Salome. "He's fun, dishy and seems exactly right for you, but marriage is huge commitment. Are you sure you're ready? You don't have much of a history with long term relationships."

"You and me both," said Amanda.

"We know why," said Salome. "Have you told him yet?"

Amanda shook her head, a pained expression on her face.

"Don't you think you should?" said Salome.

"I can't. It might turn him off me."

"Keeping secrets from him isn't a good start. What if he found out later? It would destroy any trust he has."

"I know," said Amanda. "I've been torturing myself with it."

"Has Phillip been married before?"

"Yes, to a Russian."

"What went wrong?"

"He was too busy making money. She went back to Moscow with a fellow countryman."

"Imagine how he'd feel if you let him down as well. I think you should tell him. It will be a weight lifted from your shoulders."

"But that means he has to know about your part. What if he should go to the police?"

"Then so be it," said Salome checking her watch. "It's about time it all came out, perhaps we can then move on. Come, we have to go."

Salome left some coins on the table, they helped each other back into their outer garments, picked up their bags and headed out into the plaza for their appointment.

The waiter watched them go.

Then dialed a contact on his smartphone.

"On their way," he said.

5

"Ah, Phillip," said Prado looking up from the items on his desk in the Comisaría and smiling warmly to his English friend and translator. "Thanks for coming in at such short notice but the Crown film came back last night, and I needed your perceptive analysis. I trust it is not too inconvenient?"

"No worry, Leon," said Phillip closing the door behind him and taking a seat opposite the Detective Inspector. "My business partner Richard is used to last-minute postponements. Todo por la Patria, and all that."

"And Amanda, is she too busy to support her adopted country?"

"She sends her apologies, but she's gone to an important meeting in Vélez-Málaga. How are Inma and the boys?"

"Fine thanks. Inma has been roped in by her brother in law to help with the marketing of their new bullfighting festivals."

"How is dear Juan Romero? Is their venture working out?"

"Juan is well and sends his regards. He tells me they are expanding but more slowly than they would want."

"I'm not surprised. Taking blood out of the sport has to be a step in the right direction but changing entrenched mindsets will take time."

"And so, it appears. Now, what do you make of the photos?"

Phillip went to stand behind Prado and peered over his shoulder. There were three neat rows of fifteen by ten-centimeter color prints, twenty-four of them in total. To the right of the prints stood the original film canister. Next to the canister, lay six strips of four negatives developed from the film. On the bottom of each strip was printed, 'thirty-five-millimeter Kodak'. The prints were a strange mix of colors, many stained, some faded, others with no red, but what was common to most of the images was the subject. A male in his late twenties or early thirties.

Phillip picked up one of the prints for a closer inspection. The man had a long dark untrimmed mustache and sideburns, untidy dark hair and bushy eyebrows framing dark suspicious eyes. It seemed that the photos had been taken without his awareness as the shots were not posed and the angles gave the impression that the camera had been held out from behind various vantage points. In some, part of a wall, tree or bush appeared in almost half of the image. Some of the pictures were blurred as if the camera had been moving, or the shooter had taken them too quickly. But one was a clear, sharp image of the subject's left profile. He was wearing the same jacket in each shot, but the background varied along with the pants, shirts, and shoes.

The backgrounds also told a tale. By the trees, plants, and architectural style they were all taken in Spain. One photo was of the outside of a school which included its sign by the entrance, 'Marbella International College'. Another showed a street name, Calle Toledo. Another was of an old and dilapidated single storey house. It had green window blinds, the number nineteen painted white on green ceramic tiles which were mounted by a wooden front door that desperately needed a coat of varnish.

The final image was a photo of a photo. It was a typical end of year school photo, with seven rows. Six each of fifteen pupils plus the teachers in a sitting position on the second row. The front row was of smaller boys and girls between nine and eleven years old sitting cross-legged on a tiled floor. All the children aged up to about eighteen wore a blue jacket, white shirt, grey pants, and a faded tie, probably red. A badge was embroidered on the breast pocket of each jacket. The title of the photo was printed underneath. It read, 'Marbella International College. 1984.'

Although the individual faces in the school photo were miniscule, it was still possible to identify that in the middle of the teacher's row of eleven adults, was the man featured in most of the other photos. He had trimmed facial hair and a recent haircut, but still wore his glasses and the identical jacket.

"As he's in the center of the row," said Phillip. "It implies that he is the most senior teacher, possibly the headmaster." He replaced the print back in front of Prado, moved round to the front of Prado's desk and sat back down.

"I agree," said Prado rubbing his earlobe. "But why

did Malcolm Crown keep this film for over thirty years? What was so important about it that he secreted it in his parent's farm, and why did he then point us to it, as if he wanted us to find it?"

"You mean when he said, 'Look in the darkness', what he meant was go search Cortijo Infierno?"

"It's too much of a coincidence to ignore," said Prado. "One translation of Infierno means darkness. He told us to go look in the darkness. We did so and found this film there."

"Perhaps he wants us to find this man in the photos?" said Phillip.

"Then a name would be helpful."

"Perhaps we can ask Crown's siblings? They were at the school at the same time and were cooperative when we visited them in the UK a few months ago. Can you spot the twins on the year photograph?"

Prado extracted a magnifying glass from his desk, lifted the year photo up to it and peered at each individual. "I think they are next to each other among the older students in the back row," he said after several moments of scrutiny. "What do you think?" he said passing over glass and image. "Fourth and fifth from the left."

Phillip recognized George and Georgina Crown instantly then went on to search for the other two. Malcolm was easy, he was standing almost behind the headmaster, but Patrick O'Reilly was another story. Phillip couldn't find him anywhere.

"Malcolm is behind the headmaster but there is no sign of Patrick," said Phillip.

"Perhaps he wasn't at school on the day the photo was taken?"

"Could be, or he's changed too much, or the image

is too small to identify him. Perhaps we could get an actual size photo? From the school maybe?"

"In case you've forgotten, we asked the British Consul about Crown's background during our initial investigations. The school shut down years ago," said Prado.

"But didn't it close after the Crowns had been expelled and returned to the UK?" said Phillip.

"I don't know exactly when. What's your point?"

"A couple of years back, we did an article on private education in areas of Spain heavily populated by foreigners. It's unusual for International schools to close because they are in high demand, especially in Marbella. Could we discover exactly when and why it shut down? It might tell us something."

Prado nodded, picked up the desk phone and quietly issued instructions to a detective in the serious crime squad. When he hung up, Phillip continued. "Perhaps we could send a copy of the photographs to the Crown twins in the UK?" said Phillip.

"I prefer we asked the British police to do that," said Prado. "The twins will feel more pressure to respond when dealing with the local boys. What was the name of the Detective Sergeant that took us to their cottage?"

"Er... Barker, I believe."

"Do you still have his email?"

Yes. I'll take a snap of the year photo and the best of the man with the mustache with my phone and send it to him. Perhaps the twins might recall the man's name?"

"See if they can remember any of the other names in the year photo? They might be able to spot O'Reilly."

"While I'm in contact with Barker, should I inquire about obtaining copies of the Crown siblings Marbella school reports? If I remember rightly, didn't they have to submit them to their new school in the UK?"

Prado stood, went over to the case-board by the wall and studied the notes he made about his conversations with the British Consul at the time.

"Well that was remiss of me," said Prado. "The Consul obtained copies of their reports, but I failed to request some for our records. I'll call and remedy that."

"The reports may also give details of staff names," said Phillip.

"We will see," said Prado picking up the desk phone. He found the number in his contacts list and pressed the call button. While Prado spoke with the Consul, Phillip stood, lined up the two prints, photographed them with his phone, tapped out a message to Barker and sent them off.

"Once we have mustache man's name," said Phillip when Prado had ended his call. "Should we confront Crown and O'Reilly with these photos?"

"See what their reaction is you mean?"

"That, and to ask Crown why he wanted us to find these photos."

"Let's wait to see what comes back from our inquiries, then decide."

Prado looked at his watch.

"Umm, just after ten. Breakfast on me?" he said, pushing back his chair and heading for the door.

"Now that is civilized," said Phillip joining him.

"You don't have breakfast in England?"

"Of course, but before work begins, not during."

"So that's why you said civilized. Breakfast around ten in a café somewhere is a Spanish institution. The whole country practically grinds to a halt for half an hour."

They walked down the three flights of stairs to the lobby exchanging greetings with colleagues and talking as they went.

"I read somewhere," said Phillip as they headed out the main door in the direction of Plaza de la Merced. "That modern workplace psychologists have proven that regular breaks from the work environment improve staff productivity."

"That maybe, but it can be damned frustrating if you're a client waiting for ages at the bank because half the tellers have fucked off for a croissant," said Prado almost tripping on a cobblestone. Phillip grabbed Prado's arm as he stumbled.

"Thanks, I should watch where I'm treading," said Prado. "Or I'm degrading into an old fart. Either way, I'm looking forward to my retirement in three years' time."

"What will you do?"

"We have a family plot near Ronda. We plan to raise goats and make cheese."

"Wouldn't you find being away from the cut and thrust of crime-solving somewhat boring?"

"Not in the least. Don't misunderstand me. I enjoy my job, but every day for well over thirty years, my brain has been bombarded by a seriously distorted version of humanity. The prospect of solitude, mountain views and the same daily routine free of sick-minded crooks and their crazy antics beckons powerfully."

"I think I'll join you."

"You'd be more than welcome," said Prado.

As they approached the Plaza, the delicious aroma

of ground coffee and toasted bread wafted through the air. Prado took a deep breath. "I do enjoy my coffee in the morning."

"Then why not use the office machine?"

"Phillip, please. I've probably mentioned this before, but coffee isn't a beverage to be slurped from a flimsy plastic cup that burns your fingers. It's a life-enhancing experience and should be enjoyed in a leisurely fashion, preferably sitting at a pleasant terrace table with an interesting view and discerning company."

"I love you Spaniards," said Phillip. "Priorities in absolutely the right order."

"Dead right, but it has to be good coffee. None of this powdered or filtered rubbish. Only the finest blend of Arabic beans, gently roasted, finely ground then expressed slowly under pressure to your preferred flavor and served not too hot in a pre-warmed glass or china cup. Did you know that in 1954, the owner of the Café Central here in Málaga devised a coffee index? It means you can order precisely what strength you desire, without boring the waiter to death with a lengthy description?"

"Yes, I've been there and seen the ceramic mural. I thought the *sombra* - shady and *nube* - cloudy options were most artistic. My favorite though was '*No me lo pongo*', which means, not worth bothering."

"Wow, you have learned, but don't use them outside the province of Málaga. You'll be on the receiving end of some alarming looks."

They arrived at the café and found a free table on the busy terrace. The waiter took their orders for toasted molletes and expresso coffees.

Phillip's phone buzzed while they were waiting. He

took it out of his jacket pocket and swiped the screen. "Email from Barker," he said. "He'll make an appointment to visit the Crown twins this afternoon."

"Excellent," said Prado as the waiter served their traditional Spanish breakfast. Phillip was drizzling olive oil on his soft roll when Prado's phone rang.

It was a one-sided conversation to which Prado's contribution was Si, Cuando, and Gracias.

"That was interesting," he said swiping end call and tucking back into his roll.

Phillip waited and took a sip of his coffee.

Prado finished his mouthful. "Are you free this afternoon?"

"I can be, why?"

"That was the serious crime squad. They've checked the land registry but found nothing regarding the school or the house at Calle Toledo number nineteen. The registry informed them that would usually mean the land has been absorbed into a larger plot, then referred them to the Town Hall for more information. When they contacted the Ayuntamiento in Marbella and spoke with the planning department, they were kept waiting for ages before being told that the files were locked and only accessible by the Mayor's office."

"Locked files, but surely?"

"Absolutely; planning applications should be accessible public documents, so why does the Mayor keep them to herself?"

"Covering up something, perhaps?"

"Hardly surprising in Marbella. Their Town Hall is notorious for its dodgy past. Phillip, I smell something seriously fishy here. After lunch, we have an appointment with the Mayor. Who knows what she'll have to tell us?"

6

"Has the brandy helped?" said Amanda buttoning her brown leather jacket as they walked down Calle Poeta Joaquin Lobato.

"Nope, still terrified," said Salome looking pale and unsure of herself. She shivered, even though the clouds had dispersed, and the customary clear blue sky had returned. Despite the warm December sunshine, she wrapped her coat around her and snuggled into the collar.

"Want to back out?"

"I do, but then I'll spend the rest of my life regretting it."

"Me too."

"Sorry, you must be sick of me banging on about my ancestry."

"Don't worry. After fifteen years, I'm well accustomed. Perhaps, at last, we can put it to bed."

"I really hope so," said Salome gripping her friend's arm and squeezing as they passed the Mudejar styled

Iglesia y Convento San Francisco. It was built during the sixteenth century on the site of a former mosque.

They threaded their way through a line of scooters parked outside the Mercado de San Francisco. The former municipal market had been recently and tastefully redeveloped into a popular multipurpose cuisine and cultural space. They crossed the cobbled street toward a row of mixed-age buildings; some in a semi-dilapidated condition. Others had been restored to match the original eighteenth-century facades including ornate wrought iron grills and window frames garlanded with an assortment of pot plants. Colorful hanging baskets had been cleverly integrated into the traditionally styled streetlamps. They stopped outside one of the newer buildings. Amanda peered at a small, well-rubbed brass sign set into the white painted wall next to a tall timber door glazed with a stained-glass window. 'Abogados de Vélez', it read.

Amanda pushed the door, it opened, and they went into a rather grand, spacious reception decorated with large gilt-framed portraits of serious looking, well-groomed elderly men in somber gray suits. A gray sofa was to the right by an oak door; reception straight ahead and a gloomy passage led off to the left.

An elegant woman in her late fifties with a stern face and short platinum hair wearing a smart, pink, two-piece skirt suit, stood as they entered. She waited as they approached the oak reception desk on which stood a solitary laptop computer, a phone, and an intercom system. A large photocopier was behind her against the wall, above which was a gilt-framed mirror with the name of the firm etched into the glass.

"Good morning ladies," said the woman. "I'm Sara, we've been expecting you. May I take your coats?"

"Thanks," said Salome handing it over.

Amanda followed suit.

"Before we see the senior partner, Señora Mendosa, I need to copy your ID."

Salome fumbled in her bag, extracted her purse, took out a plastic ID card and handed it over. Sara studied it, placed it in the machine behind her, printed out a copy and returned the original. "Now I'm to escort you directly to meet Señor Delgado."

She led them into the passage. A sensor brightened the lighting to reveal yet more portraits on both sides. They passed several oak doors, each with its own brass sign announcing the occupant of each office. At the far end, the receptionist knocked respectfully, didn't wait for a reply, opened the door, and led them in. She placed the copy ID on her boss's spacious rosewood desk. More portraits decorated the walls.

"Señoras Mendosa and Salisbury," she said and closed the door on the way out.

"Good morning Señoras," said Delgado in a quiet husky voice remaining in his chair. He was a man in his early eighties with wispy white hair, liver spots on his hands and impeccably dressed in a dark gray suit, light blue shirt and badly knotted plain yellow tie that appeared enormous when compared with his wizened features and slender frame. He peered over gold-framed spectacles poised almost on the tip of his nose at Salome and Amanda scrutinizing them both closely, then compared Salome's appearance with the photocopy. He appeared frail but on closer inspection, his brown eyes were alert and attentive.

"Forgive me for not standing but my legs aren't quite what they used to be," he said. "My partners keep pressing me to retire, but I tell them that while my mind still works and my eyes and hearing function adequately then I will not relinquish my position. I'm sure it drives them crazy." He cackled. "Anyway, onto business. Thank you for responding to our invitation Señora Mendosa, I had my doubts that someone in your position would be interested in such a modest affair, but you've proved me wrong."

"I've always known that I was adopted," said Salome. "And after all these years of knowing nothing about my birth family, I did wonder if it should be best left alone. However, my burning curiosity overcame my initial fear, and I've decided that I'd like to know."

"Only time will tell if that is a wise decision," said Delgado frowning before groveling around in his desk drawer. He extracted a small book and a file then passed the book over with a shaking hand.

"Your family name is Vargas, and this is the *Libro de la Familia*, family book," he said. "It contains details of your parent's marriage, birth certificates for the three of you and their death certificates. There are also locks of hair from you and your parents taped inside the book in case you want a DNA test."

Salome took them and flicked through the book stopping at the locks of silky black hair. She ran her fingers through them and burst into tears. Amanda jumped up, put her arm around Salome's shoulders. Delgado passed over a box of tissues. Salome took one and wiped her eyes.

"Sorry," she said.

"No need to apologize, Señora Mendosa," said Delgado passing over the file. "I quite understand and I'm sure there will be more tears yet to come. The papers in the file cover your adoption. Now, having satisfied me that you were born as Salome Vargas, we can move onto your inheritance. Your father was Jesús Vargas; however, our discussions today are not about him, they are about his brother Mario. Mario Vargas was your father's only sibling."

"Mario Vargas, but wasn't he?" said Salome.

"I'm not surprised that the name is familiar to you, I'll explain that later. Mario died last month on the fifteenth of November. He left a small townhouse in the old quarter of Vélez worth about eighty-five thousand Euros: some forty thousand Euros cash in the bank, and two sealed envelopes. The house and cash we can talk about at another time but without further ado here are the envelopes." He reached into the desk drawer, took out a large, heavy manila envelope and a smaller one, then handed them over. "You'll have to sign a receipt for these, but we can do that when you've absorbed what's inside and decided whether you want to accept or reject your inheritance."

Salome was about to take the envelopes when they heard a commotion outside.

"You can't go in there," shouted a woman's voice. "I'm calling the police."

The door opened forcefully and in barged a small, shabbily dressed woman in her seventies followed by an equally impoverished man some twenty years younger. The man rushed behind the desk and grabbed the envelopes still in Delgado's hands.

We'll take those," he shouted.

7

Salome and Amanda sprang from their seats and went for the man. Anger pulsed through their veins as they pulled him away from the old lawyer. Salome was particularly vicious with him and slammed his head against the wall, then made to repeat that.

"Stop Salome, screamed Amanda. "You'll kill him."

"Leave him alone," screamed the old lady moving toward them raising her arm.

Amanda stood in her way.

The old lady stopped but looked concerned over Amanda's shoulder.

Amanda turned to help Salome, but the man had slumped to the floor holding his head and moaning.

Delgado shrunk back in his chair hugging the envelopes to his chest and glaring at the intruders.

"I know you," shrieked Delgado. "You claimed to be Mario's first wife. And this pathetic example of masculinity must be your whining son."

"We are just here for our share of the Mario Vargas

estate," said the old woman. "We're entitled."

"Then ask your lawyer to submit a claim in writing to this office. You'll need to prove who you are and what relationship you had with the deceased."

"You know we can't afford to do that," said the old woman.

"Are you going to stop your nonsense, now?" said Salome to the man as he struggled to his feet still holding his head.

"OK," he said.

"Then shall we discuss this like reasonable adults."

The man nodded and went to stand by his mother.

"Send Simon to me," Delgado said to Sara.

The receptionist turned up her nose at the smell of unwashed clothes and body odor, opened the skylight behind Delgado and went back out to reception leaving the door wide open.

A muscular dark-haired man in his mid thirties wearing a white shirt and grey pants soon filled the doorway. He appraised the room calmly.

"Ah, Simon," said Delgado. "This is my investigator, also grandson. You remember these two?"

"Vaguely," said Simon. "What are your names again?"

"Cristina Ayala," said the old woman, a bitter expression on her face. "My son, Isaac."

"I remember," said Simon. "It must have been over ten years ago. We investigated your claim about being Mario's ex-wife and Isaac being his son. As I recall, you were unable to provide any proof, and there are no official documents in support."

"There are no papers," shrieked Cristina. "It was a gypsy ceremony, and we don't bother with no birth certificates."

"That's right," said Delgado. "I forgot to ask you at the time. Why didn't you make any claims to Mario when Isaac was born?"

"We lived in Sevilla," said Cristina. "We didn't know where he was."

"You could have asked a lawyer to find out," said Simon.

"You people are all the same," said Cristina. "Don't you understand, we never went to school so can't read and lived in a communal gypsy tenement under our rules, not yours."

Then the police arrived and escorted them out of the office.

Cristina's words cried, as she was dragged out unceremoniously, haunted Salome and Amanda. "If you treat us unfairly, Salome, the gypsy community of Vélez will curse you. Wherever you are, our demons will find you."

Sara returned with a fresh air spray but left the window open.

"How did they know we were here?" said Salome.

"No idea," said Delgado. "The gypsy community look after each other here. There are few secrets."

"Is there any truth to Cristina's claim?" said Salome.

"I doubt it, perhaps the envelopes may provide an answer?"

Salome sat back down, took the envelopes from Delgado, and regarded them. The large manila envelope was faded and shabby but sealed with wax on the back. On the front, hand-written neatly in pen and ink it read, 'To be opened by my niece Salome Vargas, born August first, 1986. Adopted by the Mendosa family in Madrid. September third, 1986. Contents strictly confidential.'

The second and smaller envelope, hand-written more recently, was addressed to Salome Mendosa in a similar but more spidery style to that on the larger envelope. Underneath her name was scrawled, 'Open this first.'

"How did you come by these?" said Salome.

"Three envelopes were delivered to this office about two weeks ago. One was from Mario addressed to me personally. It included the family book and adoption papers, along with a letter instructing our firm to trace and invite you here; the others were yours. Sorry, we didn't contact you sooner, but Simon took longer than anticipated tracking you down. Apparently, your agent was reticent to reveal your address."

"That I can understand. Delivered here by whom?"

"By the executor of your uncle's estate. He's a local architect by the name of Vicente Ayala."

"Isn't that Cristina's surname?"

"It's common around here."

"But they could be related?"

"That wouldn't surprise me at all."

Salome picked up the smaller envelope then looked at Delgado, eyes welling with tears.

Delgado shook his head. "I've taken the liberty of reserving a conference room for you. It will give you time to absorb everything at your own pace in private. My assistant will provide you with any drinks or sandwiches."

"Do you personally know anything about my family?" said Salome.

"Your uncle has been a client for decades. We mentioned that his name sounded familiar earlier on. That's because he was indeed the famous Flamenco dancer. He appeared regularly on TV along with your father who was a brilliant guitarist. Perhaps you've seen some of their videos?"

"Yes, I have," said Salome sniffing. "My teacher often remarked how similarly we danced but I never dreamed that we might be related."

"Why would you? At the time, they were much admired and traveled the country extensively but whenever they were in Vélez they would perform for their friends and local fans. I loved watching them in local bars during the seventies, but then in the mid-eighties for some unknown reason your father disappeared and sometime later your uncle became a recluse. I visited Mario at home on a few occasions to take instructions to dispose of various properties he owned around the town, and he would reluctantly turn up at the notary to finalize the sales. But that was it."

"My father disappeared, and my uncle became a recluse?" said Salome. "How strange, I wonder why?"

"Perhaps the answer lies in the envelopes," said Delgado. "Listen, may I suggest that you open them up and read everything? Afterward, you are bound to have lots of questions which I will endeavor to answer."

Delgado buzzed the intercom.

When Sara entered, he said. "Sara, who is actually my daughter, will attend to your needs."

They stood and followed Sara. Salome clutching the envelopes so hard that her knuckles were white, and her hands trembled. Sara led them back to reception and through the door next to the sofa. The meeting room was dominated by a huge wall-mounted painting of her father.

"Don't mind him," said Sara as Amanda frowned at the portrait.

"I'll try not to, but his eyes seem to glare at you no matter where you are in the room," said Amanda.

"The artist wanted it to be deliberately creepy," said Sara. "To encourage users of the room to be honest in their dealings, but you've just seen the pathetic creature my dad is now; he couldn't hurt a fly."

Salome put the envelopes down on a large circular oak table surrounded by black leather and chrome chairs. "Let me know if you need anything," she said as she closed the door leaving them to it.

Amanda poured glasses of water for both from an iced jug standing on a matching oak sideboard. They both sat down, sipped their drinks, and peered anxiously at the paperwork on the table.

"Before we start on this," said Amanda. "What was that back there?"

"After that night, I never wanted to feel so pathetic and weak again, so I took a self-defense course. I was just following what I was taught. Disable first, ask questions later."

"It looked like you'd lost control," said Amanda.

"I was fine," said Salome. "Can we get on now?"

Amanda stared at her friend shaking her head.

"What?" said Salome.

"Sometimes I don't know you at all."

"Nonsense," said Salome looking down at the envelopes her eyes watering.

Amanda reached out, grasped Salome's hand, and said. "You OK?"

Salome nodded several times and took a deep breath before saying. "This is weird. For as long as I can remember, I've been dreaming of this moment. At last, this is my chance to learn about who the fuck I am. Now I'm about to do just that, and it scares the shit out of me."

Salome sat still regarding the envelopes in front of her hesitantly. Bright sunshine streamed through the Venetian blinds forming stripes on the meeting room table. Amanda watched her friend carefully wondering what was deterring her. Then she remembered.

"How's your dyslexia?" she said.

"No better."

"Would you prefer that I read them out loud to you?"

"Yes, please," said Salome looking relieved.

Amanda picked up the small envelope, opened it, unfolded the contents, and held several sheets of paper in front of her. They were printed on one side only. She quickly scanned the text then began to read in a calm, steady voice.

"October tenth, 2018. Vélez-Málaga.

"My Dearest Salome,

"I am Mario Vargas, born in Vélez-Málaga in 1936. Your birth father was my only brother Jesús Vargas which makes you my niece and possibly by the time you read this, my only surviving relative. I am so sorry to make your acquaintance in this rather bizarre manner, but circumstances present me with no other choice. The reason that you are reading this now is that I am deceased, dead and no longer of this world. Hopefully, I'll be enjoying a blissful afterlife packed with nubile vestal virgins and an ample supply of crisp, fruity verdejo white wine from the Rueda wine region, we shall see.

"In 1986, I was instructed by your father to arrange for your adoption and to store various items in a safe place until after my demise. Then I was to pass them on to you so you may learn the truth of your ancestry.

"My dear friend and only contact with the outside world is, Vicente Ayala. He's a local architect who used to work with me when I developed a few properties around the town. They were all sold over the last thirty-odd years to fund my retirement. He has kindly agreed to type up this document on his laptop then print it, be the executor of my estate, and will deliver everything to Delgado the lawyer.

"Vicente is intelligent, capable and completely trustworthy. He has been a godsend to me in my later years. Apart from Delgado and his staff, he is the only other person who knows who you are and will be more than happy to help you in any way. Should you need him, Delgado can put you in touch.

"To put into perspective what follows about your parents, I propose to give you a potted history of your ancestors. Don't become too excited, it's a sad and sorry story that started during the Spanish Civil War.

"Except for a brief interlude that I will explain later, the Vargas family have lived in and around Vélez-Málaga for centuries. The land on which my home sits has been in family hands for over two hundred years.

"We are descended from the Roma tribes who were forced out of Hindustan in Northern India during the fifteenth century. Our ancestors posed as Egyptians in order to be better received by the Spaniards. The Spanish word for Egyptians is 'Egiptos' and our race was known as 'Egiptanos', which has evolved to Gitanos in Spain and Gypsy in English. We brought few material possessions with us, but our language and culture have endured, and particularly our dancing continues to thrive. Flamenco is assumed to derive from 'fellah mengu', Moorish Arab words implying 'escapee peasant.'

"We belong to the Iberian Kale group and speak Caló which is based on a mix of Spanish dialects, Romani words, and phrases. Don't worry, few speak it nowadays and you won't be expected to learn unless you marry a traditional gypsy man.

"Despite regular attempts throughout the centuries to eliminate us as an identifiable group, there are estimated to be about a million Gitanos in Spain. Most of us live in Andalucía, hence its reputation as being the home of Flamenco. Even after all this time, bigoted attitudes still prevail and we are still used by Spaniards to frighten children into obedience, like the English and their bogeyman.

"Our reputation as thieves, drug addicts, and generally untrustworthy persons is probably justified but it is mainly born out of desperation to escape extreme poverty and become upstanding members of the same society that continues to dislike and repress us. I know, crazy isn't it, and it will probably take at least another five hundred years before they judge us as equals. It is this reticence by many Spaniards to treat us fairly which partly drove me to become a recluse. I was always referred to as the gypsy dancer, but I yearned to be recognized just as a good dancer; my race should have been irrelevant. Nevertheless, by allowing ourselves to be associated with raw Flamenco and promoting it as a uniquely gypsy art to persuade customers to pay more to see the genuine article, I accept that we've probably made a rod for our own back.

"Over the years, you may have wondered about your roots. When I first saw you dance on TV, I knew instantly that you were our Salome. You had the family face, identical hair to your beautiful mother, moved as

I used to, and set your chin in a similar way while you gazed smolderingly at the audience. I blubbered like a baby every time I saw you. However, I couldn't not watch it. Seeing that you had survived the horrors of your childhood, overcome the mental turmoil of being adopted and made a success of your life somehow made me feel less guilty for abandoning you. By the way, Delgado has the family book, all certificates, and your adoption papers.

"Regretfully, I won't be around to see how you handle this issue. Now that you know you are of gypsy stock, will you include that in your marketing blurb to increase your earnings appeal, or remain as you are? No pressure from me.

"Your father was born in 1937 and died in 1991. Your mother was Rosario Luengo (1954-1991) also from a good gypsy family in Vélez. I'm going to be mentioning quite a few family members so to help you with the timeline, I'll include dates of birth and death. Both Jesús and Rosario disappeared on the seventeenth August 1986 and despite intense police investigations, were never found. In 1991, the police announced that the case was closed, and they were declared officially dead.

"The final time I ever saw your father was in my hallway. It was when he handed you over wrapped in blankets along with a few pathetic clothes, nappies, and feeding paraphernalia. He then gave me various envelopes and a file that I bundled together in the large manila envelope which I addressed to you and sealed. He then told me, rather ominously, that if he had not reported back within forty-eight hours, I was to immediately arrange for your adoption and hide everything that he had given me in a safe place.

"Initially, I refused to cooperate with such a dramatic request and pressed him for an explanation. He was adamant that I remain ignorant but reluctantly did concede that he and your dear mother were on a quest to clear up the mystery involving our father, your grandfather, Abraham Vargas (1910-1937).

"As I eluded to earlier, Abraham was accused by the Guardia Civil of doing something dishonorable during the Civil War in January 1937, after which; he disappeared.

"Abraham's wife, our mother, was Maria de la Concepcion Caracol (1916-1972) also from Vélez. Although pregnant at the time with Jesús, she suffered cruel reprisals for Abraham's deeds as twisted people, including other gypsies, took pleasure in making life hell for her. She was desperate for us to leave, but the war prevented that.

"After the war was over, and the survivors dribbled back into Vélez, this hell grew worse. These same cruel townsfolk cranked up the returning heroes who increased reprisals against us. We were spat on; fires were set regularly against our front door in the middle of the night and some shops refused to serve us. We were only young boys and didn't understand why we were hated so.

"In the end, my mother gave up trying to persuade people that she knew nothing of my grandfather's supposed crime and took us to Sevilla. We rented out the Vélez house and went to stay with friends of hers in La Triana, the gypsy quarter of that vibrant city.

"That was where I grew up, and unlike most of my fellow gypsies learned to read, write and tried to put the pain of our disgraceful treatment behind us. The reality is that such childhood trauma stays with you throughout your life and as an adopted person I'm sure you've faced this yourself.

"As we wandered around the streets of Sevilla in search of work and a purpose in life, we discovered Flamenco. I developed my passion to dance. Jesús learned guitar and we became most accomplished. The thrill of burying myself in dance enabled me to escape my childhood demons. Your father, however, continued to battle against them for the rest of his life. His recurring depression was painful to see.

"We started performing throughout the city and province and eventually all over Spain, even on TV. Now you know my name, you may even have seen old repeats. To this day, I cannot accept that we were technically that exceptional as artists; unlike yourself. Maybe audiences sensed that subconsciously we projected the pain of our youth into our performances and it added an extra dimension. Who knows? Sorry, this is turning heavy and not what I intended.

"When our mother died in 1972, we decided to return to Vélez. We were both getting tired of working so intensively, living out of hotel bedrooms, and paying rent for our Sevilla apartment which remained empty most of the time.

"We evicted the current tenants from the old family home and moved back in. There were still a few snide comments about the past but after Franco died in 1975 and democracy was quickly established, all that was soon forgotten. There was a new Spain to build and that wouldn't be possible if everyone consumed themselves with the hate of the past. Although it always lurked in the dark corners of people's minds and probably still does.

"Neither of us had found time to meet a partner yet

were eager to marry. We started teaching but also continued to perform mainly at shows and festivals around Andalucía and traveled occasionally to Madrid or Barcelona.

"Through our Flamenco lessons, I met Beatriz and your father Rosario, a young and beautiful raven-haired gypsy girl from a respectful Vélez family. We had a quiet double wedding in Convento Las Claras during the autumn of 1983. In 1985, when Rosario became pregnant with you, we all agreed that the old family home would be too small to accommodate four adults and a child, so your parents moved into one of my apartments opposite the Convento.

"I believe there were several motivating factors that inspired your father to try and solve the puzzle of Abraham.

"He had a deep appreciation of the nuns from Las Claras and their caring attitude toward the gypsy community. They had often provided shelter and food to our homeless and nursed our sick. Jesús used to gaze out of his apartment window at the church speculating about the nature of our grandfather's alleged deeds, vehemently disbelieving that any member of the Vargas family could have acted dishonorably against such a venerable institution. We were honest, upstanding citizens, not a bunch of wide boys and he was determined to prove this to the nuns and the community somehow.

"Then he found something that he thought could help him do just that. While we were reshaping my house to suit Beatriz's layout preferences, Jesús found an old wooden box bricked into a wall of the outdoor lavatory. He was most excited when he realized it must have been sealed there by Abraham, yet he refused to show me the contents.

"We had a huge row about that and eventually he did show me, but they were just various boring old things. I immediately lost interest, but your father became obsessed with trying to make sense of them.

"Several months later, about the time that you were born, he told me that he was certain that he'd solved Abraham's problem and would I join him in his search. I refused point-blank, saying it was better to let slumbering legends lie. What still pains me today, is that if I'd gone with your parents on that day, my more cautious attitude may have made them think twice before acting recklessly. Perhaps then they might have survived, and you could have been part of my life.

"So that morning, as I closed the door behind your father for the last time and handed you over to Beatriz, I felt a sense of dread wash over me.

"Needless to say, the forty-eight hours passed, and I'd had heard nothing more from Jesús. So, I followed his instructions and began adoption proceedings.

"The Mendosa family in Madrid; your adoptive parents were carefully selected by Beatriz and me, but everything was handled through a high-class private adoption agency, so they never knew who we were, or what your background was. However, we sent an anonymous note implying that one day your heritage would be revealed to you and that you should not worry about it.

"The day we handed you over to the agency was the worst day of my life. You were such a placid, cute little thing and as we had no children of our own, we would have loved to have cared for you ourselves.

"I am writing this now while my brain can still recall the main points that I need to tell you. I am eighty-two years of age, my liver is shot, and my doctor tells me that I only have a few weeks to live if that.

"Other than the envelope from your father, there may well be some additional family photos that you might wish to see. There is an outside chance that your great-aunt Marta Vargas, (b 1929) Abraham's baby sister, is still with us although approaching her nineties. Last I heard, via Vicente only last week, she was in Nerja's only care-home giving the nurses hell for banning her daily Cava allowance. If you do go and see her; she may recall some family history, but a word of caution. We told everyone that you had died shortly after birth. Cot deaths were still a regular cause of infant mortality in those days, so it was simple enough to fool people. I propose that you share your identity with the mother superior first who will advise on how best to introduce you to Marta, otherwise, the shock might finish her off. She will remember you as Salomita Vargas. She never married or had children.

"My wife Beatriz was broken-hearted after we sent you for adoption. We'd had difficulty in conceiving, so I surrendered myself to rounds of tests involving numerous plastic containers. To my horror I learned that I was infertile. This was too much for Beatriz who gradually became depressed and eventually killed herself in 1994.

"I'd been dancing and teaching regularly until then, after that I lost interest in everything and locked myself in the house here and resolved to drink myself to death. Happily, thanks to a marked improvement to the quality of my beloved country's wine selection, good genes, and an ox-like constitution, this has taken considerably longer than anticipated.

"I paid a Polish lady named Magda, to move in and

look after me, which she has done most dutifully. However, she too is becoming frail, has no desire to return to her home country, and will be worried about her future. Delgado may have some ideas about what to do with her.

"So now my darling niece, you are faced with two choices.

"Give the manila envelope containing your father's papers unopened to Delgado and tell him to burn it. Or, open it and begin a journey to uncover your ancestry however dark or light it might be.

"Knowing what I know now, I would burn it, but I am nearing death. You have the rest of hopefully many years of a fruitful life. Learning about your roots may bring some peace to your inner demons but be careful what you wish for; your grandfather and parents didn't disappear without reason. I wish you good fortune and may God bless you.

"You will always be with me no matter where the bastards send me.

"With love. Tito Mario."

"I don't recall seeing a guitarist in the videos of Mario dancing," sniffed Salome. "I'll have to find copies and see if my father appears too. How weird will that be? Salome, after thirty-four years - da da, here is your dad."

Amanda turned her chair and put her arms around her sobbing friend.

Eventually, Salome stopped shuddering looked up with mascara stained eyes. "Sorry," she said. "I'm being such a baby."

"You said it would be life-changing," responded Amanda. "So, how does it feel? Knowing who you are."

"It hasn't sunk in yet, but my initial thoughts are a maelstrom. What kind of dysfunctional mob have I evolved from? On the one hand, there's an unsolved grand paternal mystery with a poisonous shadow hanging over his reputation. That caused an awful childhood for my father and uncle. Then my parents disappear with no trace of their bodies. Add to that my aunt killing herself and my uncle boozing his way to oblivion. Then what do we do about Cristina? They could have been married but Isaac can't be Mario's son. That's more disasters than a years' worth of TV soap opera episodes. Where does that put me?"

"Try not to be so negative."

"Are you joking? Nobody could be unaffected by such a tragic family history. Two whole generations suffering such dreadful pain and sorrow. What concerns me most is that people say that subconsciously, families follow the path of their ancestors, and from what I've heard so far, it does not bode well for me."

"You can still walk away. You know, just try not to become embroiled in it."

"Not now I couldn't. You know me, I hate anything unresolved. Now I want the whole story. Not knowing would tear me apart, sort of like being half pregnant."

"Salome, you already have an idyllic existence. Personally, I would walk away from all this shit and get on with that. However, if you're sure, you want to launch yourself on what is bound to be a painful journey, we ought to get going on the rest of these papers. Before we wrap ourselves up them though; what do you want to do with your uncle's Polish lady?"

"Magda can stay rent-free in his house. I'll pay the bills and make sure she has an allowance. Should she need a care home, I'll pay for it."

"That's generous, but why?"

"I'll want to talk to her about my uncle. Best to keep her close and amicable."

"Fair enough. You ready?" asked Amanda picking up the manila envelope and handing it to Salome.

This time there were no tears or hesitation. Salome slit the top of the envelope with her nail and tipped out the contents onto the table. At first, they just looked, wondering what they were seeing. Salome picked through the jumble of items, glancing at each before replacing it back on the table in a more orderly manner, prioritizing as she went. There were several different sized envelopes. On the front of a small white one, handwritten in blue biro, it stated, 'Start here.

8

The Mayor of Marbella, Maribel Bueno was a short, striking-looking woman in her late forties with dyed blond hair, inquisitive brown eyes, and a rounded figure. She was dressed in a white jacket and dark blue pants. Maribel paced back and forth in a heated discussion with her director of planning; Carlos Jiménez, a tall, rangy, long-serving architect with grey hair, calm brown eyes and usually renowned for his patience with passing politicians; but not today.

The mayor's office was located at the *Tenencia de Alcalde* in Plaza de los Naranjos, the orange tree-lined square in the heart of the attractive, pedestrianized *casco antiguo* - the old part of the town. The four flags of Spain, Andalucía, Marbella, and the European Union fluttered gently in the mid-morning breeze from the third-floor Balcony.

After Málaga, Marbella is the largest town of the province with a standing population of just over 140,000 that swells to some six hundred thousand during the peak tourism seasons. The local electorate had long admired Maribel as a seasoned and honest politician. After many years serving the council, she'd been rewarded with the number one position on the voting list of the Partido Popular, Spain's centrist right party, which had won the last elections in 2015.

"How many more of these old illegal planning cases will keep biting us in the bum?" shouted Maribel looking at the two thick dusty files sitting on the corner of her large mahogany desk. "Every time our seedy past starts to fade from public memory, up pops another disaster to drag us back into the mire. This time the national police are involved. What have I done to deserve all this crap?"

"You're a politician Maribel," yelled Carlos. "Clearing up old cases and fuck ups from previous administrations, especially the Jesús Gil years, goes with the territory. The sins of our fathers and all that. Look," he lowered his voice to more normal decibel levels. "You're doing a good job cleaning up the town's image. But you promised the electorate that you would make Marbella great again, knowing that there is so much crap to get rid of, it will take another century at least."

"I may have overdone it a bit," said Maribel, calmer now. "At least we're no longer referred to as the Costa del Crime."

"Well, that's a start."

"What's so special about Marbella International College that the planning file was never digitized and is under lock and key?" said Maribel. "And why do the police insist on talking to me about it?

"Where do you want me to start? Bribery, money laundering, illegal planning, theft? Take your pick."

"But in 1984, it was the socialists in power. I don't recall any scandal."

"And the previous lot from your party was so clean and pure? Anyway, you were just a teenager."

"And extremely well connected and aware of what my generation was up to. It must have been smothered."

"It was buried as deep as you can get. Not a whiff escaped."

"Did you have anything to do with it?"

"I rejected the original planning application."

"Why?"

"The plot the developers had assembled was too small for the density of proposed buildings. To circumnavigate the problem, they had included adjacent national parkland to make the square meterage up to the required volume. There was no way I could sanction such an illegal application; I'd have been struck off by the College of Architects. However, I was overruled by the planning committee. Their justification for approving the project was that it was an educational facility and the national parkland would only be used for sports fields and temporary changing rooms. I objected strongly, but it was made quite clear to me by my boss that should I value my career, I should shut up."

"And as a dutiful employee, you happily complied. Were you rewarded for your loyalty?"

"I kept my job, and for that I was grateful. My wife had just given birth to our first."

"OK, point taken. When are the cops due?"

"They are downstairs waiting for you to invite them up. How do you want to handle them?"

"Do the files actually include anything

incriminating?"

"Nothing except the dodgy planning approval signed by the now long dead incumbent, but I wouldn't worry about that. Listen, despite your clean-up campaign, there are still hundreds of files that break planning legislation. If the national police were interested in corruption, they would have been here years ago."

"Then I will answer all their questions honestly and provide them with a copy of both files. If I need facts or something technical, I'll nod for your intervention." She went back to her desk, picked up the phone and said, "Please collect the officers from the lobby and then make copies of the two files on my desk."

***

Prado and Phillip followed the Mayor's personal assistant over to the elevator. He was a short, chubby, bald young man overdressed in a tight-fitting blue suit, beige shoes and sporting large black-framed spectacles.

When the elevator doors slid open, they squeezed in.

"Doña Bueno is an extremely busy person," said the assistant. "So please wait until she speaks to you before asking any questions."

"What is your name sonny?" said Prado.

"Oscar, I'm the mayor's personal assistant."

"Thank you, Oscar," said Prado. "For your kind lecture on mayoral etiquette but we are here on a murder inquiry, not a pensioners outing. We'll talk to the mayor how we fucking well like."

They studiously ignored Oscar for the remainder of the upward journey who bristled busily to himself. The door opened and they followed him along a short corridor to the Mayor's office. Oscar opened the door, didn't hold it open and walked in ahead of them.

Prado and Phillip entered, walked over to Maribel and Carlos, shook hands, introduced themselves then sat down in the indicated visitor chairs. Oscar picked up the dusty files from the Mayor's desk, stomped out and just managed to avoid slamming the door behind him.

"Don't mind my assistant, Detective Inspector," said Maribel smiling. "He's temperamental but bloody organized, whereas I am scatterbrained and dysfunctional. We make a good team."

"It would account for your daunting reputation señora," said Prado. "I'm sorry that we've disturbed your day, but we have an old case to solve and need your cooperation."

"Before I answer your questions," said Maribel. "I'd like some assurances about confidentiality. As you know we are struggling to rebuild the image of this once great tourist destination as our contribution to the growing Spanish economy. Yet another seedy revelation from the past won't help us achieve that."

"Señora, please relax," said Prado "We have no interest in, or sufficient time and resources to rake over previous town hall misdemeanors. All we are seeking is information about the backgrounds of two dangerous men currently awaiting trial in Alhaurin Jail."

"Thank you, Inspector," said Maribel looking relieved. "Oscar is making a copy of the Marbella International College and Calle Toledo files for you and will bring them in shortly. How can we help?"

"I'm intrigued as to why the files weren't readily

available through the planning department." began Prado. "After all, they are public documents."

"One of the many discrepancies of the past. I'm afraid," replied Maribel. "We keep them all in a separate strong room with access only allowed through me."

"I take it that there are some irregularities with the permissions?"

The mayor nodded to Carlos.

"Yes, only minor but still illegal," said Carlos. "The Marbella International College plot was too small to comply with planning densities. To solve the problem someone added an appropriate square meterage of National Parkland that bordered the plot to make up the difference. Said someone had no permission to grant public land for such usage."

"Are you implying that a bribe was paid by the purchaser to the said someone?" asked Prado raising his tone of voice at the end of the sentence.

"Inspector, I was a mere junior in the office at the time. I'm implying nothing but somehow a serious stumbling block to this application magically disappeared, and that would have needed the collusion of more than one person."

"Then multi payoffs. Must have been a purchaser with deep pockets. Did this situation also apply to the house on Toledo Street?"

"Actually, no. That was a zoning problem.

"Are there any incriminating documents in these files that would identify the wrongdoers?"

"Only the final signoffs by the incumbent mayor."

"Who is?"

"Long dead," interrupted Maribel.

"What can you tell us about the two properties?"

The mayor signaled to Carlos.

"They were both absorbed into larger developments during the 1980s," said Carlos.

Oscar entered and handed Phillip copies of each file, who opened the largest one and started flicking through the letters, reports, documents, and plans. Oscar left.

"Who built the original school?" said Prado.

"It was decades ago Inspector," said Carlos shaking his head. "I doubt anybody involved will be traceable. It was also a time when offshore companies could purchase property without having to declare who the beneficial owners were."

"And is that the case here?" said Prado.

"The original three-hectare plot for the school was purchased in 1974 by Education International Ltd.," said Phillip pointing to a document in the file.

"Don't tell me, a Gibraltar address?" said Prado.

Phillip nodded. "With Martin and Bayne acting as solicitors," he said then carried on turning pages.

"Did Educational International also manage the school?" inquired Prado.

"I don't think so. If my memory serves me right," said Carlos looking at Phillip with eyebrows raised. "It was run by Servicios de Escuelas S.L. A local Marbella Company."

"That's correct," said Phillip reading a document. "An opening license to run an international school providing private education for up to one hundred mixed gender students between the ages of nine and eighteen was granted to Servicios de Escuelas S.L in 1977. Classes would follow the English school's curriculum and be supervised by the British Schools Foundation. Can we identify the owners and directors of that company?"

"Their names should be in the archives at the mercantile registry office in Málaga," said Carlos."

"When did the school close down?" said Prado.

"In 1984, it was sold to a Spanish golf course developer," said Carlos. "The finished scheme included an eighteen-hole course and some nine hundred mixed properties. The developer went bankrupt in 1989."

"And the house in Calle Toledo," said Phillip.

"That too was sold to another Spanish developer as part of a hotel project in 1986, along with all the properties in that and the surrounding streets. The hotel has subsequently been in and out of various hands but is now part of a reputable major Spanish group."

"Do you have the owner's name of the property when it was sold?"

"Yes, it was a Spanish property rental company. They owned a row of six houses in the street," said Carlos. "However, that company also went bust in the early nineties, so we have no way of finding out the names of any tenants."

"Were the original discrepancies in the college planning application resolved when the golf course developers purchased it?" said Phillip.

"Yes, they insisted that the National Parkland be restored to its rightful owner," said Carlos. "The plans in the new permission clearly show that."

"You mentioned a zoning problem with the Calle Toledo property," said Prado.

"Our town plan had been approved by the Junta de Andalucía some four years earlier," said Carlos. "And that plan was already three years old. It had the area designated as residential only. Nobody had foreseen the demand for hotel accommodation at that time and developers were desperate for building land. As everywhere, money talks and the proper regulations were ignored in the interest of expanding the town's tax-paying population."

"I have to add," said Maribel. "That the town plan now accurately reflects up to date zoning regulations. The hotel land is no longer residential."

"That's thanks to your efforts ma'am," said Carlos.

"That's sweet of you Carlos," said Maribel blushing. "However, the gap between planning approval timescales and market conditions continues to yawn ever wider. It takes ten years to initiate and complete a building project, but recessions can pop up at any time. It's why there are half-finished projects dotting the skyline."

"Carlos," said Phillip. "Sorry, but I don't understand. You said that the town was booming at the time the college was built, yet the companies involved in these schemes went bankrupt. What's the explanation?"

"The town's main income is from tourism and property transactions. As the mayor said, recessions pop up with tedious regularity and are usually out of our control," said Carlos. "The United Kingdom is our largest customer. When Britain has a recession, we fall apart. Practically every company involved in property and construction went bankrupt between 1989 and 1991, then again from 2003 to 2005 and yet again from the world financial crash in 2008 until recently. Plus, we suffered close to fifteen years of Jesús Gil politics, where he and his cronies raped Town Hall coffers to finance their own nefarious activities. Consequently,

Marbella public funds have been in dire straits for years. We are only now starting to recover."

"So, what you are saying," said Phillip. "Is that tracing people that can give us accurate information about events in the early 1980s will prove difficult?"

"Nigh on impossible, except for two potential sources," said the mayor. "And they are the Sur in English newspaper, who published their first issue in 1984, and the remaining International schools."

"And your reasoning is?" said Prado.

"The largest source of advertising revenue for all English media is from in and around Marbella, particularly from property companies and the international schools that regularly publish their curriculum and results. Sur's digitized archives are well organized and searchable, but you'll have to visit their offices in Málaga."

"And the remaining schools?" said Phillip.

"Just because the college closed, doesn't mean that all the staff and pupils vanished from the area. Their education still needed to continue, and the staff would have required new employment. I think you'll find that many would have been absorbed by the other schools, most of which are still thriving."

"Would you have a current list?" said Phillip.

"I'll have Oscar prepare one for you," said Maribel. "Excuse me," she added picking up the desk phone and issued instructions to her assistant.

"Going back to the college," said Phillip flicking through the file. "I can't locate the original planning application. Which firm of architects made the submission?"

Carlos stood, went over to the mayor's desk, picked up the top file and flicked through it. "Ah," he said after turning a few pages. "Here it is. It was a firm of lawyers in Málaga who handled the application in 1976. They commissioned the architects, engineers, environmental consultants, etc. and paid all the Town Hall fees right up to and including the opening license after construction was finished in 1978."

"Well let's hope they haven't gone bankrupt," said Prado. "What were they called?"

"Sanchez and Sanchez," said Carlos. "They are on…"

"Calle Larios," said Prado. "Yes, we know them."

"May I ask what your culprit's names are?" said Carlos.

"Malcolm Crown," said Prado. "And Patrick O'Reilly."

"Crown," repeated Carlos. "For some reason, that name rings a bell."

Prado looked at him. Carlos racked his brain for a minute or so and then continued flicking through the file. Oscar reentered and delivered a list of schools to Prado.

"Thank you for the list and your cooperation," said Prado standing. "Most helpful. We'll be in touch if need be."

"A pleasure, Inspector, glad we could be of help," said Maribel looking relieved.

Phillip closed the file and joined Prado. Just as they were going out the door Carlos shouted, "Wait, Inspector. It's here, the last item in the file."

Phillip went over to Carlos and looked at a faded photocopy of a business card. On it was written, 'John Crown. Director. Servicios de Escuelas S.L. Calle Muro, 138. 29601 Marbella.' Underneath were telephone and fax numbers.

"Surely not Malcolm's father?" said Prado, rejoining Phillip.

"Too much of a coincidence not to be," said Phillip. "But what is his business card doing in the file?"

"Did Crown have any involvement with the school or golf course planning applications?" said Prado.

"Not that I recall," said Carlos.

"Then what prompted you to recognize Crown's name?" said Prado.

Carlos went back to the file, a quizzical expression on his face and turned over the page with Crown's card details. On the back were a date stamp and some handwriting.

"I made some notes on the back," said Carlos then proceeded to read out loud. "The date was February seventeenth, 1984. My notes describe Crown as attended the planning office without an appointment and aggressively demanding a copy of the planning permission granted to the golf course developer. A photocopy was issued by me at the time."

"Do you recall the occasion?" said Prado.

"Vaguely," said Carlos. "But not enough to be of any help."

"So, you couldn't describe Crown?"

Carlos thought for a moment then said. "The only thing I do recall is that he was shorter than average."

"Is the golf course permission in this file?" said Phillip.

"No, it will be in the developer's file, said Carlos. "I'll find it and email you a copy. Who was John Crown?"

"Our culprit's father," said Prado before he and Phillip headed out of the door.

On the threshold, Phillip stopped, deep in thought,

turned and asked, "Can you remember what language John Crown was speaking?"

"No," said Carlos. "But it must have been in Spanish because I can't speak a word of English."

9

"You want me to read your father's letter out loud too?" said Amanda.

"Would you mind?" said Salome passing over several sheets of wafer-thin paper typed badly on both sides.

Amanda took the document which had been written on an old typewriter and glanced through it noticing corrections and rows of xxx's over several words. She looked at her friend, eyebrows raised. Salome was gripping the table and had her eyes shut.

"Are you sure?" said Amanda. Salome nodded.

Amanda took a deep breath.

"16th August 1986," she said, then paused for a second before continuing. "My dearest Salome.

"As I sit down to write the hardest and most emotional letter of my life, you are suckling at your mother Rosario's breast and gurgling quite happily in between slurps. We are so fortunate to have such a beautiful, happy, and contented baby, but my darling daughter, we are the ones who are crying. Because in the morning we are going to deliver you to Uncle Mario with instructions that if we do not contact him within forty-eight hours, he is to immediately arrange for your adoption.

"We think it highly unlikely that anything will happen, but if it does, we think it better for your future security to leave Vélez to make a fresh start where nobody has heard of the Vargas family and our beleaguered reputation. We have agreed with Mario that when he dies, this letter and various items will be passed on to you so that you may learn of us, hopefully, understand what we were about, and can see your way to forgiving us for abandoning you. By then, more than enough time should have passed for memories of these events to have faded and for your safety to be no longer at risk.

"So why are we doing this?

"I can assure you that it is not a matter we entered into lightly.

"Ever since I can remember, I have constantly struggled to deal with the tragedy of my father Abraham's disappearance and the subsequent poisonous shadow that hung over his honor and reputation. Unlike my brother Mario, I have never been able to shake off this inner conflict. Not knowing what happened to him often tears me apart and sends me into deep spirals of depression. Finally, I have a chance to bury these demons and tomorrow, if all goes well, I should learn the truth about my father.

"Your grandfather, my father, Abraham Vargas was a religious man. He and my mother regularly attended mass at the church of Convento Las Claras. The nuns there were most supportive of the gypsy community and often provided for our homeless and nursed our sick in their own cells located to the rear of the church. As the building was extremely old, they were constantly having to prop up walls and repair leaking roofs, which with little money proved difficult; consequently, the building progressively deteriorated. Abraham, who was a competent stonemason and builder helped them as best he could to keep the place safe and habitable, but it was a never-ending struggle.

"In January 1937, during the Civil War, as Franco's troops approached Málaga, it was rumored that churches were being looted. Many started hiding their art, relics, ancient statues of saints and the contents of their treasury, but then people heard that soldiers from both sides would torture the priests, monks, or nuns to reveal their whereabouts.

"Not long after these rumors started circulating, the contents of Las Claras treasury disappeared and so did Abraham. Naturally, everyone assumed that Abraham had stolen the lot. My mother swore that she knew nothing about it and was adamant that Abraham loved the convent and would have given his life to protect it, but nobody believed her.

"I was born shortly after all this happened and was too young to remember the reprisals against us. After the war ended, we and the authorities waited for Abraham to reappear to solve the mystery, but he never did. Eventually, the police charged him with theft and a manhunt began. He was never found, but the shame on my mother and the continual hate from neighbors drove her to take us to Sevilla where Mario learned to dance and I the guitar.

"When our mother died in 1972, we returned to Vélez, moved back into the old family home and started teaching as well as performing. That was when I met, then married your dearest mother. In 1983, we shared a double wedding with Mario and Beatriz at Las Claras, and it was after the ceremony that the aging mother superior approached me with a proposition. She knew of my success and wondered if I would care to help the convent.

"That was when I learned more detail of my father's alleged crimes.

"This plain, rotund, quietly spoken nun had known Abraham and loved him dearly for his commitment to God and the help he provided free of charge. She admitted that she was shocked when their ancient treasures and relics disappeared. Abraham hadn't mentioned anything to her or showed any signs of his intent. She admitted that they had discussed the possibility of soldiers coming to loot the treasury but had come to no agreement about a potential course of action, even though Abraham had expressed deep concern about the sisters being tortured.

"The nun, her name was Dolores, showed me around the whole place including the treasury. The dusty glass display cabinets were still there, some still contained the signs that described the long-absent contents. That was when she told me something that made my heart thump and my guts churn with excitement.

"Apparently, the treasury was kept locked and only opened occasionally to extract items for specific religious services or festivals. There had been only one key, which had been kept by Dolores in her cell. Only one other person knew of its location: my father. The key had been found left in the treasury door and the police, although it was relatively new technology in those days, identified Abraham's thumbprint on the key and on several of the cabinets. It had matched the one on his toothbrush. It had been this that had convinced the police of Abraham's guilt.

"I conceded that I was also persuaded until Dolores said in such a whisper that I almost failed to recognize the significance of her words.

"I'm positive that Abraham did remove the contents of the treasury, she said. But didn't tell me for fear of us being tortured. I've racked my brains wondering how he did it because the combined weight of just a few of those gold and silver items was far more than one man could carry. He either had an accomplice or he stashed them nearby somewhere. I've always believed that they are still on the premises.

"My immediate thought was that my father must be innocent, but how could I prove it.

"Then she made her proposal.

"She explained that all the nuns were in their seventies and it was becoming impossible for them to keep pace with the demands of a crumbling building that was way too large for their needs. Plus, it was cold, rat-infested and an unhealthy place to live out their remaining years. She wondered if I might know someone that might buy the convent so they could use the money to build a new and smaller facility somewhere nearby.

"At first, I was shocked that they would want to leave their beloved home, but when Dolores showed me around after we returned from our honeymoon in Galicia, I could understand their problem and promised to think about it.

"Then while we were reshaping our house for Beatriz and Mario, I found Abraham's old papers bricked into the outside toilet wall. Once I had studied them, I was convinced that Dolores was right. The items from the treasury must still be in the convent and I think I knew where they were. However, searching would need some demolition work and create a lot of noise and mess. In order to recover them and prove that Abraham had committed no crime, I needed private and unfettered access.

"I resolved to find a solution which would also provide the nuns with their new convent. Which I did. It took a while and tested my patience beyond belief but tomorrow, after dropping you off at Mario's and picking up the convent keys from Dolores, your mother and I will go there and begin our search.

"We have no concerns that our search might be dangerous, other than from the crumbling building itself. But today's value of the treasury contents must be worth millions and my father did disappear so just in case, I've made these arrangements with Mario.

"Hopefully, all will go well. If not, then I am so sorry. Whatever you may think of us, remember that you were loved more than the world itself.

"Your father and mother."

Salome wept into Amanda's shoulder, her whole-body shuddering. Amanda held her tight and gently stroked her hair but said nothing. The unopened envelopes lay on the table, the detail of their contents waiting ominously to be revealed.

"Enough," said Salome sitting up and smiling wanly to her friend, wiping her mascara stained eyes and face with a tissue. "Thanks, I'm so glad you came."

"It was always going to be difficult," said Amanda. "Shall we order some lunch?"

"No, let's go over to the market. I need a break and

some fresh air. But first I need the washroom."

"Me too."

***

The Mercado de San Francisco was bustling with locals and a few tourists sitting at the central tables under a high V-shaped roof supported by timber beams sitting on top of brick-built walls. They were chatting loudly and munching on a range of foodstuffs purchased from the kiosks that lined the perimeter of the old market. Nobody took any notice as the two of them appraised the selection of food.

"I fancy a salad," said Salome looking pasty behind her large sunglasses. "You?"

"That will do me, but I can't see quickly which of the kiosks offer them," said Amanda. "Shall we try the restaurant Mangoa? It's late so they should have a free table."

A charming young waitress in uniform escorted them to a corner table by a tall arched window that overlooked the market. They settled down with a glass of mineral water each and surveyed the menu. Salome chose the Salad with *Bacalao* – Cod, and Amanda with *Aguacate y Gambones* - Avocado and Prawns.

"Are you up to opening the other envelopes after lunch?" said Amanda as they waited for their food.

"Yes. Then I'd like a quick look at the convent and Mario's house, just to get a feel for it. I don't want to go in or anything."

"What do you make of it so far?"

"It's emotionally draining but I'm becoming more and more intrigued. Are you available the day after tomorrow to come back to Vélez and do some more research?"

"Of course, where do you envisage starting?"

"I'd like to meet with Magda and this architect fellow, Vicente Ayala, but best to finish looking through the rest of the papers first. They may shed more light on matters."

"And your great aunt Marta?"

"I think we should go directly there when we're done here, don't you? Hopefully, she'll still be with us."

After their delicious salads, they paid up and walked back to Delgado's office. It was siesta time now; the town hall offices had closed, and the street was practically deserted as Sara welcomed them back.

"Will you want to see my father again this afternoon?" said Sara. "Only I usually take him home around four. Otherwise, he falls asleep."

"We're just about to open the final envelopes," said Salome. "We'll let you know shortly."

"Thank you," said Sara taking their coats and showing them back into the meeting room.

They sat down in front of the envelopes.

"You take these, and I'll open the others," said Salome sliding two over to Amanda.

They both attacked the envelopes, slitting them open with their nails and piled the contents in neat stacks on the table. The largest stack lay in front of Salome. She picked it up and flicked through it.

"These hand-drawn sketches appear to be an inventory of the treasury contents," she said. "We'll have to show these to the nuns to see if they can confirm that. Look, there are some notes on this one. The old script is impossible for me to read. Would you mind?"

Amanda picked up the sketch and peered at it

closely. "Oh my God," she said. "These must be worth a fortune. The notes say, 'Solid gold replicas of Columbus's three ships used on his voyage of discovery in 1492: Santa Maria, La Pinta, and La Niña. Donated to the Sisters of Convento Las Claras by the descendants of Luis de Torres, the Jewish convert who lived in Torrox, and sailed with Christopher Columbus as a translator.' The paper feels old and flimsy. Salome, these sketches must have been made by your grandfather, Abraham. Other than the ships, what else is there?"

"Chalices, crosses of various sizes, candlesticks, marble icons and various containers that could contain relics. There are also half a dozen paintings, but I don't recognize the artists' names."

"Wow, if the ships are representative of the whole collection, it must be worth a fortune."

"Yes, but it belongs to the sisters and must be returned to them. Assuming we can find it. Anything interesting in your envelopes?"

"I have this," said Amanda waving a large steel key in the air. "And an *escritura* - set of deeds. From my initial flick through, they are the deeds of the convent which is in your father's name."

"So, he purchased it to have exclusive access."

"The deal was notarized on the twelfth of August 1986, two days before your parents disappeared.

"Attached to the deeds, is a notarized copy of the *Compra-Venta* – Sales Contract confirming the sale from *Las Hermanas de Las Claras* – the Sisters of Las Claras to your father for the sum of seventeen million Pesetas, which is a touch over one hundred thousand Euros. The contract was signed two years earlier than the deeds and was conditional on your father financing the construction of a new convent on the Arenas Road for the sum of six million pesetas. When the nuns had relocated out of Las Claras, they would hand over the key and the property would be transferred to your father."

"Could that be the key?"

Amanda picked it up and took a closer inspection.

"It looks new, but the style is old fashioned. Maybe, your dad had a copy made?"

"Could be. Were there any lawyers involved in the transaction?"

"Nothing in the text to say so. It appears that everything was done directly with the notary. There is also a copy of a bank draft for the seventeen million Pesetas from Caja MonteMar dated the day before the notary appointment to sign the deeds.

"On top of that, there is a copy of a bank loan from the same bank to your father for nine million Pesetas dated the same day as the bank draft. The loan repayment schedule is also here, and there appears to be a life insurance policy issued by the same bank in your father's name covering that amount, with the first year's premiums paid in advance."

"Does that mean that I own the convent?"

"I propose we ask Delgado to inquire discreetly," said Amanda. "That's my lot. Shall we look in the last envelope?"

Salome picked it up and opened it, hands trembling. She extracted a piece of tracing paper with the number one hundred and twenty-nine in large gothic letters that hadn't been written but rubbed onto the paper with a pencil. The texture surrounding the number appeared to be of concrete.

"That's a stone rubbing," said Amanda. "Basically,

you lay the paper over the image you want to copy, angle the pencil almost flat against the paper then rub back and forth until the image is complete."

"But what does the number signify?"

"No idea but as everything else here refers to Las Claras, it must be from there."

"Right," said Salome, "What I suggest, is that we reseal everything back into their respective envelopes and mark the escritura one for Delgado to copy and work on. As I have nowhere secure to store stuff, we'll leave everything in Delgado's safekeeping and instruct him to act on my behalf to establish ownership of the convent. Then we'll head off for a quick look at the house and convent, then to Nerja. I'll call Barbara now, ask her to locate all three locations on the map, then pick us up in ten minutes."

Salome dug her phone out of her handbag and called Barbara. They had a quick sip of water then went out to reception.

Sara escorted them down the corridor to Delgado's office, opened his door and led them in. The elderly lawyer was fast asleep in his chair, head back, mouth open, and snoring gently. The file that he had been working on was still in his hand.

Sara went around his desk and shook him gently. He spluttered, opened his eyes, was instantly alert and said, "Just resting my eyes. So, ladies, how did it go?"

"We've left all the papers sealed back into their envelopes on the meeting room table. I'd like you to keep them here in your safe and access them as needed. Please look in the envelope marked 'escritura', where there are documents confirming that my father financed the construction of the new Las Claras Convent, and purchased the old one from the sisters using his own money and a loan from the bank secured by a life insurance policy. Assuming that the policy was paid out after his death, in theory, it should form part of his estate and therefore the convent should now belong to me. Could you make some discrete inquiries?"

"Of course, it will be our pleasure to work with you, Señora. Will that be all?"

"For now, yes."

"Then goodbye for now and please give Sara your bank details on the way out."

***

Barbara drove the short distance through narrow, pretty streets to the convent located on Calle Felix Lomas. She slowed as they headed down the hill with the convent to the right.

A small historical building sign announcing Las Claras (S.XVI – 16th Century) stood at the foot of three gated arches with stone steps, that led up to a full height timber door entrance. This was protected by a tiled roof and formed the center point of a two hundred meters long white stucco wall that was three meters high and topped with regularly spaced bronze sculptures of chalices sitting on decorative plinths. The paintwork was shabby but in surprisingly good condition given the lack of care and attention the building was so obviously crying out for.

Three meters in from the outer wall, the church walls rose starkly to some seven meters high. Circular leaded windows illuminated the interior and a three-storey square tower sat on top of the tiled roof just in from the entrance.

At the lower end of the wall was another gated arch wide enough to admit vehicular traffic and led to the nuns' dormitory block and the remainder of the convent. It stretched some hundred meters back from the road and was an enormous tract of real estate.

"It looks somewhat forlorn and abandoned," said Salome. "But gracious and extremely convenient for the town center. I do hope we can get access."

"I should be able to arrange that," said Amanda. "I can tell the lady at the tourist office who organized my previous visit that we missed a few points and want to do a follow-up article."

"Can we do that on Friday?"

"It's a bit short notice but I'll try. The tourist office is closed now but I'll call them in the morning."

***

Mario's house was situated back up the hill on Calle Maria Magdalena. It was a sad-looking single-storey house with a wide white painted stucco façade, brown aluminum front door and window frames with green plastic roller blinds. Opposite was Iglesia de Santa Maria la Mayor, a fifteenth-century church built in Gothic Mudejar style on top of the remains of a former mosque. Its attractive brick tower was the highest point of Vélez and could be seen from miles around.

They drove past slowly over the cobblestones but there was no sign of life. Then headed back down the hill threading their way through the maze of narrow streets and out of town to take the coastal motorway to Nerja.

***

The Casa Residencia del Buen Samaritano is located at the top end of Nerja in Urbanization Almijara III. It's the last building before the countryside begins. It nestles below the ridge of a hill overlooking the Rio Chillar and Almijara mountains. The polite description translated from Spanish is Geriatric Residence for the Third Age, but, it's a comfortable and kindly place to die.

The building is modern with clean lines and finished in white painted stucco. The nuns live on the top floor at the front, the lobby leads to admin offices, the chapel, a spacious terrace, stairs, and lifts to the three floors below that house the dining room and bedrooms. There is enough accommodation for up to eighty old folk and visiting hours are all day until seven at night.

Barbara squeezed into a parking space out front. Salome and Amanda entered through sliding glass doors and stopped outside an open administrator's door where a pretty lady in her late thirties was working at her laptop. She looked up and smiled. "How may I help you?"

"Sorry to disturb," said Salome. "But my great-aunt is a resident here. Would it be possible to visit with her?"

"Come in please," said the lady standing up and coming around to shake hands and introduce themselves. "My name is Carolina and I run the social care program on behalf of the sisters. Please take a seat. What is your great aunt's name?"

"Vargas. Marta Vargas," said Salome.

"Oh, I'm so sorry," said Carolina her face darkening. "We expect her to pass at any time."

"Is she conscious?"

"She drifts in and out."

"Can she communicate?"

"Oh yes, in her few lucid moments she still demands her daily glass of Cava."

"I'm her only living relative," said Salome. "She knows me as Salomita and thinks I died as a baby. I only learned about her this morning and desperately need to talk to her about my family history. Do you think the shock will be too much for her?"

"Probably, but she's past caring about living longer. However, she won't be that surprised about your presence here. She's always suspected that you are still alive. Shall we go and wake her up?"

10

"Did you think the Mayor was holding something back?" said Prado as he and Phillip walked toward their car parked in the Guardia Civil barracks some four hundred meters north of the Plaza de los Naranjos.

"I don't think so," said Phillip. "She seemed genuine in her bid to improve the town's image and I'm pretty sure she would have shown some discomfort if omitting important facts or lying to us."

"I agree. I sensed that the architect was being straight with us too, but what was John Crown up to? Why was a copy of the golf course planning permission so important to him?"

"When Carlos sends me the copy," said Phillip. "I'll read it through. Perhaps there's something in the detail that might lead us to an answer."

"Let's hope so. Meanwhile," said Prado taking out his phone. "I'll set my detectives loose on the Mercantile Register. Perhaps the director's names of Servicios de Escuelas S.L might tell us something?"

Prado issued his instructions as they walked back to the barracks. He hung up just as they arrived, climbed in the car, and headed north out of Marbella toward Málaga.

Just after they joined the *Peaje* - toll motorway, Phillip's phone buzzed. It was an email from Barker. He read it then translated for Prado, "Just come out of Crown twins' cottage where I spoke briefly to their gardener. They are traveling in South America and not expected back for some months. He gave me an emergency email address that they check occasionally. I've added it to the bottom of this message. Over to you."

Phillip tapped a quick thank you, then emailed the photos directly to the Crowns.

"Grr, that's three bits of information we have to wait for," said Prado. "Any other lines of inquiry we can explore meanwhile?"

"I meant to ask back in your office, were there any prints on the film canister?"

"There were four sets of old ones that we could hardly get a reading from, the oils had practically dried out; and one set of recent from Malcolm Crown."

"So, it was him that hid the film in the Cortijo?"

"Almost definitely, but there was something weird about the other four sets. By their size, they were all from younger people. Ana Galvez from forensics estimates their age as early teens, however, it was the positioning of their prints on the canister that puzzled me. Bearing in mind it's only a small object, there was a thumb and forefinger print from all four on each side of the canister as if they were all holding the canister up in the air at the same time."

"Celebrating something?"

"Could be."

"Was there enough of a print remaining to identify any of the youngsters?"

"Not enough similar points to stand up in court but one set was similar to Crown."

"Any others?" said Phillip.

"O'Reilly's were also there."

"Suggesting some kind of teenage pact between Crown and O'Reilly?"

"Plus, two others."

"All of whom could be on that class photo?"

"Four young people who had some kind of reason to photograph the man with the mustache," said Prado.

"A grudge maybe?"

"Too much detention?" said Prado.

"Or something more serious?"

Prado's phone buzzed. He pressed the hands-free and said, "*Digame* - Tell me."

"It's Fonseca, Sir. I have some information on the directors of Servicios de Escuelas S.L."

"Go ahead, Fonseca."

"The director, and major shareholder was a John Bertram Crown, aged forty-one, address at an apartment in Marbella. The administrator, and minor shareholder was a Rodriguez Sanchez Marquez, aged twenty-nine, address Calle Toledo nineteen, Marbella."

"Thank you, Fonseca," said Prado. "Anything else?"

"The company was wound up by court order in 1986 because the company had ceased trading and no accounts had ever been submitted. Their lawyers and *Gestoria* – accountants; were Sanchez and Sanchez of Calle Larios, Málaga. Their bankers were Caja de

Montes e Sierra in Marbella."

"Thank you," said Prado. "Send me the link and see what you can find on Marquez and the bank." Prado pressed end call.

"The Sanchez brothers again," said Phillip.

"Perhaps Marquez could be related," said Prado. "Is it possible that we are looking at some kind of family business here?"

"Founded by John Crown, then after his death taken on by Malcolm?" said Phillip.

"And don't forget Crown's elder siblings; the twins," said Prado. "They could also be involved despite denying any contact with Malcolm."

"Sanchez brothers too. Could they all be in this together? Sanchez taking care of the Spanish end and the Crowns moving internationally?"

"Pure speculation at this point," said Prado shaking his head. "But we don't have anybody else in the frame."

"Are we ready to confront Crown and O'Reilly?" said Phillip.

"Not yet," said Prado. "We need to be more informed about what is going on here before we talk to them again."

"But do you think we are closing in on the truth?"

"As I said this is pure speculation. I don't want el jefe to accuse me of building the evidence to suit our hypothesis. However, it's a plausible explanation but we need more evidence and should pursue this line of inquiry."

"I read somewhere recently," said Phillip. "I think it was in the Smithsonian Magazine, that, scientists can predict people's physical features from DNA samples. Would it be possible to have that done from the canister prints?"

"I heard about that in a recent police circular but apparently it's only partially accurate. However, worth a try. Call Ana," said Prado.

The hands-free whirred into action.

"Ana Galvez," she said after a few rings. "What can I do for you Leon?"

"Probably a half-baked idea, Ana, but did you lift any DNA off the film canister?"

"Yes, I have five sets," said Ana. "But the quality is poor."

"Is there any way that you can run a prediction analysis as to the owners' physical characteristics?"

"Not in my lab, but I could send them off to Madrid, see what comes back. It will take a while though. They are overwhelmed with requests."

"I understand, but could you send them off marked urgent."

"Fine, but don't expect much for several weeks."

"Thanks, Ana," said Prado ending the call.

A sign on the motorway indicated that the next junction led up to Alhaurin. It prompted Phillip to inquire, "Have Crown and O'Reilly shown any signs of knowing each other?"

"In their cell, no," said Prado. "They continue to studiously avoid any conversation."

"Have you tried microphones in the toilets, exercise yard or places they can be alone."

"That's a good idea, but I'll have to check with el jefe first. Best if I wait until I'm back in the office. With him, the personal touch is usually more effective."

"Any trial dates yet?"

"Sadly, they could take several years. Our legal system is creaking at the seams, mainly due to the increase in foreign criminals. Massive tourism may help the economy, but it also attracts all sorts of unsavory characters from all over Europe. Freedom of movement might be wonderful for business and pleasure but it's a nightmare for our authorities. We can't forecast how many prisons or courts we need, and it's strictly one-way traffic. Our criminals don't go rushing off to Poland, Russia, or Albania but theirs come here in droves. The number of shootings between drug and people trafficking gangs, particularly Irish and Scandinavian, has increased dramatically over the last few years. As fast as we deport them, new ones arrive. And then there are the illegal immigrants."

"Doesn't it irk you a bit? Spanish taxpayers having to foot the bill? Couldn't you send Crown and O'Reilly back home or bill their countries for their costs?"

"Good idea but their crimes were committed here and according to EU law they must be tried here and yes it does piss me off having to pay. But what can we do, release them?"

"What about the Spanish criminals? How do their crimes compare to the influx of foreigners?"

"We do have a few drug barons and wife killers, but most Spanish inmates have a sorry tale to tell. Dysfunctional parenting, pathetic education, poverty; particularly among the gypsies, abuse, or mental illness, all of which in a modern world, a responsible society should have resolved by now. Those are the problems politicians should be addressing. If we could create better, more inclusive communities that focus on helping the less fortunate instead of treating them as lepers, we could slash crime. If not, then we should use the time they spend behind bars to rebuild them into useful citizens. They've done it in Norway, why not here? Then we wouldn't need so many police, but more importantly, we could substantially slash bureaucracy and the bloody politicians that dream it up."

"Wow. Philosophical for a cop."

"Not really, when one has cleaned up as much shit as I have, much of it by re-offenders, you know how bad things are. It frustrates the hell out of me seeing the same old faces being processed through our police stations. Many commit crimes deliberately just for the three meals a day, a roof over their head, medical care, and social interaction, none of which they can obtain easily when on the street.

"Crown and O'Reilly don't seem to fit any of your background categories, and I can't figure what's driving them. They are well educated, not from poverty, and don't seem to be suffering from mental incapacity. Do you think they might have been abused? By mustache man, for example."

"Could be," said Prado. "It would explain why Crown gave us the 'look in the darkness' clue that led to the film in the garage at his parent's property. It's as if he wanted the police to find Marquez because they have been unable to."

"Then why not tell us everything so we have a better chance of tracking the man down?" said Phillip.

"That would reveal the criminal activities they want to protect."

"Selfish bastards. They want to have their cake and eat it. Well, they are not going to find Marquez while wallowing in their prison cell."

"That's right," said Prado. "But what about the other two sets of prints on the film canister, could the owners of those also be working with Crown? Are they also still out there hunting for Marquez?"

"Probably. Perhaps we'll bump into them during our inquiries?"

"We might have met them already, who knows."

"What do you think they want to do to Marquez if they find him?"

"Repay him for whatever pain he put them through."

"After thirty-odd years?" said Phillip.

"Revenge is a dish best served cold," said Prado.

11

Carolina led the way along the short passage, past the chapel, and into the elevator. Amanda and Salome went down two floors, through a communal seating area full of old folks in various states of degradation. Two old men, one with his head wrapped in bandages were arguing loudly about Brexit in English. Others sat staring into space, some moaned occasionally, and one Spanish lady was crying out woefully for her daughter. A uniformed young male nurse was attempting to comfort her. They followed Carolina through double doors into a long corridor with windows to the left looking out onto a central garden and a row of timber doors to the right. They walked to the far end and went in through the final door.

Inside the rectangular room were two beds, one at each end, there were wardrobes either side of the door, a shared bathroom to the right and windows with net curtains overlooked the riverbed. The bed to the left was empty but to the right, a tiny, wizened old lady with snow-white hair lay on her back, under the bed covers with her mouth open exposing several missing teeth, the remainder were misshaped and a mix of colors from almost black to dirty cream. She was completely still.

"Oh no," said Salome putting her hand to her mouth. "We're too late."

"Wait," said Carolina who went over to the bed, gently shook Marta, and spoke loudly into her ear. "Marta, you have a visitor."

Marta's eyes snapped open and she croaked in a barely audible voice, "Me, a visitor. Have they brought my Cava?"

Carolina indicated to Salome that she should approach Marta.

As she passed her, Carolina whispered. "Shout in her ear, keep it simple."

Salome drew near Marta and looked down at her only relative, the first she had ever met. She saw no familiar resemblance just a skeletal face with pale, wrinkled skin. She bent down and as instructed shouted into Marta's left ear. "Great aunt Marta," she said. "It's me, Salomita."

Marta turned her head and looked directly into Salome's eyes for several seconds. Her face lit up into a smile. "Salomita," she croaked. "Is that you? Let me see."

She extracted a bony hand from underneath the bedclothes reached up and stroked Salome's cheeks drinking in her facial detail. "You have your father's eyes, but you look just like your mother, she was such a beautiful girl." Marta's eyes began to water. "I always knew you were alive," she croaked.

She took out her other hand and held them both up

inviting Salome to hug her. They held each other tightly and wept.

"I don't have long," croaked Marta. "Is there anything you want to know?"

"My father," sobbed Salome. "What was he like?"

"He was a bit of a dreamer but played the guitar beautifully, worshipped your mother and was besotted with you. He'd always dreamed of a daughter."

"What about Mario?"

"He was no angel. He had a different girl in every town when they went on tour. He did have a big heart though and was always generous, especially to the family."

"Did he ever marry before Beatriz?"

"There was a gypsy wedding to an incredibly young girl in Sevilla, but it only lasted a few months. He couldn't keep up with her."

"Cristina?"

"Yes, why do you ask?"

"She's claiming that her and her son by Mario are entitled to part of his estate."

"She might be under gypsy law, but the son isn't Mario's, he was infertile. It's in his medical records if you need proof."

"Thanks."

"Promise me one thing," said Marta into Salome's ear.

"Anything," said Salome.

"My brother Abraham," said Marta. "Your grandfather was accused of some terrible things but Salomita," she shook her head. "You can easily prove it couldn't have been him. He was...," she breathed raggedly. "He was such a gentle and loving man." She raised a bony hand and pointed at Carolina. "It's all…

it's…"

Then Marta rasped once and was still.

Carolina immediately pulled Salome off her, grabbed Marta's wrist and tried to locate a pulse but after several attempts shook her head in frustration. She tried again with the other wrist, and on her neck but found nothing. Carolina turned to Salome. "I'm sorry but she's gone."

"Shouldn't we call an ambulance or a doctor?" said Amanda.

"There's no point. It was her time. She was eighty-nine years old with absolutely nothing wrong with her. She was just old and ready to go, was happy to do so and dying in her relative's arms would have been most comforting."

"But I had thousands of questions for her," sobbed Salome. "Now I'll never learn about my roots."

Carolina went over to the wardrobe, rummaged around at the bottom, lifted a heavy brown leather album, brought it over, presented it to Salome and said, "You might not be able to ask her, but she has been preparing for this moment all her life, just in case you materialized. It's all documented here. Photos, family tree, events, newspaper articles, thoughts; everything. I helped her put it together. I probably know your family history better than you."

Salome stopped her crying, took the book, and flicked through it.

After a while, she looked up at Carolina. "Thank you, this is perfect. Is there anything else?"

"You're welcome to look through her wardrobe, it's all she had but it's only old clothes, bags and shoes most of which she hasn't used for years. The Residencia will be happy to find a home for everything should you prefer, but in the safe, I do have her jewelry. I insist you take it."

"Thank you, please take all the wardrobe contents. What about her funeral, does she have any money to pay for it?"

"No, she lived here at the expense of her pension and a top-up from social services. Normally, they would pay for basic disposal but now that she has relatives, that will be down to you I'm afraid."

"Have you a number we can call, preferably a local company?"

"There's only one but they are most helpful and efficient," said Carolina laying Marta out flat, closing her eyes and covering her face with the bedsheet. "Shall we go to my office? I'll dig out her papers and we'll finalize everything there?"

"I appreciate that your home is run by Catholic nuns," said Salome as they went up in the lift. "But was Marta religious at all?"

"She believed in God but couldn't be bothered with the rituals of worship," said Carolina.

"Did she leave any instructions as to her funeral?" said Salome.

"She was happy with a cremation."

"I understand she came to Nerja just after the war but never married. Do you know what she did for all those years?"

"It's in the album but it was nothing special. She worked in the Town Hall as an administrator until she retired. She'd had a new hip in her seventies but had to have that removed after a fall in her mid-eighties. She's been here ever since and was a hell of a character. Feisty if things weren't going well but a great laugh most of the time. We're all going to miss her. Sorry, but don't I recognize you from somewhere? Oh my God, you're the Flamenco dancer."

"Yes, but I'm here on a family matter and would appreciate your discretion."

"Of course, Salome, everything that happens here, stays here. You'd be surprised how many famous people have passed through our humble establishment. Only last week one of the investors in the Trivial Pursuit Game died here. He helped the Canadian journalists who were in Nerja on a sabbatical during the early eighties, when, in between hangovers, they developed the game's concept on Burriana beach."

They arrived back at Carolina's office where she opened the safe, passed over Marta's ID card and papers plus a small box. Inside were some exquisite rings. Salome took out the single diamond in a simple gold setting out and put it on her wedding finger. It fitted perfectly. She sniffed, placed it back in the box and slipped it into her handbag.

Carolina called the funeral director and agreed to have the body collected and cremated. Marta's ashes would be ready for collection from the *Tanatoria*-Funeral Parlor, on the Frigiliana Road in three days' time. Salome used her phone to transfer the two and a half thousand Euros to the undertakers.

"Thank you so much for taking such excellent care of Marta," said Salome. "I didn't know her, but somehow in our brief time together I connected strongly with her. Now I feel some inner peace knowing that she was as happy as her circumstances could allow and at the end, passed painlessly."

They stood, hugged, and exchanged cheek kisses.

"Gracias Carolina and Adios," they all said together. Amanda carried the album to the car, and they headed back to Málaga.

Salome began to flick through the album but after a few kilometers, the hum of the motor and the warm interior had its effect and the two of them dozed.

Barbara woke them outside Amanda's apartment. The streetlamps were on and a light drizzle dampened the pavements. People scurried back and forth, umbrellas up as they headed home.

"What will you do this evening?" said Amanda gathering her things.

"Room service and read the album. Can we meet tomorrow lunchtime briefly?"

"It will have to be early, can you come to the market?"

"Sure, where?"

"Bar de Pescado, the fresh fish is out of this world."

"Fine, see you there at twelve-thirty. Goodnight," said Salome as her friend opened the door. "And Amanda; thanks."

They hugged before Amanda clambered out and dodged through the crowd to her apartment block entrance. At the door, she paused and looked back at Barbara trying to barge her way into the stream of traffic. Horns blared, eventually she edged in front of a delivery van.

Salome waved at Amanda, her expression pained and sorrowful. Tears were streaming down her face.

Amanda waved back, sticking her thumb up in the air. Trying to say to her oldest and dearest friend. "Don't worry, it'll be fine." But as the car disappeared around the corner and Amanda unlocked the front door. A feeling of dread shuddered through her as if someone or something was walking over her grave.

12

Amanda gazed at Phillip's face as he lay sleeping. She had hardly slept worrying about whether to tell him about the Madrid incident or not. In her heart she knew she should but was terrified about what his reaction might be. Then his eyes opened, and he smiled lovingly. "What?" he said.

"Sorry?"

"Why are you watching me with such a sad expression. Am I that bad?"

"I was just thinking about something."

"Want to tell me?"

"It's just work, it can wait."

"How long?"

"Long enough," she said drawing him to her and kissing him deeply.

They made tender love slowly, and afterwards lay in each other's arms saying nothing but treasuring the afterglow.

"How's it going with Salome?" said Phillip.

"It's an emotional journey full of drama," said Amanda going on to explain what had happened the previous day.

"How did this Cristina find out about Salome being at the lawyer's office?" said Phillip when she'd finished.

"We guessed she must be related to Mario's executor, this architect Vicente Ayala."

"What about her son; did he look like Mario?"

"We don't know what Mario looked like."

Phillip reached for his phone and searched on YouTube. Seconds later, he showed her an old video.

"This is Mario Vargas at a Madrid theater in 1973. Could that be him?"

Amanda sat up and looked more closely. She watched fascinated by the dancing and the man playing the guitar on a chair at the back of the stage. There was no doubt it was Salome's uncle; the facial resemblance was uncanny. "And that must be her father Jesús playing the guitar. They're good and no, Cristina's son looked nothing like Mario."

"Has Salome said what she should do about Cristina?"

"We haven't discussed it. What would you do?"

"Until I knew for certain about their marital status, I'd try and keep her sweet. Meanwhile, don't go wandering around any gypsy neighborhoods in Vélez on your own. It could be dangerous. Sorry darling, but we need to get on with the wine bodega project before we meet Salome. Shower, some fruit then home office?"

"Can't we snuggle a little bit longer?"

"At this rate, you'll be pregnant by the weekend."

"I hope so."

***

"When did Salome say she finishes her stint at the Cervantes?" said Phillip as he and Amanda crossed the busy road that divided Amanda's apartment block from The Mercado Central Atarazanas.

"Tonight," said Amanda as they walked holding hands through the imposing Arab archway and into the bustling market. "And just to remind my forgetful old fart, she has a week off before rehearsals begin for her new show in Barcelona. She wants to use the time to deal with her inheritance. We start again Friday morning with a visit to the convent with my contact in the Vélez Tourist Office."

"Sorry, I switched off when the shopping talk started at the restaurant. Will helping Salome take all of your time my love? Only, tomorrow morning, Prado wants me to go with him to interview Crown in prison."

"I don't know, let's ask her," said Amanda spotting Salome perched on a barstool at the fish bar drinking mineral water.

Salome didn't look happy but brightened on seeing the two of them.

They exchanged cheek kisses, sat down, ordered more waters and a ration of grilled Málaga Bay Prawns. The bar formed one end of a fresh fish stall. The other was made up of display fridges packed with wriggling crabs in a basket, a wide variety of whole and partly cut fish laid on an ice-covered slab, on top stood a tank containing live lobsters and crayfish.

"Did you read the album?" said Amanda.

"Couldn't put it down," said Salome. "It was just what the doctor ordered. Now I know more about my bunch of weirdos than I'll ever need to. Somehow, I feel less different."

"That's fantastic," said Phillip. "Did the album contain anything that might throw some light on the good character of your grandfather?"

"Actually, yes. There was one newspaper cutting from 1930 published in *Renovacion*, a bi-monthly Vélez newspaper which I found compelling and added weight to the information we have so far that describes my grandfather as a good citizen."

"What was it about?" said Phillip.

"It was an article about a Max Augustin. He was a German soldier who served in the fifth army on the Western Front during the First World War. In December 1916, when the French recaptured some fort or other near Verdun; Max was one of six thousand prisoners taken.

"Conditions in the POW camp were atrocious, so to brighten things up for the Catholics among them, Max reverted to his skills learned as an apprentice restorer of religious artifacts in the magnificent Baroque churches and cathedrals of his homeland in Bavaria. Out of what was basically trash, barbed wire, and dried mud, he made them a statue of the Virgin Mary then painted it by mixing flower petals with chalk and water. It was so beautiful that all the camp marveled at his creation, including a local French priest.

"This priest arranged for Max to be released into his care to restore the many damaged and ignored artifacts in Verdun church. Now he could work with proper materials, the quality of Max's work was outstanding. When a visiting Bishop saw what Max had done, he was transferred to Reims where he repeated his magic.

"By now the war was over and Max was being well paid for his services and enjoying the delights of the many widowed ladies, their delightful cuisine and wine. Each completed project led him to another and slowly he headed south toward the Spanish border where he was discovered in Toulouse by a Spanish bishop from Barcelona.

"And so, the process repeated itself. By the time that he'd reached Andalusia, Max had amassed a not inconsiderable sum. When the project he was working on in Granada came to an end, he headed for the coast for a well-earned rest. Hearing about how desperate things were in Germany, he was more than happy to continue his preferred Mediterranean lifestyle and balmy climate, especially when at an evening of Flamenco in Vélez-Málaga, he met and fell in love with Josefina, a local gypsy girl.

"They married in 1920 at the Convent Las Claras and as a thank you to the Sisters he made an amazing *retablo*, a backdrop to the altar plus an outstanding Virgin Mary. While he was working on-site, he expressed a desire for a nearby workshop, so the Sisters granted him a free lease on part of the land on what was then their vegetable garden.

"He built a small brick structure with the help of a young gypsy laborer who was a school friend of his wife. This laborer was Abraham Vargas. Max was so impressed with the quality of my grandfather's work, his diligence, and honesty that he offered him a full-time job as his apprentice. He then set about building an international business that created new and restored old artifacts.

Salome paused and looked at her friends.

"What do you think?" she said.

"It's a great character reference for Abraham," said Phillip. "And as you said, adds weight to the likelihood of his innocence. However, it's still speculation. The only way to really clear his name is to find the treasure or at least discover what happened to it."

"Is that what you want to do?" said Amanda. "Search for it and rescue your grandfather's name?"

"I know I promised my great aunt," said Salome. "But after the call I had earlier from Delgado, I'm not sure I'll be able to deliver on that."

"What did he say?" said Amanda.

"He's completed his searches in the Land Registry and the Town Hall."

"Is it bad?" said Amanda. "Only you don't look too happy."

"The current deeds are exactly as the copy included in my father's papers," said Salome. "Which apparently is good and makes a strong case for me to prove any claim should I wish to make one. However, there are a number of complications that might make that difficult, the first being that my parents never made a will."

"That shouldn't be a problem," said Phillip. "There are strict laws in Spain how an estate should be divided up. As the only inheritor with no children of your own, you would automatically be entitled to the first refusal on everything."

"Thanks, Phillip, but I am familiar with our probate laws however, there are other issues to consider," said Salome. "Caja MonteMar, the original bank that helped my father to finance the building of the new convent and to acquire the old one, was only a small local Building Society. Nine years ago, it went bust and its assets were absorbed into Inmobanco, a new state-owned corporation established to mop up the millions of bad property loans from the 2008 crash. Inmobanco took a charge against Las Claras, on which interest has been accruing. That sum is now around the same as the current estimated value of the property."

"Which is?" said Phillip.

"Three hundred and seventy thousand Euros."

"That's extremely low for such a large plot in a town center location. Why did the bank take out a charge?" asked Phillip.

"My father never repaid the loan," said Salome.

"Wait," said Phillip. "Amanda told me that there was a life insurance policy to cover that loan. Did they not pay it?"

"Apparently not," said Salome.

"That is complicated," said Phillip.

"Hold on, there's more," said Salome. "The workshop built by Max and my grandfather is still there and has been expanded quite substantially over the years. The business is now run by Max's granddaughter Sonia. Sonia, bless her, has offered to buy the convent from the bank."

"Why would she want to?" said Amanda. "It's a crumbling old ruin."

"I don't know and normally, I wouldn't care," said Salome. "But as of this morning, her offer is a pain in the butt."

"Why?" said Amanda.

"In the early hours of this morning, while I lay staring at the ceiling in my hotel room thinking about the convent, I had an epiphany moment about what I could do for the future. You know I've spent the last dozen or so years traveling the world performing in most of its iconic theaters. One of the consistent conversations that crop up during the after-show get-togethers, especially when I'm in Japan or the USA, is where can students learn to dance like me?"

"And?" said Phillip.

"In a tailor-made Flamenco University.

"Amanda, Phillip; Las Claras would be perfect. A striking town center property with onsite accommodation, a world-renowned teacher, an ample supply of musicians from the buoyant gypsy community. It would fulfill a huge demand and provide me with an opportunity to work until the end of my days doing something I feel really passionate about."

"That's a brilliant idea," said Amanda. "And it would help put Vélez firmly on the global map."

"That's why I'm dejected about Sonia'soffer. I have to stop her from buying the convent. Could you and Phillip help me?"

"Of course," they said in unison.

"It's an exciting project," said Amanda.

"We'll have to work out how you will be paid for your efforts," said Salome.

"Thanks, but…," said Amanda.

"No buts, I insist that we keep this on a commercial footing," said Salome.

"I agree," said Phillip. "However, our first challenge is to deal with Sonia. From what I've heard, I don't think that Delgado is up to the mark on his own, plus he's too involved with the Vélez local administration, which may well divide his loyalties. What we need is a completely independent rottweiler to sit alongside him who will represent you and you alone."

"You're right. Do you know someone?" said Salome.

"Oh yes," said Amanda. "Lisa Gabaldon will be perfect, she specializes in property and inheritance. However, she's incredibly busy."

"This will be a high profile case," said Phillip. "Right up her street."

"Do you know her?" said Salome.

"We've met briefly a couple of times at social functions," said Amanda. "However, Richard, our business partner has worked with her."

"I'll call him now," said Phillip.

Phillip extracted his phone from his jacket pocket and headed outside to call Richard.

"Are you sure you want to do this?" said Amanda stroking her friend's hand.

"Half of me is terrified about where this might go," said Salome. "The rest of me though is champing at the bit."

The waiter placed their order of king prawns on the bar in front of them. They looked and smelled delicious. Neither of them noticed and continued to sip their waters in quiet contemplation, minds wrestling with the conflicting emotions of excitement and uncertainty.

"Lisa is in court," said Phillip reaching out and helping himself to a prawn. The shell fell off easily as he peeled and popped it into his mouth. "Mmm, sooo fresh and the taste?"

"Typical man," said Amanda. "Oblivious to the mood of the moment and thinking only of his stomach."

"Life goes on," said Phillip. "But you do have an appointment with Lisa at her office tomorrow morning."

"Brilliant, I can't wait," said Salome looking much more certain.

"What about Cristina?" said Phillip.

"I don't know," said Salome. "Any suggestions?"

"No, but she is a gypsy living in a town with a large population that will support her claim irrespective of its validity. I understand it's the gypsy way. If you want to build a Flamenco university in a town full of them I suggest that you involve her, recognize her and get her on your side. Then all the others would follow you and not Sonia."

Salome absorbed Phillip's suggestion, head nodding and said. "It's a bit early yet to say for sure, but that's good advice and I'll bear it in mind."

"Wherever this project is going to take us," said Amanda. It will involve a lot of kicking things around as we evaluate the best way forward. Purely for the sake of convenience, why not move into our guest suite for the duration."

"Great idea," said Phillip. "And you wouldn't be so lonely."

"Let me think about it for a microsecond," said Salome. "It's kind of you but you don't need to…"

"Nonsense," said Amanda. "We insist."

"Then I'll happily accept."

13

"Ah, Señor Crown. Sit down please," said Prado indicating the chair opposite. The escorting officer removed the prisoner's handcuffs, closed the visiting room door, and stood at attention outside. His bulky shoulders just visible through the frosted glass panel.

Prado had driven Phillip up to *Penitenciario de Málaga*-Málaga's super modern and spacious prison located some ten kilometers west of the city and to the north of Alhaurin de Torre. They had stopped for coffee at a small roadside café on the way where they discussed their interview strategy for Crown and O'Reilly. They would see them separately and talk to Crown first, presuming that he was the weaker personality of the two.

Malcolm Crown, in blue pants and a gray T-shirt, was a short, skinny, effeminate man with slender hands and greasy unkempt dark hair. His gaunt grey face, chin, and neck were covered by several days' stubble. He glared hard at the two of them through bloodshot blue-gray eyes then leaned indolently against the wall by the door.

"You look like shit," said Prado smiling. "Prison life suiting you?"

"Vete a la mierda - fuck off," said Crown in perfect Spanish.

"Happily, said Prado. "But first a few home truths and then a surprise."

Crown shrugged.

"Since you've been enjoying our Michelin Star accommodation, somebody has transferred your money from Gibraltar. It's gone to an account in the name of CVS Holdings Ltd., in a bank located in the Turks and Caicos Islands. We've also discovered that a data center based in Mumbai, India, is also an asset of the same company and provides web design and hosting to one of Spain's largest hotel groups. Anything you can tell us about this relationship?"

"No comment," said Crown covering a yawn with his hand.

"As you have no contact with the outside world, someone else must have transferred your funds and I was wondering," Prado paused and extracted a photo from his inside jacket pocket and placed it in front of Crown. "If it was this man?"

Crown couldn't resist and glanced at the photo.

Phillip watched astounded as Crown's demeanor changed from contrived apathy to white rage. With blood vessels about to pop, he rushed over to the table, snatched up the photo, ripped it apart and scattered the remnants over the table. He sat down and slumped over the table, head buried in his arms, and shuddering.

"Likeable fellow was he, Señor Marquez?" said Prado.

Crown sat up and collected himself and used the front of his shirt to wipe the tears from his eyes and the snot from his nose. "You found the photos then?" said Crown.

"Thanks to your cryptic nudge in the right direction," said Prado.

"And him?" said Crown nodding at the ripped photo.

"Should we be looking for him?" said Prado.

"He's worse than evil," said Crown.

"Last time I looked, being evil was not an indictable offense," said Prado. "Perhaps you have some incriminating charges that we could use to justify the use of police resources in finding him?"

"I don't even know if he's alive," said Crown.

"I take it then that he has nothing to do with CVS Holdings," said Prado,

Crown shook his head.

"Then perhaps Marquez was your headmaster at school," said Phillip staying in Spanish.

"He was also supposed to be our art teacher," said Crown staring down at the table. "We stole his camera to take the photos in that film."

"Who are 'we'?" said Phillip.

"Never mind," said Crown. "The most important reason to find him is that he stole money from my father."

"Was he the administrator of the company that managed the school?" said Phillip.

"Right," said Crown.

"And as such, he would have been heavily involved in the negotiations to sell the school to the golf course developer?" said Phillip.

"He was, and the bastard stitched us up royally."

"How?" said Phillip.

"It was the days when the seller and purchaser agreed to keep the property price low on the deeds and pay the rest of the actual sales value in cash. Both parties would attend a notary appointment to seal the transfer of property. After signing, Marquez would receive a five percent commission, the remainder was due to the school's outright owner; my father. Dad was only five minutes late for the notary appointment to complete the transaction. He assumed that as usual, they would be kept waiting. But Marquez had brought the meeting forward by an hour. He'd signed the papers on his own, which as administrator, he was entitled to do, and gone straight to the bank to withdraw the cash. By the time my dad reached the bank, Marquez had disappeared."

"And you've never seen him since?" said Prado.

"No, despite employing the best detective agencies."

"How much did Marquez steal from you?" said Phillip.

"Under the original terms of the deal, we would have received just over two million. However, my father discovered from the planning office that the permission granted to the developer was for a bigger project that included nine hundred properties, not four hundred. It had substantially increased the value of the school plot. Marquez hadn't informed my father about these modifications, or that he'd agreed a much higher cash element of the deal. He walked away with over six hundred and sixty-four million pesetas, some four million Euros of our family's money."

"Did your father report this to the police?" said Phillip.

"No," said Crown.

"Why not?" said Phillip.

"At the time, my father never spoke of it. I only learned years later that his business activities in Spain at the time tended toward the dodgy and he didn't want to raise his profile with the authorities. Shortly after Marquez vanished, we all went to England."

"That still doesn't explain," said Phillip, "why you and whoever, went to the trouble to steal a camera and take clandestine photos of your art teacher."

Prado reached into his pocket, extracted more photos of Marquez showing him outside the school and his house. He placed them before Crown and nodded to Phillip.

"I'll speak in English," said Phillip. "In case your answers may cause embarrassment in front of the Inspector." Phillip paused and scrutinized Crown's bloodshot eyes. However, Crown had fully recovered his senses and stared back saying nothing.

"These photos," said Phillip. "Tell a story about Marquez. Where he lives, his habits and lifestyle. There are no pictures of a wife, so I assume you were implying that he was single. Why did you take them, what message are they supposed to tell us, and why did you want the police to find them?"

"Enough," said Crown in Spanish, standing and striding over to bang on the door. "This interview has just ended."

The prison officer opened the door, raised his eyebrows to Prado who nodded. Crown was re-cuffed and taken away.

A few minutes later, another officer appeared with Patrick O'Reilly, also in prison garb. He limped over and sat down opposite Prado. He was a mean-looking man, with a dour expression, cold hard grey eyes and had a small scar running down the side of his lip. His nose was crooked as if it had been left alone to mend after being rearranged. There was a hint of gray in his cropped black hair. Stubble covered his face and neck. He was a big imposing man and despite initial appearances, Phillip thought he looked a lot fitter and more muscular than when he last saw him a few months previously. The generously equipped prison gymnasium was obviously serving him well.

Prado reached into his pocket for a duplicate photo of Marquez and held it face down on the table in front of O'Reilly.

"I'll tell you what we asked Crown," said Prado still holding the photo. "Concerning CVS Holdings, their ownership of the data center in Mumbai and one of their largest clients Pablo Bosque."

O'Reilly raised his eyes from the desk and stared inscrutably at Prado then Phillip.

"Not interested," he said.

"Thank you, Crown was as equally helpful." Prado flipped the photo and said, "Both of us want to find this man. What can you tell us about him?"

O'Reilly glanced at the image, stared hard at Prado and Phillip then stood and banged on the door without saying a word.

Prado let him go.

As they walked toward the car park, Phillip said, "At least our visit cleared up why Crown senior went to the Marbella planning office that day and why he was so angry?"

"And we know that the photo is of Marquez," said Prado.

"O'Reilly behaved just as I expected," said Phillip.

"But I was surprised by Crown's reaction to the photos. I assumed that he would have his emotions about Marquez under control after all these years."

"Obviously not, any ideas why?"

"It must have been as we thought. Marquez was abusing Crown?" said Phillip.

"Him, and by the number of different prints on the film canister, three others," said Prado. "One of which was O'Reilly."

"Any traces of Marquez?"

"Nope, not a damn thing."

14

"I've been an avid fan of yours for years," said Lisa Gabaldon welcoming Salome and Amanda at the doorway of her roomy office. She led them over to a large picture window that overlooked Calle Larios, Málaga's principal shopping street that was swarming with people. They lowered themselves into comfortable leather armchairs surrounding a timber coffee table covered with legal and fashion magazines. "Coincidently, I thoroughly enjoyed your show at the Cervantes earlier in the week. It was the first time I'd seen you live, and it's a privilege to help you in any way I can."

Lisa was a little older, about the same height but more slender than Amanda, with short dark hair, brown eyes and dressed casually in black jeans and a plain bottle-green blouse. However, her direct gaze was disarming, when she spoke her voice commanded attention, and she oozed confidence from every olive-skinned pore.

"Thank you, Lisa," said Salome. "My current lawyer for this matter is Delgado in Vélez-Málaga. He's well established, professional and efficient but I suspect that he is too intertwined with the business and political community there to totally focus on representing my interests independently from local pressures."

"I understand," said Lisa. "And you need an out of towner to rattle their cage. What do you want to achieve?"

"Mendosa is my adopted surname. I've only recently discovered that my birth name is Vargas and that I've inherited property from my late uncle Mario Vargas in Vélez-Málaga. Also, my late father; Jesús Vargas is the current owner of a plot of land, church and Convent buildings in the center of Vélez known as Convento Las Claras. According to the deeds, it is by rights mine to inherit but the bank is claiming otherwise. All I want is to accept my inheritance without any strings attached by the bank."

"What do you want to do with the convent?" said Lisa.

"Convert it into an international Flamenco University."

"That's a great idea. It's bound to attract enormous political support both in Vélez and here in Málaga. If the convent is yours to inherit, why is the bank not accepting that?"

"Something about unpaid interest. However, there was a life insurance policy to cover my father's loan. Somehow, the bank has conveniently forgotten about that."

"I see. Happily, I've worked with Delgado and his family in the past and we have a good relationship, but

I will need you to instruct him to send me copies of the relevant documents. Then, I'll study them closely and if it all stacks up as you say it does, I'll take whatever action necessary to counter the bank's claim."

"That would be great, however, there is another tiny complication," said Salome.

"There usually is," said Lisa. "Tell me."

"About a hundred years ago, the nuns granted a free lease in perpetuity to Max Augustin on part of the land to the rear of the property. It was for him to build a workshop for the manufacture and restoration of religious artifacts. They made this offer in exchange for him restoring the convent free of charge which, over a period of years he did a magnificent job. Max's granddaughter Sonia now owns the company and continues to use the workshop free of charge. Recently, she made an offer to the bank to buy the convent which the bank has accepted."

"But how could they do that when the deeds are in your name?" said Lisa.

"That is for you to find out but more importantly to stop the transaction from going ahead."

"That shouldn't be a problem," said Lisa. "Now that an heir to the convent has appeared."

"So does that mean," said Salome. "That it will be necessary to mention the Vargas name?"

"Why wouldn't you want to use it?"

Salome glanced at Amanda with eyebrows raised. Amanda nodded and smiled.

"It's a delicate matter, I'm afraid," said Salome. "Concerning my grandfather and the disappearance of the convent's treasury during the Civil War. The Vargas name might still generate negative reactions among those that still remember the story. Until I've uncovered the truth about that, I'd rather keep my relationship with the Vargas family out of the equation. Will that matter?"

"That depends," said Lisa. "On whether you want to inherit the property or compete with Sonia to purchase it."

Amanda and Salome exchanged frowns.

"The property will cost you a fortune to refurbish," said Amanda. "Competing with Sonia to buy it will add yet more to the bill. Why not just come straight out and admit that you are Salome Vargas, the convent is yours by right. Then Sonia will simply be taken out of the equation."

Salome looked at Lisa, who nodded then said, "Amanda's right. "It'll be quicker and cheaper to publicly announce who you are and why you want the Convent."

"So what you are advising," said Salome. "Is that I should accept the inheritance now."

"It will make my job less complex," said Lisa.

Salome stood and paced around the room. She stopped at the window and gazed at the shoppers below breathing deeply.

"OK," she said turning back. "Let's do it. I want the convent. Whatever my family may or may not have done is all in the past, and has absolutely nothing to do with me."

"Atta girl," said Amanda. "Do you need anything from us?"

"Just your contact details. Listen, there is something you should know about me. I have my own way of working which some clients have difficulty accepting. I can assure you that I will be working hard on your case but what that means is, I won't be stopping every five minutes to give you a progress report. If I don't call you, it means nothing is happening. As soon as I start achieving, you'll be the first to know."

"That's fine, but if I call you," said Salome. "It'll be with new information or instructions and I'll expect you to be available for that."

"Then we should work well together," said Lisa, standing.

They shook hands, had their documents copied by Lisa's personal assistant and left.

***

Barbara picked them up at the end of Calle Larios and headed east toward the motorway.

"It's likely that Gabriella, our guide for Las Claras will repeat a lot of what was in the letters from Mario and your father."

"That's expected," said Salome. "Be interesting to hear if it what she says varies from what we've learned already."

Barbara drove to the center of Vélez-Málaga where she parked illegally by a kiosk outside the Ayuntamiento in the charming tree-lined Plaza de las Carmelitas. Amanda jumped out and ran over the wide pavement grinning cheekily at the local policeman sitting on his motorcycle at the far end of the parking bay which was reserved for local officials. The cop shrugged and continued to consult his mobile phone. She returned with a slender, well-dressed lady in her early fifties. Barbara opened the front door and the lady climbed in.

"This is our guide, Gabriella," said Amanda as Barbara pulled out into the stream of traffic.

"Hola Gabriella," said Salome.

"My friend Salome," said Amanda. "She's working with me on a Flamenco project and was keen to see the convent if that's OK?"

"Salome Mendosa?" said Gabriella turning around with an astonished expression. "Wow, I'm a great fan. It'll be my pleasure to show you around."

Five minutes later, they arrived at Calle Felix Lomas, where Gabriella climbed out waving a bunch of large rusty keys and headed for the entrance that led to the rear of the Convent. Gabriella opened the black wrought iron gates and guided Barbara through.

Beyond the narrow entrance, the concrete passageway widened. Citrus trees and single-storey outbuildings lined the left-hand side and at the far end, in front of a high white wall, there was room enough to turn the car around. They climbed out, Barbara locked the car and joined Gabriella waiting at the entrance to the nuns' quarters.

"Before we go inside," said Gabriella pointing beyond their parked car. "On the other side of that wall is the workshop of Restauraciones Augustin. Until the nineteen twenties, the space used to be the herb and vegetable garden of the convent, but it was too much labor for so few nuns, so they leased the space out free of charge in perpetuity. I don't think that I mentioned this during your previous visit Amanda, but in case you didn't know, their tenant was Max Augustin, a former German soldier from Munich. Before he was conscripted into the First World War trenches, he was a talented religious artifacts craftsman. He was captured by the French, and somehow his skills were discovered by a visiting preacher to his POW camp. He was released and put to work restoring French churches. After the war, he worked his way down to Granada and ended up in Vélez for a holiday. While here, he met and married a local gypsy girl and stayed. In his spare time, Max restored the Las Claras church adding a new backdrop to the altar plus the magnificent icon of the Virgin Mary, which we will see later in the tour. The nuns were so grateful they offered him this amazing tenancy.

"Max's company expanded and today has several factories scattered around Vélez. Regretfully, the demand for religious artifacts has tumbled and Max's granddaughter Sonia, who runs the Company, wants to bring all its activities under one roof to save costs. They are selling their other buildings to fund the outright purchase of the workshop and convent. She has also offered to restore the church and donate it to the town in return for being allowed to knock down the cloisters to expand the workshop."

"That makes for an interesting article on its own," said Amanda. "Perhaps I should meet this Sonia?"

"I'm sure she'd be happy to talk," said Gabriella. "Any positive publicity that helps her acquire the convent would be welcome. I'll give you her number."

"Thanks," said Amanda. "There's one thing that puzzles me though. If the workshop is permanently rent-free," said Amanda. "Why would Sonia want to purchase it?"

"Nobody can envisage what will happen to Las Claras in the future," said Gabriella. "Yet it is deeply entrenched in the hearts of generations of Vélez townspeople. Many were married here, had their children baptized, or their parents interred in one of the memorial plots. No one wants to see it go. Sonia wishes to make sure it stays."

"That's a powerful argument in Sonia's favor," said Salome. "What's the gossip on the current Convent owner?"

"It's common knowledge that Inmobanco has assumed ownership even though the property is still registered to the late Jesús Vargas. He was a famous homegrown Flamenco musician back in the sixties and seventies. When he disappeared in the eighties, the bank took over responsibility for the building. I have to request approval from the local manager to show people around and obtain the keys."

They climbed a step up into a musty room with a high beamed ceiling. Several faded religious prints in shabby frames decorated the walls, but all the furnishings had gone leaving a bare uneven stone floor dotted with items of litter including an old paper coffee cup and an empty sticky tape dispenser. In the center of the end wall was a small fireplace, its shabby grill still intact containing the remnants of some kindling. It looked like newspaper. Amanda couldn't resist and went over to look at the date.

"2012," she said after moments fumbling with a corner. "I assumed it would be older."

"The convent was still in use for various functions right up until its final safety inspection about six years ago," said Gabriella walking over to another door, turning the handle and giving it a firm shove. The old timber door squeaked open. "Sadly, it failed the test and the whole building was condemned and declared unsafe for public use. And yet it's as dry as a bone everywhere even after the heaviest of rains, so the roof must be in good condition."

"I better put that in our article," said Amanda. "It's a shame that such a grand old building can't be put to some sort of use. All she needs is some tender loving care."

"And some serious structural repairs," said Gabriella. "The church walls, especially the tower, need major work according to the engineer's report."

"Could I see that?" asked Amanda. "Just so I can be accurate in my descriptions of its current condition."

"I'll email you a copy," said Gabriella.

Gabriella led them out into the cloisters. A rectangular green space with a cracked and empty fountain in its center was surrounded by a covered walkway supported by seven arches along the length and five at each end. The gardens were unkempt and overgrown, but it was still possible to appreciate the peace and tranquility enjoyed by the nuns for so many centuries. They walked through the garden to the far cloister.

"Why do the flagstones have a number on each corner?" asked Amanda as they walked along the cloister toward the rear entrance of the church. "For example, this one reads two hundred and seven, the next two hundred and eight, etc."

"They are memorial stones," said Gabriella. "There are three hundred and forty-two of them around the building. After they ran out of space inside, they used the treasury and then the cloisters. Some have urns underneath; others are just in memory. As the stones are quite small it was thought better to chisel them with a number rather than lots of tiny text. There used to be a directory that linked the numbers to the names of the deceased but that disappeared during the sisters' relocation to the new convent on the Arenas Road."

"They do that number thing for memorial stones in

several churches," said Amanda. "The cathedral in Pamplona particularly, but they still have their directory."

Gabriella opened the door and they stepped down into the church.

Although it was gloomy and musty, Salome gasped at its faded beauty. An arched white ceiling soared above their heads decorated with dusty ornate moldings, but the chandeliers had been removed. On both side walls, were mounted grey marble panels that commemorated local families. The plinths on which the icons used to stand were empty, they'd been transferred to the new convent. Some of the original carved timber fittings such as the pulpit remained in place, but the diamond-patterned black and white tiled floor had been cleared except for a couple of wooden bench seats and some individual high-backed chairs. At the far end of the floor, two steps led up to a decorous stone altar sitting before a backdrop of four granite columns decorated with religious paraphernalia. Sitting between and set back from the two central columns was a magnificent statue of the seated Virgin Mary.

"I can understand the reluctance to knock this down," said Salome her voice echoing around the empty church. "Who would dare wield the first blow and incur the wrath of the spirits guarding this holy place?"

Amanda looked at her friend astonished where this appreciation of religious wrecks had sprung from.

Salome shrugged and headed toward the altar. Gabriella walked alongside her. "Where does that go?" said Salome pointing to a tall timber door tucked into a recess in the wall to the right of the altar.

"The old treasury," said Gabriella. "Do you want to

look?"

"Is it open?" said Salome.

"Of course, nothing there to steal nowadays," said Gabriella. "Have you heard the story?"

"Tell me," said Salome.

"All the contents disappeared during the Civil War."

"Stolen?" said Amanda.

"It was never proven because the suspected perpetrator vanished at the same time. However, evidence was later discovered linking Jesús Vargas' father Abraham to the crime. Eventually, the courts declared Abraham guilty in his absence, but not everyone was convinced it was him. Apparently, he was a well-respected citizen."

"Do people still talk about the disappearing treasure?" said Salome.

"Nowadays no. But for a while, the story blew hot and cold. After the war, everyone was too busy surviving to bother with it but the mystery was rekindled during the early 1980s when Jesús helped out the elderly nuns by funding the construction of a new, smaller convent out on the Arenas Road and purchasing this one. Everyone admired him for that but wondered how he'd made enough money from his Flamenco activities to be able to afford it. People were relieved when the new convent was finished, and the nuns relocated but were astonished when Jesús and his wife then vanished into thin air. Many were concerned about what would happen to the old convent without Jesús around to complete its refurbishment. However, as the years went by and the older generations died people forgot about it. The bank would occasionally hold open days to celebrate Easter and our local Saints

Day but each year fewer and fewer bothered to attend.

"When Abraham's eldest son died recently nobody mentioned it at all. Therefore, I think we can safely say that today, people associate the convent's ownership with Inmobanco. Any association with the Vargas name means nothing to the current generation. Generally, I believe that everyone will be happy when a permanent solution is settled on that makes sensible use of the space, such as the offer from Sonia Augustin."

"How do the nuns in the new convent feel about that?" said Amanda.

"None are alive from those days. You'd have to ask the current occupants, not that there are many."

"I'm surprised that there are any at all," said Salome.

"There are only a couple of elderly Spanish nuns left," said Gabriella. "The remainder are from Kenya."

Gabriella leaned against the heavy treasury door and shoved hard. It squeaked open. They walked through into a light and spacious room with a high beamed ceiling. The glazing in the large window was surprisingly clean. Spread around the floor space was an untidy arrangement of different sized dusty glass display cabinets. Some of them still contained the faded printed tags describing their contents. Barbara went over to the largest case in the center of the room and gasped as she read the tag out loud. "Santa Maria, La Pinta, and La Niña. The ships of Columbus. What were they doing here?"

"They used to be the centerpiece of the collection," said Gabriella. "The miniature golden statues were donated to the nuns during the late nineteenth century by the descendants of Luis de Torres, a Jewish convert who lived in Torrox. He'd sailed with Christopher

Columbus as a translator and on his return had them cast in Toledo with his share of the profits. They must be worth a fortune today."

"Is there anyone still around that would know more detail of the inventory?" said Amanda.

Gabriella thought for a moment, shook her head, and said. "The town librarian might have various newspaper cuttings but with the passing of Abraham's last relative, I'm pretty confident that any remaining information went with him."

Amanda and Salome exchanged discreet glances then wandered around the room checking out the memorial stone numbers. They both glanced at number one hundred and twenty-nine which was in the far corner next to a window that overlooked the cloisters. Other than its different numbers, it was identical to those surrounding it.

They left the church and walked toward the remaining rooms. Two floors surrounded each side of the cloisters. Their footsteps echoed on the creaky wooden floorboards as they trailed after Gabriella through the upper floor where the nuns sleeping quarters had been. The ground floor was of stone and had been home to the kitchen, pantry, refectory, laundry, and some offices for the more senior nuns.

As they walked back to the car, Amanda noticed that Salome was quiet and reflective.

"I hope you enjoyed the visit," said Gabriella on the way back to the Town Hall. "Did you discover enough to write an update article?"

"I did thanks, Gabriella," said Amanda. "Especially when I receive the engineer's report from you and I'm definitely interested in doing something on Sonia's father."

"I'll email you everything as soon as I'm back at my desk," said Gabriella. "It was my pleasure to show you around, Salome. Will you be in the area for long?"

"If all goes well, about a week. Why?"

"The mayor will kill me if I don't invite you to our Peña de Flamenco tomorrow tonight, just to see how we do things here. I'm confident that you'll be pleasantly surprised at how good our performers are."

"Will the Mayor be there?" said Salome.

"Oh yes, he goes every week," said Gabriella. "Usually, about ten o'clock when things have livened up a bit.

"Then please confirm that I am happy to attend," said Salome.

"Thank you, Salome, I will. It will also be a good opportunity for you to meet Sonia Augustin."

"Why?"

"She and her husband manage the Flamenco club. He is also one of our best dancers," she said dreamily. "Such a handsome man."

As soon as they had dropped off Gabriella back at the Tourist Office, Salome exploded with enthusiasm. "Amanda, dearest friend," she said. "I love Las Claras. It's perfect for my Flamenco University. We have to tell Lisa. I must have it, whatever it takes."

"Are you crazy? It will be super expensive."

"Actually, from what I've seen today, it shouldn't be that bad. We'll need an architect to survey everything, design some concepts then estimate a scope of works and a budget."

"Look, Salome," said Amanda. "I would love for Las Claras to be renovated and given a purpose but your scaring me with this gung-ho attitude. Are your pockets deep enough? I would hate to see you wiped out financially. It would mean your lifetime's work going up in smoke."

"Amanda, calm down. Believe me, I have enough for this. Now, help me find an architect."

"Sorry, I'm not being obstructive, just protective."

They hugged. "I know," said Salome, and thanks. Architect?"

"How about your uncle's friend. What was his name?"

"Of course, Vicente Ayala, but what if he is related to Cristina?"

"Then you'd be seen to be supporting the gypsies, which can only be good. We just have to make it clear to Vicente that he keeps all project information confidential. He's a professional and will put clients first. He won't want to risk his license by being indiscrete. Shall I call Delgado and arrange to meet Vicente?"

"For tomorrow morning?" said Salome.

"Makes sense," said Amanda. "It was interesting to hear Gabriella's comments about the Vargas family."

"Yes," said Salome. "Sounds like it's all water under the bridge."

"At least now you won't have to worry about any recriminations against you because of the Vargas name," said Amanda. "But how do you feel about meeting Sonia? Especially, if all goes well with Lisa and the bank. How is she going to react knowing that you've stolen the convent from beneath feet?"

15

"Hola Lisa," said Salome into her mobile phone. She was perched on a stool at the kitchen island opposite Amanda and Phillip enjoying a leisurely bowl of fruit for their first breakfast together in Amanda's apartment. "How did it go yesterday?"

"More difficult than I thought," said Lisa, her voice booming on Salome's speakerphone. "I spoke with the Mayor who loved the idea of your Flamenco University, so I don't envisage any planning objections but Inmobanco is being most obstructive. They are sticking to the terms agreed with a local buyer and aren't prepared to delay the final notary appointment due next week for any reason."

"So that's it?" said Salome, shoulders slumping.

"Not by a long shot," said Lisa. "Late last night, I spoke with the president of the bank in Madrid."

"And?" said Salome.

"I told him who you were and advised him to make inquiries as to why the bank refused to pay out on your father's life insurance policy. Then I threatened him with media exposure if he couldn't come up with a valid reason. Remember, this is a state-owned bank. Politically, it would be a disaster if one of Spain's best-loved Flamenco stars has been ripped off by the establishment."

"Let's hope your shock tactics work," said Salome. "When will you hear?"

"He's calling me back sometime today."

"On a Saturday?"

"Otherwise, I've promised him it will be all over the Sunday front pages."

"Do we know how much Sonia Augustin has offered the bank for the convent?" said Salome.

"I don't know," said Lisa. "I've had my accountant analyze her last published accounts. She's fairly sure that Sonia is practically bankrupt and unless she completes the sale of her other factories before next week's notary appointment, she won't have the funds to buy the convent."

"How near is Sonia to selling her other factories?"

"Pretty close," said Lisa. "Why?"

"I'm thinking of letting her buy the workshop plot from me at a discounted price. I want a good relationship with her and will need some of her craftsmen for my restoration work."

"How much are you asking?"

"I thought around seventy thousand Euros," said Salome.

"That is generous, and I'm sure that it will help with my discussions with the president of the bank. I'll suggest that they could provide bridging finance until Sonia receives the money from the sale of her factories."

"If you could, it means all this can be wrapped up within a day or two," said Salome.

"And it will save faces all round," said Lisa. "Which means that whatever bad things people may recall about the Vargas name will be replaced with the good things that you are doing for the town and one of its most respected businesses."

"That was my intention," said Salome.

"Wish all my clients were like you," said Lisa. "Ok. Leave it with me. I'll call you as soon as I have an agreement with all parties."

"Hopefully, before I meet Sonia at the Flamenco club tonight."

"I can only do my best," said Lisa. "Where will you be?"

"Various meetings in Vélez."

"OK," said Lisa. "I'll call when I know something definite. Hasta lluego."

***

Vicente Ayala cut a forlorn and solitary figure sitting at the window table in Café San Francisco. Several locals attempted to exchange greetings and banter but failed to make contact.

One shared his exasperation with the waiter who was overheard saying. "The lights are on, but nobody is home."

Vicente was a tall, slender, good looking man in his mid-forties with trimmed black hair, soulful hazel eyes, and a couple of day's stubble. He was dressed in blue jeans and an antique tan-colored leather jacket over a blue checked shirt.

Salome wasn't his only concern.

He was worried about his ex-fiancée. She'd dumped him the previous day complaining that he was always working and not paying her enough attention. "I don't understand her problem," he muttered to himself as his mind rambled around the ups and downs of their ten-year relationship. "Was I that bad a boyfriend?"

He stood as Salome and Amanda entered, shook himself mentally and almost smiled as he helped the ladies with the coats, seated them and took their drink requests.

Salome raised her eyebrows at Amanda, as Vicente went over to the bar. "Looks good," she whispered.

Amanda grinned.

"How did you meet my uncle?" said Salome, as Vicente returned to his seat.

"We lived next door during my childhood," said Vicente feeling more enthused now he was on familiar ground. "My parents were killed when I was eleven. My divorced aunt from Sevilla and her son who was only a few years older than I moved in to look after me. However, it was Mario who stepped in as a replacement father, we sort of adopted each other. We would chat every day and he was most supportive. He became concerned that the local school wasn't pushing me enough, so kindly paid for my education and then for architectural studies at Granada University.

"Naturally, I was extremely grateful but that wasn't all he did for me. He taught me how to dance. It started when I used to watch him practice. Eventually, he coaxed me to join in. It was amazing. Just imagine how I felt. It was every boy's dream to be taught by one of Spain's most famous dancers and there was I receiving free lessons.

"Thanks to your uncle, I am who I am and do what

I do."

"Is your aunt still alive?" said Salome.

"Sadly not, but her sister is."

"Is her name, Cristina?"

"I'd heard you met her at the lawyers."

Vicente laughed as he saw their puzzled expressions and said. "It's a small town, the gypsy network works even faster with social media."

"Then you'll know what happened after the police hauled them out of Delgado's place." said Amanda.

"They were released without charge after promising not to molest you further."

"How did she know we would be there?" said Salome.

"I don't know but I can guess."

"Enlighten us, just so we know how it works here in Vélez," said Amanda.

"I was recently engaged to the daughter of Cristina's neighbor. The neighbor is the cleaner at Delgado's office and mine. Between their natural curiosity nothing is missed. Oh, and the waiter here is Isaac's son."

"Where do Cristina and Isaac live?"

"Isaac, his wife and family live in social housing on the edge of town, but Cristina stays everywhere and nowhere. It depends who is asking. Last week it was with my cousin. This week with someone else. But if you wanted to meet with her, I could arrange it."

"Are you gypsy?" said Salome.

"My family have been here as long as yours."

"Cristina claims that she and Mario had a gypsy wedding and that he was Isaac's father," said Salome. "Is that true?"

"It's well known gossip, and has always been

Cristina's story, but only she and Mario would know the truth of it."

"Did you know that Mario was infertile?" said Salome.

"I know that he and Beatriz couldn't have children, but we never discussed the matter. It was too painful a memory for him."

"There is one way to resolve any doubt," said Amanda.

"How?" said Vicente.

"A DNA test for Isaac. Nowadays they can pinpoint family lines precisely," said Amanda.

"Should I let that be known?" said Vicente.

"Could you," said Salome. "And tell Cristina that if it proves positive, I will recognize her claim to a proportion of Mario's estate."

"And if it's negative?" said Vicente.

"We'll deal with that when the results are known, but my motivation is to secure good relationships with the gypsy community, after all, I am one of them now."

"Where do they go for a DNA test?" said Vicente. "And how would you ensure it was actually a sample from Isaac?"

"If they agree to a test, I will take Isaac personally to a laboratory," said Salome. "Providing he has a shower and puts on clean clothes."

"Ha," grinned Vicente. "OK, I'll put the question and see what comes back but you need to also consider how Cristina can save face."

"Sorry," said Salome.

"If Isaac is Mario's son, she will allow him to be tested. If not, the whole community will know that her story is bullshit and she'd be ragged silly. That would make her a bitter enemy, something best avoided among gypsies."

"If she can show me any kind of proof that she married Mario," said Salome. "I don't care what type of ceremony. I will treat her fairly. If not, she can stew in her own juice."

"That should do it," said Vicente. "And may I say if this is how you do business it will be my pleasure to serve you any way I can."

"Salome looked at him tenderly, smiled and said. "Earlier, you mentioned, that because of Mario, you are who you are. Thank you for repaying him by looking after him in his dotage."

"I loved him like a father, so it was my duty, but also a pleasure. However, I began to repay him straight after I qualified as an architect. Not because I felt obligated but because I wanted to keep our relationship going. He liked building things with his money, so I introduced him to several development opportunities. He even admired my rather oddball design concepts and together we built a number of apartment blocks around the town."

"Did you meet my father?"

"On occasions. My memories of him are fleeting but I recall a quiet and kindly man. Your mother though was wonderful. After they were married, they used to pop round to see Mario and Beatriz. My aunt was always complaining about how hard it was to care for two boys of different fathers so your Mum would come and take me out for a walk. We chatted a lot even when she was pregnant with you. I even held you when you were a baby. Then, poof, you were all gone."

"That must have been painful," said Salome.

"The worse thing was not knowing where or why. I couldn't find any closure, so I blamed it all on myself.

Mario tried to compensate with his many amusing stories of him and your dad as they traveled around the country performing. But I could sense that their disappearance had upset him as dreadfully as I, so we sort of mourned you together. Then when Beatriz killed herself, he fell apart. It was painful to watch him go downhill but even at his most inebriated he was still kindly toward me."

"Do you still dance?" said Salome leaning forward and touching Vicente's arm laying on the table.

"Nowhere near your standard, or your uncles but good enough for a juerga or two. I'll be performing at the local club tonight as I do every Saturday. Perhaps you'd care to join me?"

"Wait," he shouted. "Sorry, did I just invite one of Spain's most famous dancers to come and dance with me? What a fool, a damned..."

"Vicente," said Salome squeezing his arm. And smiling warmly at him "I'd love to dance with you this evening."

"Would you, er wow. That would be, er, amazing. Thank you, but surely that wasn't why you wanted to meet me."

"Actually, I, I mean we," indicating Amanda. "Are both going to the club tonight, I have to meet the Mayor, and if possible, Sonia Augustin."

"Oh," said Vicente with an expression of disappointment. "For a moment there I thought my long-forgotten charm and magnetism had returned."

"Were you ever married?" said Salome.

"No, but I was engaged for ten years, actually until yesterday. My fiancé accused me of putting my work before her."

Amanda and Salome nodded.

"We've both been there," said Salome. "But that's not why we asked to meet you. I wanted to thank you for delivering my uncle's papers to Delgado and for being such a good friend to him. In his letters, he was most grateful."

"Really, I never saw what was in the envelopes. I assumed it was old photos and things, you know family stuff."

"Most of it was," said Salome.

"Did you get to see your great aunt?"

"I did," said Salome sniffing. "Sadly, she died in my arms only minutes after meeting her, but I did receive a detailed album about the family which was most informative. It helped me understand where I came from."

"It must have been distressing."

Salome paused to compose herself. Amanda grasped her other arm and squeezed it.

"One final thing," said Salome moving closer to Vicente and lowering her voice. "Have you heard the story of my grandfather?"

"Of course," said Vicente.

"Have you ever discussed it with anyone?"

"Only your uncle."

"What's your opinion?"

"I can only judge Abraham on what I've learned from Mario; that he was a decent citizen who was only trying to save the treasure from looting soldiers."

"Have you heard what might happen to the convent?"

"Word on the street is that Sonia is buying it."

"You know Sonia?"

"Since she was a baby. She and her husband are friends, but mainly from a Flamenco perspective. We meet at the Flamenco club and occasionally travel together to see Flamenco shows."

"Did you know that my father purchased the convent?"

"Mario did mention it."

"In theory, I could make it mine. Should I choose to accept my inheritance and subject to discussions with the bank."

"Will you be selling it to Sonia?"

"Maybe her bit, but the rest I want to convert into a Flamenco University and bring students here from all over the world."

"Wow, that would be brilliant for Vélez. How can I help?"

"I need some realism before going ahead. We have a copy of the last engineer's building survey which doesn't seem too bad. However, I want a rough idea of how much it would cost to restore the church into a dance studio and convert the nuns' accommodation into a spa hotel with a fine dining restaurant."

"We'd need to see it together so you can outline your ideas?"

"Are you free now?" said Salome. "Only I need an idea of conversion costs before I commit to accepting my inheritance."

"Do you have keys?" said Vicente.

"No, but we know where to obtain them," said Amanda picking up her phone from the table and dialing Gabriella.

***

Vicente listened carefully to Salome's ideas as

Gabriella led them around the convent making notes on his tablet computer. Using the camera app on his phone he measured off the dimensions of each room and the thickness of load-bearing walls.

"Does this mean that you are buying the convent?" said Gabriella burning with curiosity.

While Vicente and Salome continued their survey, Amanda took her to one side and explained what Salome's intentions were. Gabriella was thrilled to be taken into their confidence. Amanda smiled as she could see Gabriella itching to phone her friends, but she restrained herself during their tour of the convent. However, as soon as they had said their goodbyes at the gate, Gabriella had her phone to her ear and was talking animatedly as she walked down the hill back toward the Town Hall. By the time they arrived at the Flamenco club that evening most of the important citizens of Vélez would know about Salome and her intentions.

They walked back to the café San Francisco, ordered coffees, and sat down. Amanda and Salome chatted while Vicente played with his online drawing software and calculator. Half an hour later, Vicente turned his tablet around and presented floor plans and rough cost estimates of the Flamenco University.

"The lower figure would be using medium quality materials," said Vicente. "The higher for the best, and I haven't included furnishings or specialist recording studio equipment."

"That's more than I thought," said Salome. "But still affordable. All we need now is to hear from Lisa."

Amanda picked up her phone and dialed Lisa's number. There was no reply.

"Excuse our impatience," said Amanda to her

voicemail. "We need to know what the bank says before we meet Sonia at ten o'clock tonight. Please let us know as soon as you can."

16

Phillip and his business partner Richard Daniels, a convivial American in his early sixties were in the final stages of a meeting with their major supermarket advertiser at their modern offices on Alameda Principal in central Málaga when Phillip's phone rang. It was Prado.

Phillip didn't answer but texted that he'd call back in five.

Please hurry, texted Prado. I need you urgently.

They wrapped up their meeting, said their farewells to whom were now friends, headed down the stairs and out onto the bustling street. The streetlamps had just come on, the sky was darkening, and a cool breeze was teasing the few remaining leaves from the platano de India trees lining the street. They paused outside the historical Málaga wine bar, Antigua Casa de Guardia.

"Happy with the outcome?" said Phillip.

"Another year's contract," said Richard in his tangy drawl. Even after twenty-odd years in Spain, it was still as broad as the day he arrived from Boston, Massachusetts. "Who wouldn't be? My only problem is that Ingrid and I would prefer to slow down a bit. We want to travel before we are too old to enjoy it."

"Have you thought more about Amanda's and my offer to buy you out?"

"Believe me, we are both giving it serious consideration but it's a difficult decision to sell our lifeblood after all these years."

"I understand."

"It's not the money, but we can only do so much traveling. What else would we do?"

"Dig out the garish golf shorts?"

"It's been too long to start all that again, I couldn't hit a ball to save my life."

"From what I've seen, you wouldn't be so different from the rest of them. How about Bridge?"

"You're kidding me, right?"

"Ingrid loves it."

"And that's how it's going to stay. Actually, I've been thinking about writing a novel. I've even made a start but it's so different from writing articles. Richard peeked inside the famous old Bodega and admired the row of Málaga wine barrels. It was busy, but there was room for them at the end of the long bar. Want to join me for a tapa and discuss it?"

"Love to, but sorry, the call at the end of the meeting was from Prado. He needs me to translate something urgently. Care to join us?"

"I promised Ingrid that I wouldn't be late. She likes me to take her out to dinner on Saturday nights."

"Then let's take a raincheck and talk again tomorrow. You need to make a decision sooner rather than later, otherwise, you'll be coming to client meetings on a mobility scooter."

"I'm not that decrepit."

"No, but you'll win a better deal selling out at the top."

"Tell me about it."

They shook hands and went their own way.

Phillip walked along the recently widened pavement to Calle Larios and turned north for the Central Comisaría.

***

"This is a report from the Gibraltar Police," said Prado waving Phillip to sit down opposite his desk. "It's in response to our International all-points bulletin requesting information about the man that we now know as Marquez. It's in English which is why I needed you urgently."

Phillip took the document and glanced at the top of the front page. It was entitled, RODRIGUEZ SANCHEZ MARQUEZ.

Phillip speed read the document and then summarized it in Spanish.

"They say that on February sixteenth, 1984, Marquez deposited a huge sum in peseta notes, which equated to just under five million UK pounds, to an account in his name at Hispano-Commercial Bank on Main Street, Gibraltar."

"It's unusual for banks in Gibraltar," said Prado. "To reveal client account details."

"There's a qualifier on the final page informing us that the bank closed in suspicious circumstances during 2003. While the police were able to rescue the records, they can't guarantee the validity of these documents. They've attached photocopies of all the Marquez account transactions, which are only a few lines. They confirm that about a week after depositing the money, he made a payment to a Gibraltar citizen for almost the entire sum, then withdrew the remaining balance and closed the account. The citizen, now deceased, confirmed that Marquez had purchased a large sailing yacht from him. Three days later, he lodged a voyage plan for the Azores with the harbormaster and sailed away on February twenty-fifth."

"And from there to anywhere on the planet," said Prado. "Where he sold the boat and lodged the money in some offshore bank with a new identity. We'll never find him now."

"Probably not. Do you want to tell Crown this?"

"Straight away, are you free?"

"Yes. Amanda is in Vélez-Málaga and won't be back until late."

Prado stood, picked up his hat and said, "Then let's go. I'll drop you back home afterward then head back up to Ronda."

"Any plans for the weekend?" said Phillip as they climbed into an unmarked car parked under the Comisaría.

"Just a quiet Saturday night at home with Inma."

"I expect she's used to your antisocial working hours," said Phillip.

"She is nowadays but how about you? Don't you ever stop working?"

"I don't see it as work. When you're self-employed, it's a way of life."

"Is that what you envisaged when you first came to Spain?"

"As you know, I sold my business in London with a view to a quieter lifestyle. However, the business model here is completely different from London. There I had long commutes, office rents, bickering staff, banks and investors always badgering me. Here, it's just me and few equal minded friends having fun doing what we love and getting paid for it. Couldn't be better."

"I hope my untimely interruptions and instant need of your services don't bug you too much?"

"It's inconvenient sometimes I have to admit, but it's most satisfying. I feel as if in some small way, I'm giving something back to my adopted country and it certainly fuels the integration process. I learn so much from you. Not just about police work, but how you think. It helps me understand you guys better and it becomes easier to fit in."

"You're a rare beast, Phillip. Most foreigners are only here for our great weather and cheap booze."

***

Crown looked wary as he entered the visitor room at Alhaurin prison and saw Phillip and Prado sat at the desk so soon after their previous visit. He looked pale and was perspiring heavily. Phillip wondered if jail time stress was exacerbating a pre-existing condition.

Prado handed Crown the Gibraltar report.

Crown read it slowly through once, and then again more quickly as if he couldn't believe what he'd seen the first time.

"The amount stacks up," he said. "But I didn't know he was a sailor."

"Did he have any other interests?" said Phillip.

Crown's face hardened and he glowered at Phillip before saying, "He was an obsessive voyeur particularly when youngsters were involved and gambled excessively on the outcome of bullfights. That's my final word." With that, Crown stood, walked over, banged on the door, and waited patiently until the warder came to collect him.

"Wow," said Phillip after Crown had left. "What a breakthrough."

"Sorry," said Prado looking puzzled.

"We must have touched a raw nerve."

"Still not with you?" said Prado rubbing his ear lobe.

"It can't be a coincidence," said Phillip.

"What?"

"Our two biggest cases are both linked to Crown's list."

"You mean voyeurism, then gambling on bulls?"

"Yes, and both involved websites provided by the mastermind we are assuming to be Crown's boss."

"Are you suggesting that in an attempt to flush out Marquez they are deliberately tempting him with his favorite obsessions."

"I would bank on it."

"How do you know Crown is being honest?"

"Until now," said Phillip. "Crown has only revealed one clue to us. 'Look in the darkness' he said, just before you wheeled him off to Alhaurin. So, you deduced that as his parent's Cortijo was called 'El Infierno' or 'Darkness' that we should search there and bingo we found the film which revealed Marquez. Thus, establishing Crown's truth credentials."

"And your point is?"

"There aren't two separate issues involved here.

There's only one thing going down and that is the hunt for Marquez."

"Wait," said Prado. "Are you suggesting that all the planning of this criminal complexity, money invested, all those people involved, victims exploited, people killed and never mind the risk exposure, is all to flush out Marquez?"

"Don't forget, they also made a fuck of a lot of money in the process. But yes, this is all about the hunt for Marquez."

"It could also mean that there is no mastermind. It's actually Crown himself."

"Except he came to Spain with no money," said Phillip.

"Then it must be one of the others whose prints were on the film canister."

"If it is, they must still be out there looking for Marquez."

"That's a whole bunch of people obsessed with finding Marquez. I'd love to know what he did to these guys."

"Me too," said Phillip. "Crown called him evil. I know that equates to the pot calling the kettle black but for them to focus all this energy and money in finding him, it must have been really bad."

"It would have been really helpful if Crown had revealed Marquez's other interests."

"Wouldn't it just but as you said before, he's unlikely to incriminate himself by telling us what their next caper is going to be. Have we had any luck on flushing out former colleagues of Marquez?"

"I received Crown's school report from the British Consul, yesterday but the only staff name on it was Marquez. We've been to all the other international schools but not had any response. I arranged for an appeal for information about the school, and former teachers and pupils. It was published in Sur in English yesterday and it's been in the Spanish version today."

"Fingers crossed that something comes from it," said Phillip.

"It better because we're fast running out of ideas."

17

Barbara dropped Salome and Amanda off outside Mario's house and drove off to park the car. Vicente rang the bell. It took a few minutes to register that the faint croaking sound coming from somewhere within was Magda inviting them to enter. Vicente turned the door handle and pushed gently. The brown aluminum door creaked eerily as it swung open to reveal a dingy hallway.

"That's the first time she hasn't been able to come to the door," said Vicente, a concerned look on his face. He led the way in, heading past an empty coat stand and a chest of drawers, above which a dusty timber-framed mirror was hanging on the wall. Through an open door, Amanda could see an unmade bed and there was an overwhelming smell of urine.

They found Magda in the kitchen, come living room at the back of the house sitting in an armchair with her legs up on a footstool. She was white-haired, had a pained expression on her bony wrinkled face, was as skinny as a rake and looked exceedingly frail. A stained woolen blanket covered her from the chest down and the huge wall mounted flat screen TV was showing flash floods in Valencia. Vicente picked up the remote from Magda's lap and turned it down

"Thank God, it's you, Vicente," said Magda in heavily accented Spanish then bursting into tears. "I can't get up from this chair and I'm desperate to go."

Vicente didn't hesitate, he removed the blanket, bent over, picked her up out of the chair as if she were as light as a feather and rushed her to the bathroom door to the right of the kitchen units. He came out on his own a few minutes later.

"Too late," he said quietly shaking his head and walking toward the bedroom. "She can barely stand but can just manage a sit-down shower. I've left her to it, but she'll need some clean clothes."

He returned a couple of minutes later with a selection of garments and went into the bathroom without knocking.

"She can't live on her own like this," he said coming out a few seconds later. "Her legs are too weak, and her coordination is shot. I'm worried she'll set fire to the place."

"Would she go to a care home?" said Salome. "Only, I know that many old folks prefer to live at home."

"I don't know," said Vicente. "We've never discussed it but her biggest problem is that she's never paid into the Spanish social security and has no pension or healthcare. She has no choice but to stay here."

"But would she go if money wasn't a problem?" said Salome.

"I think she'd prefer anything to wallowing in her

own piss," said Vicente. "She's a proud woman and has always kept a spotless house."

Amanda looked around while they waited for Magda to finish in the bathroom. A glazed door provided access from the spacious kitchen to a walled yard. Terracotta pots containing dead plants hung from the jaded white walls. A washhouse and storeroom were to the right. Several different colored towels were hanging stiffly from a line suspended from one side to the other. A green painted table and two aluminum chairs stood in a corner with a dusty empty wine bottle lying on top of the table.

Was this where Mario did his drinking? She wondered.

Magda reappeared hobbling along ponderously holding onto the kitchen work surfaces. She looked embarrassed.

Vicente went over and hugged Magda tightly for a few seconds. He then helped her back to her chair and settled her back into it. Satisfied that she was comfortable, he turned and said. "This is Salome and her friend Amanda."

"My pleasure dear," she said sobbing. "Sorry that you had to meet me like this but it's my legs you see. They're worse than useless, I can't get out to do the shopping and it's difficult to dress myself. The neighbor helps out as best she can, but I'm afraid that I really need some help if I'm to stay here alone."

"Have you considered a care home?" said Salome.

"Yes dear, but I can't afford that."

"My uncle explained how grateful he was to you for all those years of caring for him and it's only right and proper that I now return the favor. Do you remember my great Aunt Marta?"

"I never met her, but I know of her, there are some pictures of her somewhere." Magda waved her arm indicating the many photos mounted on the wall and covering every horizontal surface. "Sorry, but I can't see so well. How is she, your Aunt?"

"Sadly, she died a couple of days ago, but she was living in a wonderful place in Nerja. Would you like us to find a room for you there? The nurses are exceedingly kind and will take excellent care of you."

"That's very kind of you dear but I couldn't possibly impose."

"Nonsense, it's my pleasure."

"But I couldn't ever repay."

"Magda. It's what Mario would have wanted, and it would please me greatly to make your life more bearable. Shall I call them now and book you a room. My driver could take you straight there and you wouldn't have to worry about any more housework or shopping."

"But what about this place? Sorry, but it needs a bit of a clean."

"We'll take care of that."

"Well, only if you're sure."

"Excellent," said Salome. "You'll be well looked after. I'll call them now."

"I'll go with her," said Vicente. "Make sure she's settled in."

"Is there anything you'd like to take with you?" said Amanda.

"Just my photo album, a few scraps of jewelry and some clothes. There's a suitcase on top of the wardrobe and my washbag is in the bathroom."

Amanda fetched the washbag from the bathroom and took it through to the bedroom. She fumbled through Magda's things and packed the remaining clean clothing and a small jewelry box into the battered old suitcase. The well-thumbed album lay on the bedside table. She flicked through it quickly, but it was full of black and white photos of complete strangers in unknown places so placed it on top of the meager quantity of clothing, shut the case and headed back to the sitting room.

Opposite Magda's room was another door. Amanda put the case on the floor, opened it and walked in. It was Mario's bedroom. Mounted on one wall under glass, was a large color photo of what must have been the double wedding of Mario and Jesús at Las Claras. She resolved to show it to Salome and headed back to the sitting room where Salome was talking on the phone.

Ten minutes later, Barbara dropped off a small bag with their change of clothes for the evening along with Salome's dancing shoes. Vicente helped Magda to her feet and half-carried her to the front door where the old lady turned and paused. She took a final look at what had been her home for the last thirty years, and grimaced but seemed resigned to leaving. Vicente helped her gently into the back seat then climbed in, shut the door, and opened the window.

"This shouldn't take too long," he said. "I'll see you later at the Flamenco Club at around ten."

The two girls waved until the car had turned the corner and went back inside.

"Come and see this," said Amanda grabbing her friend's hand and leading her into Mario's bedroom.

Salome stood stock still in front of the well-preserved color image. Tears rolled down her cheeks as she absorbed every nuance of her family. Amanda hugged her and rocked her back and forth for several minutes.

"Thanks," said Salome sniffing and wiping her eyes with her hands. "I'll take that to my apartment in Madrid and try to get to know them better. Have you checked the cupboards and drawers?"

"No, I assumed that Magda had emptied them."

Salome started opening the drawers. "Nope, they're still full," she said. "You try the wardrobe."

Amanda opened the large timber cupboard. It was still full of Mario's clothes. She rifled the pockets of the jackets and a large full-length black coat, but they yielded nothing as did the shelves crammed with shirts and sweaters smelling of mothballs. She dragged a chair from the side of the bed, placed it by the wardrobe and jumped up onto it. She could just see something on top and reached for what was a black plastic tube.

It was smothered in a thick layer of dust. Amanda sneezed as she brushed off the worst of it. The tube wasn't particularly heavy and its top unscrewed easily. Inside were some old rolled-up drawings, she pulled them out then twisted the papers around until she could see the faded handwritten legend - 'Floor plans of Las Claras Convent, 1872'.

She pushed the papers back into the tube and clambered down from the chair, pulse racing. Why hadn't Mario included these with the items that went to the lawyer? Had he forgotten them, or they were too high for him to access?

"Nothing in the drawers," said Salome. "What have you found there?"

"I think they are old drawings of the convent," said Amanda.

"Let's have a quick peek," said Salome.

"They are extremely fragile and faint."

"But they might tell us something. Why else would Mario keep them?"

Amanda eased out the drawings and laid them on the bed. She took a pair of shoes out of the wardrobe and placed them on either side of the top drawing to prevent them from curling back up. They looked at each drawing in turn. Amanda took a photo of each with her phone.

They spotted nothing of interest but on the fifth and final drawing of the chapel, they both gasped. On the left was a ground floor plan but on the right was a hand-drawn vertical sketch showing that there was far more to the church than they had seen in the flesh. Deep under the ground floor was another space. In the center was a handwritten word that was difficult to read. Salome looked around the room and spotted a pair of reading glasses on the bedside table. Amanda saw them and went to pick them up. She gave them to Salome who placed them over the word and peered hard through the lens.

"What does it say?"

"I'm not certain, but I think it says CRYPT."

18

"Do you think that the drawings will be safe on top of the wardrobe?" said Amanda her hand on the front door handle of Mario's house.

"I don't see why not. They've been there for donkey's years without hindrance."

"You're probably right but next time we're here we'll take them back to my apartment."

"Good idea, and we should change the locks."

Salome closed the front door to what was now her property and locked it with the key that they had found hanging on a hook in the kitchen. She placed the key in her purse, picked up the bag containing her Flamenco clothes and shoes and they headed off in the direction of Mercado San Francisco.

It was a ten-minute walk down the hill under a star-studded jet-black sky. The pretty streets glowed salmon-pink under the halogen lights and with the sun long gone, the temperature was dropping to an almost chilly eleven degrees centigrade. The girls linked arms, thankful that Andalusian winters didn't come much worse than this.

The friendly uniformed waitress at Restaurante Mangoa, took their coats then settled them into a corner table where they ordered light salads and mineral waters.

"Nothing from Lisa," said Amanda after checking her phone. "I wonder where she is."

"I'm sure she'll contact us as soon as she has anything to say," said Salome. "Meanwhile, I'm fascinated by what the crypt might have in store."

"Gabriella didn't mention it on any of her tours."

"Perhaps she didn't know about it. There was no sign of an entrance anywhere."

"Maybe that is where your father is pointing us with the numbered stone rubbing and key."

"You could be right, but we could spend weeks solving his puzzles, what we need are more practical modern tools that can see through concrete. Vicente was well equipped with modern technology. Perhaps he has a scanner?"

"Maybe, however, I don't think we should mention this to anyone just yet. Not until we know for sure that we can acquire the convent, obtain the keys and search on our own. We have no idea how many people might have copies of keys or old drawings."

"True. Are you including Vicente?" said Salome with a faraway look in her eye.

"Especially, Vicente? He's a local gypsy first, friend and care giver to Mario second. We've only just met him, and as yet don't know where his loyalties lie, or do I detect an ulterior motive?"

"Er, well," said Salome.

"I thought so, and I agree he is, er definitely your type."

"And available."

"But still freshly wounded."

"I'm not rushing him."

"No, but until you know him better, let's keep the crypt under our hat."

The waitress served the food and they picked at it with their forks.

"What do you plan to say at the Flamenco club?" said Amanda between bites.

"My main objective is to woo the audience with my dancing, and then tell them the story of who I really am."

"Are you going to mention the Convent?"

"That depends on what Lisa has to say. If she doesn't come through before my little speech, I'll say nothing. If she does, I'll announce it."

They finished their supper; Salome paid the check and they headed out to the Flamenco Club. It was just after ten.

The club was a five-minute walk from the restaurant. They could hear the hubbub of lively conversation emanating from the bar as they approached. Just as they were about to enter, Salome's phone rang. They paused a few meters distance from the entrance, Salome fished it out of her bag and looked at the screen.

"It's Lisa," she announced beckoning Amanda close to her so she could hear. "Talk about last minute."

"Sorry, I've been elusive," said Lisa. "But I've been on the phone all day between Sonia's lawyer, the bank president, and the Mayor. I've only just reached an agreement with all parties."

"Agreement?" said Salome frowning.

"Yes," said Lisa. "The bank has accepted that you are the official owner of the convent and won't be making any claims for your father's unpaid debts."

"That's brilliant," said Salome smiling.

"If only it were that simple," said Lisa.

"What do you mean?" said Salome.

"Sonia thinks that your seventy thousand price for her plot is way too expensive. Her best and final offer is forty thousand."

"Bit of a cheek," said Salome. "Especially when she's not in a strong position to negotiate. Do we know the square meterage of her plot?"

"I agree, she is pushing it but as she's desperate she probably thinks she has nothing to lose. And sorry, I don't know the size of the plot."

"Then I suggest a meeting with Sonia on site tomorrow morning with my architect to agree on the boundaries, measure up and discuss a mutually acceptable price."

"You want me to tell her lawyer that?"

"Please do it now, so that when I speak to her in about ten minutes she knows about my proposal."

"Fine," said Lisa. "Anything else?"

"What was the mayor's reaction to my project?"

"He was delighted and will ensure any planning applications are appraised favorably and rapidly."

"Excellent. Just one more thing. What was the bank's position should Sonia fail to sell her factories in time to buy the plot from me?"

"They are happy to provide bridging finance to Sonia up to seventy thousand."

"So, she could afford my asking price?"

"She could but wants to see some downward movement on your part. Salome, if you can drop the price a little tomorrow, you could sign a pre-sale agreement with Sonia on Monday morning, collect the keys from the bank by lunchtime and start designing your refurbishment in the afternoon."

"Wow, that makes tonight more interesting," said Salome. "Does she know that I am going to dance?"

"Her lawyer assures me that she is looking forward to meeting you and seeing you dance. Apparently, her husband is one of the best local performers and is beside himself with excitement to dance with you."

"Really?"

"The mayor assured me that everyone in the room would be keenly awaiting your arrival," said Lisa. "The club has attracted a few good artists over the years, but nothing compared with you. I wish I could be joining you; it sounds like a promising night.

"I hope so," said Salome.

"I'll call Sonia directly, now rather than go through her lawyer," said Lisa. "Anything else I can do for you?"

"Thanks, but no. I think Delgado is more than capable of handling the rest. So, we won't need you anymore?"

"Great. However, as you make progress you might want to consider involving a hotel chain to lease the accommodation elements of your project. If that is of interest, I can introduce you to a client of mine."

"I'll bear that in mind. Meanwhile, thank you, Lisa, most satisfactory and sorry if I was a little abrupt with you earlier."

"It's my pleasure to serve you Salome, and don't worry about how you talk to me. I'm a lawyer. It goes with the territory. My bill will be in the post shortly."

Salome ended the call and replaced the phone into her coat pocket. She and Amanda looked at each other, grinned like Cheshire cats about to enjoy a saucer of double cream, then hugged, and twirled around in the middle of the pavement shrieking like a couple of teenage girls. Much to the amusement of passersby.

"Wait," before we go in," said Amanda getting her phone out of her bag and swiping the screen. "I have to tell Phillip."

"Where are you?" said Phillip.

"We're just outside the Flamenco Club. You?"

"Having a tapa with Prado. He says Hola."

"Say Hola back. I just wanted to let you know that the deal is ninety percent agreed. We have one meeting in the morning to discuss a price for Sonia's plot. On Monday we can pick up the keys. We're going to need you for at least Monday and Tuesday to help with some secretive work on site. Please say you'll be free."

"We've reached a bit of an impasse with Crown so it shouldn't be a problem."

"Thanks, darling. Listen I have no idea what time we'll be finished here, so don't wait up."

***

Although Salome and Amanda had calmed down, they still failed miserably to mask their excitement and entered the club riding an emotional high. It was buzzing. They squeezed between several rowdy English pensioners and jostled their way to the bar. Nobody took any notice of them as they joined the queue for service, which was slow.

There were only two people working behind the

bar: a tall athletic man in his late thirties with long dark hair and handsome features, and a slim, elegant, attractive woman about the same age with long blond hair. Both wore tightly cut black shirts and pants.

Amanda surveyed the scene while Salome tried to attract attention.

A row of Serrano hams hung from a rail over the timber bar. A stuffed bull's head was mounted over the blackened fireplace, which was fronted by an ornate wrought iron grill, an array of brightly colored ceramic pots stood behind it. The business end of several large Tio Pepe sherry barrels filled the opposite wall, signed by many Spanish celebrities in white chalk. Beaten copper vessels of various shapes and sizes were suspended from the black wooden ceiling beams. Old posters of bullfights and photos of Flamenco musicians both alive and long dead hung on the walls, which were decorated in mainly ochre and white mosaic tiles. The place reeked of tradition and an aura of expectation bounced around the room.

At the far end of the bar was an open archway that led into the performance area. It was furnished by high backed Andalusian chairs in serried rows surrounding all three sides of a small space covered with a timber rectangle some four meters wide by three meters deep. It would be loud, up close, and personal. Three high backed chairs stood against the wall at the back of the stage. Over the left was draped a black Cordoba hat; a red handmade lace shawl - *Manton de Manilla*, over the right. A guitar sat on the middle one. Rows of photos of various artists hung on the wall above the chairs.

"What can I get you?" said the blonde bar person as Salome managed to attract her attention.

"Somewhere to change and a couple of waters,"

said Salome indicating Amanda.

The blonde looked puzzled for a second then twigged who she was talking with.

She approached holding out her hand with a hint of a smile. "I'm Sonia, pleased to meet you, Salome," she said. "Go through the door to the left of the stage marked private and I'll let you in." She shouted at her coworker. "Anton, hold the fort while I take Salome to the changing room."

Anton stopped what he was doing and tried to look at Salome but there were too many heads in the way. "I said hold the fort, not rubberneck the visitors," said Sonia just as loudly. She grabbed two water bottles out of the fridge, added ice and slices of lemon to a couple of glasses and headed toward the archway at the end of the bar.

As the girls excused their way through the crowd, they were spotted by Vicente who was talking with a balding man at the end of the bar. He nodded to acknowledge their arrival, proffered his excuses to the man, and made his way toward them. The girls paused at the stage door and waited for him to catch up.

Amanda smiled as she noticed her friend appraising Vicente now dressed in tight black pants and a frilly white shirt, his hairy chest peeking through the top two open buttons. He moved close and stood between them. "Magda is all safely ensconced," he said.

"How did she take it?" said Salome.

"Relieved at not having to be on her own. I'll go and visit her from time to time," said Vicente.

"That's kind of you," said Salome.

"After all she's done for me, it's only fair."

"I understand," said Sonia. "Listen, there have been some developments with Sonia, and it looks like we have a deal on the convent."

"That's great news."

"It means we have to split the plot. We have a meeting in the morning at her workshop to agree on the boundaries and a price. We'll need drawings to submit to the town hall. Are you available to help us?"

"Fine, let me know what time."

"Is the mayor here?" said Salome.

"That was him I was talking with at the bar," said Vicente. "He's keen to meet you."

"Me too, but after the dancing. What routine did you have in mind?"

"The musicians are in the changing room. Let's go work it out together."

The stage door opened, and Sonia beckoned them through. Ahead was a narrow passage with coats hanging on hooks to one side, crates of bottles were stacked along the opposite wall and there was a faint smell of stale beer. Sonia led them to a door halfway along. She knocked and went in. Two attractive women were standing in front of a brightly illuminated, wall mounted mirror preening their long dark hair. One was a teenager, the other almost identical but older. Both were dressed in tight black pants and red leather jackets.

"Say hi to Bibi and her daughter Isa," said Sonia, then turning to Salome and adding. "Did your lawyer manage to contact you?"

"Yes, what time will suit you tomorrow morning?" said Salome.

"Shall we say ten-thirty?" said Sonia, relieved.

"OK, I'll be bringing my business partner," said Salome indicating Amanda. "And Vicente who has agreed to prepare the drawings."

"Excellent, excellent," said Sonia. "I better get back to the bar. Otherwise, that useless husband of mine will be chatting up the young girls instead of serving. Your waters are on the dressing table."

The audience now seated around the stage, hushed as the door opened and Isa entered. She walked over to one of the chairs against the wall, picked up the guitar, strummed it a few times, retuned a couple of strings and began to strum a slow melody. The music was captivating, and it wasn't long before the audience was enthralled by the sadness of the tune and the enchanted playing of the beautiful teenager. Her mother entered to tumultuous applause, as the music ended.

Bibi sat down, smoothed out her dress with the palms of her hands and began to sing. Flamenco isn't just music. It's an expression of mood designed to take the listener on a journey of emotional highs and lows. Each number is performed to varying levels of intensity expressing tranquility, solitude, grief, love and joy in languorous ballads or raucous celebrations that can be inspiring, devastating or uplifting. The audience can often end up as mentally exhausted as the performers are physically drained. And so it was with Bibi's singing.

Her voice was angelic, her range incredible and unusually for Flamenco singers, the words were clear and mostly understandable. Halfway through her second song, Vicente entered through the stage door and strutted onto the wooden platform. The metal plates on his Cuban heeled dancing shoes clicking as he walked over the stone floor.

Bibi paused. Isa strummed and as one Bibi restarted, and Vicente moved.

His initial gestures were with his arms, waving them around his upper body, hips swaying as his eyes smoldered at everyone yet nobody in the audience. Then his feet began to drum. Toes and heels vibrating against the floor like the roll of a drum growing progressively louder. Then he twirled and stamped his right foot once only.

The audience gasped at the intensity of emotion in his body language. He stamped his foot once more, raised his right arm and guided the audience like a bullfighter with a cape toward the stage door. The door opened and there stood Salome. She'd changed her shoes, swopped her pants for a long red skirt and taken off her jacket to reveal a tight cut sleeveless black T-shirt. The audience applauded and whistled with unbridled enthusiasm.

Salome glided toward Vicente her eyes burning into his.

Amanda slipped in behind her, closed the door and leaned against it. It was the only space remaining. She watched spellbound as Salome stopped almost cheek to cheek with Vicente and paused. The music changed to a more light-hearted but distinctly rhythmic melody and they danced a Sevillana. A traditional folk dance for couples originating in Sevilla that most Spanish children learn as soon as they can walk. It's elegant, fluid and when danced well by a loving pair exudes romance and sensuality. The audience tapped their feet in time to the beat.

Vicente and Salome had only just met, yet the ambiance between them as they swirled, twirled, waved their arms, and interchanged positions while gazing into each other's eyes, presumed a long and deep relationship. They bowed to the audience when done and received a standing ovation.

Amanda seethed with envy. After years of Sevillana lessons, she still resembled a waddling duck. Vicente and Salome danced for another fifteen minutes before exiting through the stage door.

"You move well for an architect," said Salome as Sonia held the door open for them.

"Thanks, but after years of coaching and encouragement from Mario, I ought to."

"Oh, I thought it was your appreciation for fine lines and sensuous structures."

"Very flattering but I know my limits. After the break, you'll find Anton far better than me."

"Anton? Isn't he the guy behind the bar?"

"Sonia's husband yes. He used to dance professionally until a few scandals forced early retirement. You'll need to watch his clinches. He takes more than a few liberties with beautiful women."

***

Vicente was right. Anton was a brilliant dancer.

He and Salome performed three successive Fandangos that brought the house down. Salome assumed that Sonia must have warned him to behave himself because he was a perfect gentleman right until the end when under the excuse of putting his arm around her to present her to the audience, he pinched her backside. She 'accidentally' stamped her foot on his toe in a final flourish, twirl, and bow. Anton limped off wincing and the musicians left Salome alone on the stage. Vicente came to stand next to her.

She waved her hands indicting silence. When the noise was bearable, she began to talk.

"Thank you, everyone, for your warm welcome and enthusiastic appreciation of our dancing and the excellent musicians. Your local performers sure know their stuff and you should feel extremely proud of them." She paused while the crowd cheered in agreement. She waited patiently for them to calm down and then paused again as if she was struggling to say something of importance. A few women shushed the room into total silence, and everyone waited for Salome to continue.

After a couple of false starts she said, "Until a couple of weeks ago, I'd never heard of Vélez-Málaga. Then one morning at my apartment in Madrid, a letter arrived from a lawyer summoning me to the reading of the will of my birth relative at his offices opposite your San Francisco market. This was the first time I'd heard about having any real family, so it came as quite a shock. Yes, I had been told by my adoptive parents that they had taken me in as a baby but other than that I knew nothing of my ancestry. Now I'm delighted to say that I do.

"Some of you may have heard the rumors but this week." Salome paused and glanced around her. There was total silence which she dragged out for several seconds before continuing. "I discovered that I am the daughter of Jesús Vargas, the granddaughter of Abraham Vargas and the niece of Mario Vargas."

The room remained totally silent.

"I have no idea if the legends surrounding my relatives are true or not and frankly it doesn't worry me. It was a long time ago and whatever crimes my grandfather was alleged to have committed are long forgotten and had nothing to do with me personally. You can imagine that hearing the will of my birth father was a nerve-racking event and so it proved. I won't bore you with the details other than to inform you that I have inherited this beautiful town's grandest old lady. Convento Las Claras."

Now there were some murmurs.

"As you know Flamenco dancing at this level is a young person's game and I'm no longer the flexible slip of a lass I once was, so I've been thinking of my future. What I'd like, and hopefully you will approve, is to refurbish the convent into a Flamenco University with onsite accommodation. I propose to provide residential degree courses on a global basis particularly to the biggest fans of our Andalusian tradition, the Americans and Japanese. First, though, I must refurbish the building and no this is not a request for donations. I will finance the project from my own funds. What I will need are craftsmen accustomed to working with ancient monuments and I'm confident that Sonia Augustin can help in this respect or point me to the right people. My first dancing partner tonight Vicente has agreed to be the project architect and together we want to make everyone proud of this abandoned old dame. That's all I wanted to say. Thank you for your time."

It started slowly but within seconds everyone was standing and applauding Salome. She acknowledged their support and made to leave but before she had a chance a tall, slender, balding man in his mid-fifties wearing a grey jacket, black trousers with an open-necked white shirt stepped forward.

"It's the mayor," said Vicente when Salome looked at him with raised eyebrows.

The Alcalde de Vélez-Málaga, Antonio Ruiz, representing the Spanish Socialist Party - PSOE, had overseen the Townhall since 2015. He shook Salome's hands, then stood on her other side.

"Great speech," he said.

"Thanks, I was terrified," said Salome.

"You didn't show it. Listen we need to meet sometime and discuss the finances of your project. There may be some grants we can raise through the national government and the EU that I can help arrange for you."

"That would be wonderful," said Salome. "Let me complete my preparations, plans, and costings then Vicente and I will stop by your office."

The mayor nodded, held his hands aloft and gestured the audience to retake their seats. When they had settled, he spoke in a clear and commanding voice. "I'd like to thank Salome for a wonderful performance this evening. Obviously, you enjoyed it."

Good-natured jeers all round.

"I only learned of Salome's real identity the other day," said the mayor. "And am delighted to support her plans for a building that has been causing all of us a lot of headaches for decades. Finally, a vital part of our town center can thrive once more and even better in the capable and generous hands of one of our own. All I will say, Salome, is that during the building work, should you find the odd bit of religious treasure, we'd like it back."

During the braying and dissonant laughter, Salome exchanged cheek kisses with the Mayor and Vicente, waved at everyone as she went toward Amanda who was holding open the stage door. As Salome went through it, she failed to notice Sonia scowling at her from behind the bar with an expression of pure unbridled hatred.

19

"Thanks for your time today," said Prado as he double-parked outside Amanda's apartment blocking the evening rush hour traffic behind him. "I like your ideas about all this being a hunt for Marquez and you're probably right but there's one other matter that we haven't yet explored and that's the golf course developer. What if Marquez was in cahoots with them? They could have colluded to rip off Crown senior."

"You mean Spaniards ripping off Johnny foreigner?"

"Regretfully, many visitors are so gullible about how matters work here, some of my less scrupulous countrymen just couldn't resist parting them from an easy peseta or two. Did you receive a copy of the golf course planning application from Carlos, the Marbella architect?"

"It's in my inbox but I haven't had time to study it yet."

The vehicles behind honked their horns

aggressively but Prado remained unperturbed. Phillip grabbed the door handle and made to open it.

"Let them wait a minute," said Prado. "I'm going back to the Comisaría for a bit, could you send me the planning application and I'll start a search on director's names, see if that turns up anything."

"Great idea," said Phillip. "How long will that take?"

"An hour or so why?"

"Are you still heading back up to Ronda tonight?"

"Not now. I need to work on this?"

"Won't Inma object?"

"Almost certainly, but she knows me. I'm like a terrier after a rat when I'm onto something."

"Amanda is out late in Vélez-Málaga. Fancy a tapa and we could chat about the golf course people?"

"Even better idea. Where?"

"Somewhere a tad more tranquil than the usual Saturday night bedlam, how about La Tranca?"

"Perfect, see you there in an hour."

Phillip shoved the door open and ambled over to the main entrance of Amanda's apartment block. He picked up the mail from their box, shuffled through a few envelopes and leaflets, discarded the promotional trash in the bin provided and walked up the seven flights of stairs. It was the only exercise he'd had all day.

Phillip poured himself a glass of verdejo and went out onto the terrace with his laptop to see what he'd missed during his time with Prado. He forwarded the golf course stuff then called Amanda, but she wasn't answering. He texted her with his evening plans and browsed the remaining emails.

Richard confirmed that he and Ingrid were keen to

progress the buyout and they should meet tomorrow to see if they could reach an agreement.

His sister Glenda wanted him to phone her urgently.

The remainder was the usual business stuff that could wait until tomorrow.

He suggested a breakfast appointment in Nerja for Richard then called Glenda.

"Hi bro," said Glenda.

"What's cooking sis?"

"All good with the tribe, girls desperate to see you as usual but the reason for my message is that something weird has arrived in your post box."

"How weird?"

"I think it's a letter from your ex-wife, Valentina."

"You think?"

"It reeks of perfume and looks like her handwriting. It's postmarked Berlin, dated four days ago."

"Berlin? I thought she was in Moscow."

"That was six years ago, times change. Do you want me to open it?"

"Please."

Phillip heard a tearing noise and the rustle of paper then silence as Glenda read the contents. "It's in English," said Glenda. "And is just a short note saying, Phillip, I need to see you urgently. Will be in touch."

"That is weird. Is there a number or address?"

"No."

"Nothing I can do about it then."

"Looks like. Are you coming to Nerja soon?"

"Tomorrow to meet Richard and Ingrid, I'll pop in sometime, say hello to the monsters."

"They'll be at Sunday football in the morning, why not join us for lunch?"

"With pleasure. You were right to call this through but what the hell it means I have no idea. Valentina is the last person on Earth I ever want to see again."

"Especially with your forthcoming nuptials. What will Amanda think?"

"No idea, no point in alarming her about it until we know something more definite."

"What about you, how will you react to seeing Valentina again?"

"I'm well over her now, but that's not the problem, I'm so busy, I don't have the time or inclination to deal with her drama. See you tomorrow."

Phillip showered, changed, and headed down in the lift to meet Prado.

***

La Tranca is an intimate tapas bar on Calle Carretería, a tranquil one-way street some two hundred meters north of Plaza de la Merced. It fitted well with Prado's ethos of eating within walking distance from whichever base he found himself.

Beamed ceiling, timber fittings, old olive oil containers, and sherry bottles lined wooden shelves mounted just below ceiling height. Posters and photos depicting Spanish cultural history, celebrities and fiestas decorated the walls.

Prado was already seated on a barstool at a sherry barrel located in a cozy niche at the far end opposite the entrance. He was biting into the house specialty of the day, an enormous *empanada atún* – tuna pastry. A glass of chilled vermouth straight from the barrel stood next to his plate. His expression was ecstatic. He acknowledged Phillip's arrival, nodded for him to take the other stool then indicated the papers lying on the table.

Phillip picked them up and scanned the document. It was a planning application dated 1983 to build an eighteen-hole course, driving range, clubhouse, and nine hundred mixed housing units on 230 hectares of land to the north-west of Marbella known as Greentrees. Developer: Greentrees Development S.L. Declared bankrupt in 1989. Company Directors; A.S. Barrio; deceased. J.M. Salvini; deceased. M.S. Carrera; deceased. P.T Marquez; deceased. R.S. Marquez; status unknown.

"Wait," said Phillip. "Is this the same R.S. Marquez?"

"Dates of birth and NIF are identical, so it must be."

"How old was he?"

"When Greentrees was founded he was thirty-three so now he'd be sixty-eight."

"And this other Marquez?"

"His elder brother, and what's more there is a younger sister. Still alive and living in Marbella."

"Can we go and see her?" said Phillip.

"The locals are scoping her out first. They'll report back as soon as they've been to the house."

"Won't that alert Marquez? Assuming he's still in touch with her?"

"They won't be mentioning Marquez, just discussing a neighbor's complaint about excessive noise. I want to know the sister's circumstances to see if they fit with their lifestyle. If the wealthy brother is still around, maybe some of his money found its way to them in the shape of a fancy car or luxury apartment. You know us Spaniards, families tend to share things, not hog everything to themselves."

"Good idea. So, it appears that Marquez conspired with his fellow directors to rip off Crown senior. Together with the abuse of Crown junior and classmates that is a pretty strong motivation for Crown and colleagues to go to extraordinary lengths to flush him out."

"It adds weight to your theory that this is all about the hunt for Marquez."

"How did you trace the sister?" said Phillip.

"Through the deceased brother's funeral directors."

"When did he die?"

"Eighteen months ago."

"Were there any suspicious circumstances about his death?"

"No, but to be fair, I haven't inquired."

"Worth taking a look?"

Prado looked at Phillip and rubbed his earlobe. He extracted his phone and spoke briefly to the duty night shift officer in charge of the Comisaría."

"They going to contact the doctor who signed the death certificate," said Prado ending the call. "So, we'll probably not hear anything until Monday at the earliest."

"Good," nodded Phillip. "Maybe, the brother left some papers or something on his computer?"

"Possibly."

Phillip's phone rang. He glanced at the screen and said. "It's Amanda, I better take it," Phillip spoke a few words in English and ended the call.

"That was brief," said Prado.

"She's about to go into a Flamenco Club with Salome Mendosa."

"The Salome Mendosa?"

"The one and only."

"You two do move in exclusive circles."

"Not really, they were roommates at uni. She's going to be the maid of honor at our wedding."

"Then I'll meet her?"

"You will."

"Inma will be ecstatic. Why are they going to a club in Vélez?"

Phillip began a brief summary of Salome's story but after a few seconds, he stopped. Prado was only asking to be polite; he was too preoccupied with Marquez to pay serious attention.

"Have you decided, sir?" said the waiter interrupting them.

"Cheese platter and a glass of Ribera del Duero," said Phillip then turning back to Prado, "On the way here, I was putting myself in Marquez' shoes back when he was planning his disappearance."

"I've been thinking about that too but in this respect, I'm too Spanish. Beyond the Canary Islands and the occasional trip to Morocco, I'm not as well versed in global bolt holes as you are. Where do you think he could have gone?"

"Mmm… Money laundering legislation was much more relaxed in the 1980s, but he'd still have needed somewhere whose regime wasn't fussy about how he came about his wealth. He was only thirty-three so wouldn't want to maroon himself too far from opportunities to enjoy his perversities. The principal language would probably be Spanish, so he could blend in easily."

"I think that's too strong an assumption. The guy was a teacher in an International school. His English should have been perfect otherwise his school wouldn't have been approved by the British Schools Foundation."

"Fair point, but his first port of call would have been somewhere he could easily convert the value of the boat back into cash to fund his lifestyle there or elsewhere. Once the boat was sold, he could settle down at his final destination and live like a king. In those days interest rates were between twelve and fourteen percent on long term deposits. He wouldn't have to touch his capital and wisely invested he could have increased it substantially."

Prado thought for a while. Took a sip of his vermouth and rubbed his earlobe. "So how can we trace him?"

"The boat. Can we find out the name?"

"Possibly, but wouldn't he just change the registration?"

"Probably, but it's not that easy because buyers of expensive boats are fussy people. They like to know the pedigree of their toys and certainly wouldn't want to touch anything that wasn't licensed and registered with a recognized state authority. Otherwise, they wouldn't be able to moor it where they can broadcast their wealth and supposed importance. Also, Marquez would know that he would lose money when selling the boat. If it weren't properly registered, its sale price would be rubbish and he needed to sell it for as high a price as possible."

"So, you think he would have sold the boat openly?"

"It's the only way he could maximize the sale price," said Phillip. "Could we try tracing the transaction? It should still be in the mercantile registry."

"It's a lot of work tracing a boat. Every country has

its own registry and licensing authority."

"And they are all accustomed to requests from global police forces tracing elusive citizens."

"In that case," said Prado. "I'll ask the Gibraltar police to send us the boat name and we can make a start. I should have thought of this earlier."

"I should have mentioned it earlier. Finally, there's just one more thing bugging me on this case."

"Care to enlighten me?" said Prado.

"It was over thirty years ago that we think Crown was abused at school and Marquez disappeared. Why have they waited until fifteen months ago to start hunting him down?"

"We don't know that they began recently," said Prado. "They could have been at it for ages but eventually after years of no results, their anger faded or perhaps the search costs were too much so they gave up, concentrated on building their business, and kept a weather eye on the Marquez brother and sister."

"Then did the death of Marquez's brother retrigger their efforts to find him?"

"The timing certainly fits. Let's bear it in mind."

20

Phillip rose quietly and crept to the guest bathroom hoping not to disturb Amanda. The girls had arrived back well after midnight and in his semi-comatose state, he had only half absorbed his beloved's description of their exciting day.

The morning traffic was thin as he headed east out of Málaga toward the coastal motorway. The sky was lightening in the east and a few clouds dotted the horizon. Out in Málaga bay, the lights from several anchored container ships flickered as they rocked on the gentle swell waiting their turn at the giant gantries in the docks. A massive cruise liner was moored at Muelle Uno, but the cabin lights were out.

Forty-five minutes later, he drove down the ramp into the underground garage located under Nerja's central square; Plaza España. He parked, walked under the town hall archway, onto the iconic *Balcón* de Europa and across to his favorite café, Don Comer by the church. At that precise moment, the sun peeked its head above the horizon. At the far end of the Balcón, several budding photographers stood near to the bronze statue of King Alfonso XII clicking away madly at the stunning natural phenomenon.

A cleaner chose that moment to start the motor of his jet spray and began his daily ritual of cleansing the Balcón of the detritus remaining from the night before.

"Nothing changes," said Phillip nodding at the cleaner, as Manolo his old friend and café owner came out from behind the bar.

"Including your order, I expect," said Manolo a short, rotund man with a shaven head in his early forties with a Real Madrid Tattoo on the back of his neck.

"Absolutely," said Phillip. They hugged, slapped backs and Phillip took a seat on the terrace. He nodded at several familiar faces and let his mind drift back to the previous May when Juliet used to work here as a waitress. And that led him to Valentina.

What did she want with him?

"Penny for them?" said a booming voice in American English.

Phillip turned. It was Richard.

"Worth a lot more than that dear friend," said Phillip as Manolo served his favorite toasted mollete, drizzled with olive oil and grated tomatoes accompanied by his customary double expresso.

"Are we talking Manolo's delightful breakfasts or something more cerebral?" said Richard as he sat down.

"Manolo isn't the only breakfast maestro. We have plenty in Málaga. Actually, until your rude interruption, I was relishing the good times we had when Juliet worked here."

"Not too painful?"

"Not anymore, although something related has come up to impede my nostalgic moment."

"Ex-wives on the horizon?"

"How did you know?"

"Ingrid bumped into Glenda at the pharmacy."

"So now all of Nerja knows, fucking brilliant."

"Bullshit, they spoke in German, nobody would have understood."

"Whew," said Phillip relaxing. "Anyway, enough of my paranoia; have you and Ingrid come to a decision about the business?"

"Yes, I'll come straight to the point. We want a complete sale in one hit."

"What? No fancy earn-outs, golden goodbyes, extended terms?"

Richard paused while Manolo delivered his usual coffee. "Too complicated. We want to hand everything over to you guys and walk away."

"Are you sure?"

"Positive."

"What will you do?"

"We'll travel, and to keep our brains engaged, we want to write."

"Both of you?"

"Together, yes. Ingrid will cut down on her bridge and we'll write cookbooks."

"Well, that's a surprise, although I hardly think there's a market for your overdone burgers."

"Ha. Ingrid will do the recipes; I'll make the photos. We're going to focus on Spanish cuisine and wine pairing. Plus, how to make tapas, choose hams, cheeses, etc and I'll only ask one thing from you."

"Wow, sounds great, how can I help?"

"Promote them on Nuestra España for free."

"Providing they meet our editorial quality."

"Cheeky bastard," said Richard laughing."

Phillip grinned. "What price did you have in mind?"

"Initially, we agreed ownership was split one third to you, and two thirds to Ingrid and me. When Amanda joined, we changed it to one quarter each and thanks to her and your contribution, the value of the business has soared. So, my offer is that you pay us what the company was worth when Amanda joined us. That is sixty-five thousand Euros."

"Wow, that is generous. Are you sure?"

"I don't want to load you with debt going forward. You should be able to pay that in a one-off settlement and then we are rid of each other."

"Then I, er… sorry, we accept."

"You're sure Amanda will be happy with that?"

"She'll be delighted."

They stood and hugged, then shook hands.

"It's been a thoroughly enjoyable journey," said Richard. "Thank you, and I wish you and Amanda well with the business."

"Look forward to seeing your first book."

"Me too."

"At least let us take you out to dinner tonight. Name your restaurant."

"You don't need to."

"I insist. It's a major milestone in both our lives. We should at least get plastered to celebrate."

"Anywhere?"

"Yep."

"Then let's have the best fish in town at Puerta del Mar. Bring your bank manager."

"Perfect and actually, Salome Mendosa will join us

if you don't mind. She's staying with us while we help her through the trials and tribulations of her uncle's inheritance."

"Wow, Ingrid, will enjoy that. She loves Flamenco. OK. Well, that's that. My life in Spain auctioned off like a herd of cattle," said Richard knocking back his coffee then standing. He paused, rested his hands on the back of his chair back and said. "At least I know the business will be in good hands." And with a tear in his eye, he turned and headed toward the town hall.

"Is he all right?" said Manolo coming to clear the table.

"He's fine, he's just agreed to sell me their share of our business."

"Wow, that is a big change, how long was it since he started the magazine?"

"Over twenty years."

"That's a huge slug of life."

"Ain't it just," said Phillip watching Richard disappear under the town hall archway. He felt elated but tainted by a twinge of sadness for his dear friend and now ex-business partner. He knew how big a wrench it would be for Richard no longer to be involved in the daily cut and thrust of their virtual guide to Spain. It had been his and Ingrid's baby and now he was walking away from it with what in real terms was a small payment in return for all the energy, creativity, and advertising revenue he had brought to the table. He would miss their banter and sense of fun, but their baby would live on without him.

Phillip finished his breakfast and paid the bill before walking up to the butcher's shop at the top of Calle Cristo to buy Iberian pork ribs. He headed back to the car park via the greengrocers on Calle San Miguel then drove to the bodega opposite Supersol supermarket to pick up cases of Albariño and Arzuaga, his favorite wines. As the car wound its way up the Frigiliana Road, he relished the outstanding rare winter panorama of snow-topped mountains set against the clear blue sky. He couldn't help but compare it against the stark brickwork chimneys of Bedfordshire in middle England, his last military posting in the British Intelligence Corps. He smiled grimly at the memory, blessing himself that coming to live in Spain was the best decision in his life; and, he'd met Amanda.

At Urbanization Cortijo San Rafael, he turned off in the direction of his countryside villa. Back in the 1960s the whole area was a farm, but the landowner sold parts of it, plot by plot to the increasing number of foreigners who wanted to build their dream property with amazing sea and mountain views. One of these foreigners was Phillip's grandfather.

Phillip and his elder sister Glenda had been born on a British Army base in Germany and grown up speaking German. They had been visiting their grandparents since they were babies and spent entire school holidays there when they used to play with the farmer's children which is how they learned Spanish. Glenda had married the farmer's only son Jose and lived on the still substantial remnants of the farm next door to the villa which Phillip had inherited when their parents had died. In his absence, she picked up his mail from the boxes at the top of the lane and checked that everything was in order with the property.

Phillip and Amanda tried to spend every weekend at the villa but recently, the pressure of work had kept them at Amanda's apartment. He pulled into his driveway and entered via the front door turning off the alarm as he went in. He grabbed a bottle of water from the kitchen and spotted his mail left in its customary place on top of the fridge. He glanced through the bills and then came across the letter from Valentina. Seeing her handwriting, sparked a flashback of her lying on their bed naked and taunting him. He recalled their passionate lovemaking. It had been good, exceedingly good and he'd loved her madly despite her drama queen behavior. The memory unnerved him.

He shook his head and yesterday's world vanished into a far corner of his mind and was replaced by his current life with Amanda. A glow of pleasure pulsed through him and he headed to his study. Life was sweet just as it was, the past is dead. Farewell.

He sat down in his comfortable office chair, turned on his computer and surveyed his collection of old, mainly Apple technology while it booted up. There was a time when he was proud of them but now, they were just old machines cluttering up his study. He decided to replace them with pictures of the people in his life.

He drafted up a sale agreement and emailed it off to Richard.

Then an email from Prado arrived marked urgent. It read, 'Please translate this email from the Gibraltar police received late last night.'

Phillip scanned the attached document.

It was brief and to the point. The Marquez boat was originally registered in 1983 in the Azores Archipelago, a Portuguese Autonomous Community in the mid-Atlantic. It was named, Graciosa.

Phillip sent off the reply to Prado, closed the machine, refreshed himself in the bathroom and went through the communal gate to join his sister's family for lunch.

21

Amanda was propped up in bed, phone in lap working her way through numerous emails when Salome knocked on her door.

"Come," said Amanda.

"I've been thinking," said Salome parking herself on the bed next to her. "If I can arrange some cleaners to sort out the house in Vélez, I could move in there for the rest of the week and not be bugging you two. Would you mind?"

"Not at all but why bother? It will take until Monday to locate some reliable cleaners, Tuesday before they start work, and as it's so disgusting the place will need a day to air to get rid of the stink. And, do you really want to sleep on Magda's old sheets?"

"Ever the Miss practical but point taken. I'd like to get it cleaned up anyway so I may as well make a start. With some minor modifications and a lick of paint, it would be at least bearable as a base during the refurbishment of the convent. Then I could leave my stuff there and not have to worry about dragging a suitcase everywhere."

"Phillip has good constructor contacts. They did a great job to his villa. You'll see what I mean this afternoon."

"If I leave you guys with a key and some basic instructions, would you be able to let the builders loose and keep an eye on them?"

"Sure. When are you finished in Barcelona?"

"The show is on for a fortnight, then that's me done except for a few selective appearances such as at the Soho Theater. What are we doing after Sonia?"

"Drive to Nerja. Tomorrow Phillip will cook one of his barbeque specials for lunch, they're superb. His sister lives next door, she'll be joining us with her husband and kids. They'll be at the wedding too."

"Sounds idyllic and Phillip cooks as well, awesome."

"He's extremely adept with his hands."

"I bet," said Salome sighing. "I wonder if Vicente cooks."

"You can ask him later."

"Mmmm. Maybe. What clothing should I take for the weekend?"

"Just your lotions and potions, you can use what you want from my wardrobe, but you'll need to bring your own pants, mine are still a tad short for you."

"Great, thanks. We should leave for Vélez in about an hour. Can I buy you a coffee before we meet Sonia and Vicente?"

***

Barbara drove through the open double sliding gates into the yard of Restauraciones Augustin. The yard was cluttered with a smart liveried Mercedes van, a wide variety of shabby statues, and dilapidated icons of Virgin Mary's and saints awaiting attention from Sonia's craftsmen. Everyone climbed out and walked toward the semi-glazed door marked, 'Oficina'.

It opened as they approached and out came Sonia and Vicente.

"They seem overly friendly," said Salome watching Sonia smiling at the architect as he offered his hand to help her down the steep office step."

"Don't overreact," said Amanda. "He's only being gentlemanly."

"He better be," said Salome frowning.

They shook hands and headed for a double-width sliding door that secured the entrance to the *Taller* – workshop. They entered through a door cut into one of the larger doors that opened into a dusty workshop.

Here were the works in progress.

Nearest the door and half-packed for shipment was a large seated enigmatic Virgin Mary. All the visitors gasped at the beauty of the finished piece.

"Today is Saturday, so none of the workers are here," said Sonia. "Which is just as well as the noise and dust are unbearable. We have an efficient extraction system but it's still not enough to cope. Everyone must wear headphones, eye protection, and facemasks.

"The large left-hand prints hanging on the wall at the back of the workstation show the piece's condition on arrival from the front, rear and side elevations. The ones to the right show its original. As you can see, the Virgin has been completely reshaped and repainted and now matches the original perfectly. This one is in timber, but we can also work in sandstone, granite, marble, and any metals the customers send our way. This section repairs the timber, the next stone, then metal. The pieces can be fonts, statues, icons, plaques, altarpieces, altars, pulpits, pews, in fact, anything that churches need to function."

Sonia waved her hand in the direction of two doors set in the rear wall next to a large empty bay. One was heavily secured with an outer gate of metal bars a large padlock.

"We also have two studios. One where paintings are cleaned, touched up and reframed. The other ultra-secure unit restores artifacts such as gold and silver chalices, crosses, reliquaries, etc. And the workshop at the back of my office is where we repair tapestries, drapes, altar cloths, etc. The biggest part of our work though is restoring processional thrones. Nowadays, we do the work in situ to avoid transport difficulties so at any time I have some eight craftsmen scattered all over the country. It's particularly busy now just before Christmas and Three Kings and then again building up to Easter."

"What about stained glass?" said Amanda, fascinated by the wide range of crafts Sonia's team provided.

"We used to have our own glass factory, but I sold that about ten years ago to a competitor. There wasn't enough volume for both of us.

"What do you produce in your other factories?" said Salome.

"Nothing," said Sonia. "The requirement for brand new products isn't what it was so I've brought it all here under one roof. Today over ninety-five percent of our work is restoration. Occasionally, we manufacture a special commission, but the Far East has stolen the production of new items. Their craftsmen aren't anywhere near as good as ours and work for peanuts, but I also must concede that they, the Chinese in particular, use more modern methods of manufacturing with automatic lathes, presses, and spray booths, etc.

"At least we retain the bulk of the available restoration business. Most of the work is in Europe and is mainly handwork by skilled craftsmen repairing one piece at a time. If the Chinese discovered how to take that from us, then we're buggered. It's why I have to cut our costs and why buying this workshop is crucial to our survival."

"How much would you be prepared to pay for it?" said Salome.

"Regretfully, it's not a question of how much but how little. Have you given any thought to reducing your seventy thousand price?"

"Yes," said Salome. "Sorry, but I'm not prepared to reduce it. It's already a rock bottom valuation. However, I don't want to deter you from the deal so am prepared to accept an immediate payment of forty thousand with the remainder in two years' time. It should give you more than enough breathing space to sell off the other factories."

"That would help me tremendously," said Sonia barely disguising her relief. "I accept."

They paused and shook hands.

Salome gazed at Sonia directly in the eyes and smiled, but Sonia couldn't bring herself to do the same.

"However, there is one condition on the deal," said Salome not letting go of Sonia's hand.

"What?" said Sonia grimacing at Salome's firm grip.

"Approximately how many square meters are we

talking about for the plot?"

"Roughly, four hundred," said Vicente.

"I want to use your services during the restoration of the convent, and it will need some new pieces that reflect dancers, not religion. Is there enough room to take on the extra production?"

"We'll do our best," said Sonia appearing relieved. "We've never done anything other than religious works, but we'll try. It might help us open up new markets."

"Then you can use the convent as your showroom," said Salome. "However, I will expect exceptionally keen prices."

"Of course," said Sonia almost smiling. "And thank you, Salome."

"You're welcome. I'll instruct Delgado to draw up a contract for Monday," said Salome. "Can you meet us there around midday to sign the papers?"

"And afterward we can go to the bank to conclude the financials," said Sonia. "If all goes well, you should be able to take the convent keys with you."

"In that case, I'll start measuring the boundaries," said Vicente tapping the App on his phone and pointing it at the far wall."

"Do you need us to help?" said Amanda.

"No. I can manage," said Vicente.

They shook hands, clambered back in the car and Barbara drove them off to Mario's house to meet the cleaners and collect the new keys from the locksmith before continuing to Nerja.

Sonia watched them go completely disarmed by Salome's generous offer. "Why is she being so nice to me?" she said under her breath then went over to assist Vicente with his measuring.

22

After a fun light lunch with his family, Phillip treated himself to a leisurely siesta on his favorite Eames lounge chair looking out over the garden before starting on his food preparation for Sunday lunch. He was going to use his recently acquired Sous Vide water bath to tenderize the ribs and needed to vacuum pack the meat into individual portions with a spicy marinade for them to bubble away overnight.

He was in the kitchen stirring the marinade on the hob when he heard the girls arrive in Amanda's Prius. They opened a bottle of crisp verdejo and sat around the island chatting about Salome's proposed improvements to Mario's house while he finished his culinary preparations.

Amanda went to the fridge to replenish the wine and noticed the opened mail on top of the fridge. She picked it up and flicked through it.

"What's this?" she said after reading the letter from Valentina.

"Apparently, my ex wants to see me," said Phillip tasting the marinade.

"How do you feel about that?" said Amanda looking concerned.

"I'm more worried about how you might feel," said Phillip.

"Sorry," said Salome. "Would you prefer that I leave you two alone to work this out?"

"No, no," said Amanda and Phillip.

"It's no big deal," said Phillip. "Just a mystery. I don't understand why she wants to see me after all this time?"

"How does she know where you live?"

"We came here often to visit my parents, despite my mother detesting her. 'Decorative drama queen' was how she referred to her, but I was blinded by her beauty and couldn't see what Mum meant until long after the divorce. Anyway, let's not dwell on Valentina. For the moment, we have no idea if or when she might turn up, and it looks like we're in for a great weekend. Weather forecast is superb until Monday morning and we have lots more positive stuff to talk about. Tell me, what's new about the convent?"

The girls brought Phillip up to date.

"Wow, a crypt, you say."

"We think so," said Amanda. "But we need a scanner to make sure and to help find the entrance."

"How deep is the crypt?" said Phillip.

"I'm not good at reading drawings," said Salome. "The distance between the floor of the church and the roof of the crypt seems quite long on the drawing, at least three meters down."

"That's unusual," said Phillip. "Normally, crypts form an integral part of the main building's foundations. A three-meter gap implies that the crypt was tunneled out before the church was built."

"Perhaps it was an Arab graveyard or tombs underneath a mosque?" said Amanda. "That's often the case in these ancient towns."

"Possible", said Phillip. "Anyway, the builders of the church must have known it was there. Otherwise, it wouldn't have been on the drawings. Either way though, three meters down, especially through solid rock is too deep for most scanners to penetrate," said Phillip. "Better to drill a small hole and feed an endoscopic pipeline inspection camera down. With a high res screen, spotlight and 360-degree lens, we should be able to see what is down there and locate the entrance."

"Won't that need a powerful drill?" said Salome.

"Yes, but we can hire one along with a generator."

"And the camera?" said Amanda

"That too. When can you pick up the Convent keys?"

"Latest Tuesday morning," said Salome. "Will we have time to collect Marta's ashes on Monday? I thought we could scatter them in the convent courtyard before we begin work."

"Yes, of course, and what a great idea," said Phillip. "She can watch over the place during the refurbishment."

"From the little I know about her," said Salome. "She'll haunt us until we deliver regular supplies of cava."

"Ha," said Phillip. "Then when the ribs are underway, let's organize our spy in the crypt kit."

"Great, how did it go with Richard and Ingrid?" said Amanda.

"Surprisingly well, my love. We've agreed on a deal which I think is most generous. Basically, we give them sixty-five grand and they walk away."

"That means we don't need to load ourselves up with debt."

"Exactly. You'll have the opportunity to thank them both tonight. I've invited them to Puerta del Mar."

"Yummy, live lobster and Cava," shrieked Amanda. Her eyes lighting up with excitement. "Salome you'll love it and darling, it'll be a great excuse to get some oysters down you."

"I don't think it's right for me to intrude…"

"Nonsense," said Phillip. "Ingrid is one of your biggest fans."

"Then Amanda, we better take a look at your wardrobe."

The girls went off arm in arm to the main bedroom. Phillip vacuum-packed the marinade and ribs, loaded them into the Sous Vide, turned on the heater and then went through to his study. He sat back down at his machine, booted it up and searched for generators, cameras, and long robust drills to rent.

23

It had taken most of Monday morning for Salome and Amanda to complete the formalities with Sonia at the bank and notary on Calle Canelejas.

"Would you care to join us for lunch," said Salome, as they shook hands outside.

"Sorry, but I have to return to the office," said Sonia. "Thanks once again for your flexibility. It will really help us through these difficult times. Good luck with your refurbishment project. I'm sure it will be a great success."

She tossed her head, turned, and headed off.

They watched her go. The tall striking blond attracting admiring glances as she went.

"She's saying all the right things," said Amanda. "So why do I have a nasty feeling about her?"

"Really," said Salome. "Then my radar must be tuned into another station, because I'm only receiving good vibes from her. I've just saved her bacon. Perhaps she feels too embarrassed to be too gushy with her gratitude. She's a proud woman."

"Perhaps," said Amanda. "Do you want to go and see your new toy?"

"No, I've done enough looking. I'd rather wait until we all go in the morning and can start searching for the elusive crypt. Shall we go up to the mercado for lunch? We can pick up the envelopes from Delgado and then walk up to Mario's house to meet the cleaners and builders."

***

A local police car with flashing lights was parked outside Mario's house as Salome and Amanda walked up from the market. The door was wide open and one fresh faced officer was guarding the door. Several people were gathered near the officer exchanging lighthearted banter with each other. They stopped and adopted serious expressions as the women arrived.

"What's going on, Officer?" said Salome.

"We've had a report from a neighbor, ma'am. About half an hour ago, they heard noises inside and called us. My colleague is looking around."

"May we go in?" said Amanda.

"When my colleague returns," said the officer.

"Salome?" said a voice behind them.

Salome turned to see a young, slender woman with short dark hair wearing a striped housecoat.

"I'm Conchi," said the woman. "The cleaner."

"Hola, Conchi," said Salome. "Thanks for coming, although I'm not sure what's happening."

"That's OK," said Conchi. "Paco the builder is also here, but he's just parking his pick-up."

The other officer: a short man in his forties with a

salt and pepper mustache, came out of the door and said in a raised voice. "Did anyone see anything?"

"I saw someone from my kitchen window," said a lady at the back. "He ran off like a scalded cat about twenty minutes ago. He was wearing a hoody, blue sport shoes and was carrying a black tube."

"Did you recognize this person?" said the officer.

"No, but it looked like a young lad. He wasn't noticeably big."

"This is the owner," said the young officer.

"I'm Mario's niece," said Salome.

"It's OK, Salome," said the older officer. "We know who you are. Come with me, please."

They followed him inside.

"There is no sign of a break in so whoever this was must have had a key," said the officer. "Have you given a key to anyone?"

"No, officer. I've only just inherited the place."

"The witness outside mentioned a black tube. Does that mean anything to you?"

"It certainly does," said Salome. "We'll just check in my uncle's bedroom. It was kept in there on top of the wardrobe."

"I should warn you," said the officer opening the bedroom door. "It's not pleasant."

Salome walked in, screamed, buried her head in her hands and burst into tears.

The glass protecting the large photo of the double wedding had been smashed and a large X slashed through the image. Over the top, a message had been sprayed in red paint. It said, 'Go back to Madrid.'

Amanda climbed onto the same chair as before and looked on top of the wardrobe.

The drawings were gone.

24

It had taken most of Monday afternoon to check the rest of Mario's house and complete statements at the police station. As far as they could ascertain, it was the just the drawings that had been taken. The only suspects Salome could think of were Cristina, or members of her family, but the police disagreed. After being arrested at Delgado's office, Cristina and Isaac had sworn not to molest Salome further. The interviewing officer was adamant that they wouldn't have been so dumb to have broken their promise but at least agreed to question them.

"Was it, Cristina?" said Salome, as Barbara picked them up from the police station. "Or is this a new threat. And what have I done to upset them?"

"Maybe, there are still some people in town that blame your grandfather for the disappearing treasure."

"After all this time?"

"Sadly, some parents condition their children to continue family hate and resentment."

"But what do they hope to achieve by ruining the only large photo I have of my family?"

"Maybe, it gives them some sort of satisfaction to cause you pain."

"But why?"

"To drive you out of town and away from the convent."

"Then I feel sorry for them. To live with such bitter, twisted perceptions of the past and take it out on complete strangers. They should seek counselling."

"That is typical you," said Amanda. "Always looking for a logical justification for people's motives. Why can't you just accept that people want you gone because you're getting in their way."

"You mean Sonia?"

"Yes, but not just her, there could be others. Perhaps they have other plans for the convent?"

"Or maybe it's hiding something more than just the answer to my grandfather's alleged crimes?"

"That's more like it," said Amanda, as Barbara pulled up outside Mario's house. The crowd had gone and there was police tape over the front door. Conchi was just arriving but there was no sign of Paco.

"Do you know an emergency locksmith," said Salome as they clambered out.

"You want me to call him now?" said Conchi. A slim, short lady in her forties with long, curly, titian hair. She was still wearing the same striped housecoat.

"We may as well," said Salome.

Conchi made the call, the locksmith agreed to come in ten minutes.

Then Paco pulled up in his pickup truck and they all went inside.

Paco, a short, well built, jovial man in his late forties

with a thick mane of silver hair and dressed in blue overalls, frowned when he saw how upset Salome was about the vandalized photo.

"I know someone that can fix that," he said. "As good as new?"

"Then please go ahead," said Salome. "Whatever it costs."

They continued walking around the house, Salome explaining what she wanted while Paco made notes. The locksmith arrived and installed new locks to the front and back doors. Salome paid him in cash and handed one set of keys over to Conchi.

She agreed to clear everything out and either sell or dispose of it depending on its condition. Paco promised a quotation by the end of the week.

They returned to Nerja via the funeral home to pick up Marta's ashes then back to Phillip's.

He'd just returned after a long day's drive to Granada and back. The nearest hire center that could provide all their equipment was based on an industrial estate located on the fringe of the city.

They opened a well-earned bottle of verdejo and enjoyed a light supper.

***

Early on Tuesday morning, Barbara arrived to take them all to Las Claras. They loaded everything into the spacious trunk of her SUV and drove to Vélez. Salome was in the back with Amanda. Marta's urn between them.

It was just before nine when they pulled up outside the convent. Salome opened the side gate; Barbara nursed the vehicle through the narrow entrance and

Salome locked up behind them while the others clambered out and looked around them.

"At last, we're alone here," said Salome extracting the urn from the back seat, tucking it under one arm and holding the convent keyring in her other hand.

"And it's all yours," said Amanda. "How does it feel?"

"Not sure yet. Can't wait to start looking for the crypt though."

"I wonder if it will solve the mystery of your grandfather?" said Phillip opening the trunk.

"Let's hope so," said Salome opening the convent back door. "Before we unload, shall we dispose of Marta?"

"Good idea," said Phillip extracting a cold bag and draping it over his shoulder. "I've bought some cava to send her off and to celebrate your new venture."

"Thank you, Phillip," said Salome. "How thoughtful."

"Nonsense," said Amanda. "It's just an excuse for him to start drinking early."

They trooped through the former convent office and out into the overgrown courtyard.

"How about here?" said Salome stopping by a raised flower bed containing roses and weeds.

"Do you want to say anything?" said Barbara, as Salome placed the urn on the dilapidated low concrete wall surrounding the flower bed and unscrewed the plastic top.

"Not sure," said Salome. "I've never done this before. I suppose I should say something."

"Was she religious?" said Barbara.

"A bit, but rarely went to church," said Salome.

"Then why don't you say what you want," said

Barbara. "Then I'll pray for her."

Salome unclipped the plastic bag inside the urn, tentatively inserted her hand and grabbed a handful of ash. She grimaced at the unfamiliar texture and sprinkled bits of Marta over the flower bed. "I know," she said taking another handful. "Let's all take turns at her distribution and then raise our glasses to her when she's, er, all, what's the word; gone?"

They gathered around Salome, digging alternative hands into the urn and sprinkling ashes around the flower bed evenly. Birds were twittering, there was a faint rumble of passing traffic and an airliner passed overhead.

When the urn was empty, Phillip opened the chilled cava, poured it into five plastic champagne glasses handed them around, and said. "Let's raise our glasses to Marta, may she rest in peace."

They all took a sip and echoed, "To Marta. Rest in peace."

"I only knew her for a few minutes," said Salome. "But at least I had that precious time with the only relative, I've ever met. In honor of that, whatever we do with this courtyard I want to name it after her."

"It would make a great tapas bar," said Phillip. "Or terrace restaurant."

"There you go again," said Amanda. "That stomach of yours will be the death of you."

"What else is there?" said Phillip. "Apart from…"

"Now, now," said Salome. "Decorum, you two. Remember where we are, but I love the name for a catering establishment of some sort. So, my toast is Marta's Courtyard and the Las Claras Flamenco University."

"And on a more serious note for a Christian lady,"

said Barbara. "May the road rise to meet you. May the wind be always at your back. May the sunshine warm upon your face. May the rains fall upon your fields. And until we meet again, may God hold you in the hollow of His hand."

"Thank you, Barbara," said Salome finishing her drink. "That was lovely. Now, shall we unload and start work. I can't wait to see what this regal old lady has hidden within her bosom. Do we have a hammer and chisel? I want to dig up the memorial tile."

"We do, but it's in the toolbox underneath everything else," said Phillip, smiling at her impatience. "If we all help unload, the quicker you can start."

They returned to the car and when each had picked up something, they headed in a procession with Salome at the front, eager to start work.

They arrived at the rear entrance to the church and paused in horror at the top of the steps.

The floor had been covered in red spray paint.

25

'Salome go home,' was repeated again, and again from the altar at the far end to the steps where they stood.

Salome burst into tears.

"Stop crying," screamed Amanda grabbing Salome's arm and shaking her gently. "Don't you understand? That is exactly the reaction they want to achieve."

"It's not your name, they're abusing," screamed Salome shoving Amanda away much harder than necessary.

"Just because you've had self-defense lessons doesn't entitle you to push me around," yelled Amanda. "Don't you understand, that's exactly what whoever this is trying to achieve. Disharmony among us to cause delay or to deter you from your objectives. To me, it shows that whoever it is, must have something to hide and are too cowardly to confront you directly."

Phillip went down the steps and placed his gear in

the middle of the church floor.

"Amanda's right, Salome," he said. "I know it must be painful to see your name like this, but most people have been friendly and supportive of you and your project. Whoever did this and the damage at Mario's house either has a personal grudge against you or your family or they are trying to deter you."

"Your probably right," said Salome, reaching out to Amanda. "Sorry, I hope I didn't hurt you."

"Just my pride," said Amanda hugging her friend.

"Everything was locked when we arrived? Do you think they have keys to this place as well?"

"More than likely," said Phillip. "we'll have the locks changed but for now we need to get on with the drilling. I must return all this gear, tomorrow. We can speculate who 'they' are when we have more time."

Salome reluctantly allowed Amanda to lead her down the steps to join Phillip and place their packages next to his.

They needed several trips to transfer all the gear into the church including print outs of the photos that Amanda had taken of the stolen drawings, copies of Abraham's sketches, the stone rubbing and the key from Jesús.

By the time Salome had deposited her final load, she'd stopped sniffing but remained tight-lipped and morose.

"I think we should drill in the center of the floor," said Phillip. "Then the camera light should be able to illuminate the entire crypt so we can see where the entrance is."

"OK," said Salome, smiling wanly. "Let's get on with it. Give me a hammer and chisel and I'll lift memorial stone number one hundred and twenty-nine.

Barbara, can you give me a hand please?"

Phillip handed them the tools. Salome and Barbara strode off to the treasury where urgent banging and the occasional curse was soon heard.

Phillip mounted the drill into its rig. It would ensure that the hole was bored precisely vertical. He then slotted the diamond drill-bit into the chuck and connected the machine to the generator. Amanda set up the endoscopic camera and its monitor.

"How long will the drilling take?" said Amanda.

"No idea," said Phillip. "Depends if we're drilling through rock or sandstone." He topped up the tank on the petrol generator and pulled the cord to start it. It purred into life. He tested the drill a couple of times. Satisfied it was in order, he positioned the bit on the grout between one of the black and white diamond-shaped floor tiles, checked that the angle was exactly vertical then pulled gently down on the drill lever. The drill head disappeared into the grout, which spewed out to the side. After the first twenty or so centimeters, the drill bit bored substantially faster.

Amanda stood by him fascinated by the rotating drill. She adored his handyman skills. Eventually, its one-meter length had penetrated the floor. Phillip attach the next meter long extension. He reversed the drill a little which as it ascended slowly back out of the floor deposited a powdery substance on the tiles surrounding the borehole.

"We're in luck," he said rubbing the powder between his fingers. "Sand not rock."

"Brilliant," said Amanda. "I wonder what we'll find."

"What do crypts usually contain?" said Phillip grinning as he lowered the first drill-bit section back into the hole, paused with a few centimeters remaining and attached the first extension piece.

"Bastard," said Amanda punching his arm lightly, eyes twinkling. "I mean other than old bones."

"Hopefully," said Phillip setting the drill going again. "We'll discover that shortly. What was it with the self-defense thing?"

Amanda froze, unable to look at him.

"Later," she whispered. "I promise."

"Amanda, Phillip," shouted Salome. "Come, see."

"I can't leave the drill," said Phillip.

Amanda squeezed his arm and went over to the treasury.

Salome and Barbara were bending over something on the floor in the far corner by the window. Memorial stone one hundred and twenty-nine was leaning against the wall. At its base, bits of broken grouting lay surrounding the hole that it had left behind. Amanda peered over their heads and saw a small metal box set in the earth. Salome was scratching at it with her hands to try and extract it, but the box was proving stubborn.

"Wait, mind your nails," said Amanda. "Loosen the earth surrounding the box with the chisel."

Barbara picked up the hammer and chisel and followed Amanda's instructions.

It didn't take long before she was able to lift out a shallow rectangular tin some twelve centimeters long. A faded design described pipe tobacco as its original contents. She eased off the lid to reveal a folded paper. Salome stretched her arm and picked it out delicately. Underneath was another steel key that initially appeared identical to the one that came with her father's will. The paper was folded in two. Salome opened it carefully. A rectangular outline was drawn roughly in pencil. At the left-hand end of the rectangle was a square box marked with what looked like stairs. Numbers were written against each side elevation. Forty; along the top. Twelve, along the side. Four, along each side of the square box.

"Dimensions?" said Amanda.

"But of what," said Salome.

It has to be the crypt?" said Barbara. "It's roughly the same size as the floor space of the church, seems a bit smaller though. The square box could signify that the entrance is by stairs at the western end."

"But what do these two squiggly blue lines abutting the center of the top edge mean?" said Salome.

"Looks like they were added to the sketch at a different time with a felt tip pen," said Barbara

"What do they signify?" said Salome.

"Possibly that there are two entrances to the crypt," said Amanda.

"And this key?" said Salome holding the newly discovered one up to compare with the one from her father's envelope.

"Same size, same metal but different bits.

"Yes, I can see that, but what are they meant to open?"

"Let's go show Phillip," said Amanda.

Phillip was adding the final section to the drill to extend its reach to four meters. He set the machine going again, took the drawing from Salome and inspected the sketch and keys.

Phillip looked around the church roughly calculating its dimensions. "Yes, I think it's an outline of the crypt," he said. "It's definitely a smaller footprint than the church. Probably so the weight of the outer walls was supported by solid ground. The keys may well open the entrance." He looked at the rotating drill, a concerned expression on his face. "Let's hope we breakthrough soon; otherwise we're stumped."

It took three and a half meters of drill bit before the drill suddenly slowed. Phillip pushed down harder on the lever. "We're into rock now," he said. "Or maybe the crypt has a brick roof."

Three minutes later, the pressure changed, and the drill motor went faster.

"We're through," said Phillip. "He stopped the drill, turned it into reverse and the bit slowly reappeared. He removed the extensions and finally the drill bit itself. Amanda handed him the camera cable which he threaded into the hole.

Amanda turned on the camera light.

They could see the sandy sides of the hole on the monitor as the cable wormed its way downwards. Salome was beside herself with excitement jumping up and down resembling a teenager at her first pop concert, all negative thoughts about nasty messages disappeared without trace.

The camera burst out the end of the hole. Phillip eased the cable up and down so that it moved freely. He then jiggled it to shake off any dust in front of the lens and lowered it further. Gradually, more and more of the space below became illuminated by the camera's light.

They were all glued to the monitor, spellbound by what was being revealed to them.

A brick-built arched ceiling was supported by four thick stone arches creating five separate chambers each about eight meters wide. The end walls were of the same brick construction except the one to the left contained a large timber door. Niches containing what appeared to be religious artefacts were set in rows into both side and end walls. The floor was covered with rows of coffin sized stone slabs except in the center which resembled a solid pathway from the door to the far end. It appeared to link all five chambers.

On top of the slabs in chambers one and five were rows of glass display cabinets. In chambers two and four were two large solitary tombs, and in the center was a large throne hard up against the north wall overlooking more display cabinets.

"What the fuck," said Salome peering at the screen in shock. "I don't understand."

"What did you expect?" said Phillip.

"It's a crypt," said Salome. "Shouldn't there be more tombs, catacombs, piles of skulls, rats maybe, but not display cabinets and that throne thing?"

"Let's have a closer inspection," said Phillip shoving the camera cable further into the hole.

"The dust from the borehole is obscuring the contents of the cabinet immediately below," said Amanda. "But those in the adjacent cabinet resemble chalices. Each one has a label in front of it, but they are impossible to read."

"Is that the entrance at the far end?" said Salome.

"I believe so," said Amanda. "Just where it indicated on the sketch you found underneath the memorial stone."

"How do we find our way inside?" said Salome, scampering toward the altar. Amanda close behind. "The door has to be somewhere underneath the Virgin."

The others followed more circumspectly. They stepped up onto the altar surround and walked to the rear of the housing that protected the Virgin. Barbara crossed herself as they passed the incredibly beautiful icon.

They found Salome standing by a solid white wall abutted up against the outer wall of the church, she was scratching her head and looking irritated.

"The entrance should be here," she said. "Perhaps this is a false wall?"

Phillip knocked along the width of the wall and then again at varying heights. It was solid as a rock.

"Not here," he said. "Let's try the other side."

They traipsed around to the left-hand side of Virgin and found an identical wall. It was equally as unmoving.

"What about inside the housing?" said Salome.

They returned to the front and examined the structure more closely. The Virgin was set back from the waist-high front wall of the housing by a meter or so. A row of five circular marble columns supported the front of the housing's roof and there was an ample amount of room inside the housing on both sides of the Virgin. Phillip heaved himself over the wall into space to the left of the icon. It was surprisingly dust-free.

He took out his phone, switched on the flashlight and pointed it around the dark recess. He stood up but had to stoop as he rested his head against the top of the recess and inspected the narrow space at the back of the Virgin. To the left was a timber panel. Phillip knocked on it. It sounded hollow.

"Nothing so far," he said. "I'll try the back of the Virgin's head.

"There doesn't seem to be anything here either," he said running his hand over the back of her head then shoulders. "Wait, there's a niche between her shoulder blades. I'm feeling inside. Wow, there's a small lever. I'll try and move it." A few seconds later, he said, "No, I've pulled it and tried to push it sideways in all directions, but it won't move. It appears to be stuck solid."

"Try pushing it in," said Salome. "It has to do something otherwise what's the point of the damn thing."

"OK, pushing now," said Phillip.

There was a loud click followed by a whirring sound. The Virgin began to vibrate gently then edge slowly away from the back of her housing on what must be some mechanism underneath her. She stopped automatically, after a meter or so. Phillip flashed the light into the gap she had left behind her and saw that the timber panel formed the top part of a door.

"Amanda pass me both the keys please."

Amanda squeezed in beside him, handed him the keys and gasped. "There's a secret door behind the Virgin," she said.

"Let me see, let me see," shouted Salome attempting to pull them out of the way.

"Wait," said Phillip. "Stay calm, we don't want to overload the recess. Salome, climb down for a moment and let us out. Then you can come and try the key in the door."

"No, no, you do it," said Salome.

Phillip inserted the first key into the keyhole and turned it clockwise. It moved easily and after a quiet click, the door opened. He directed the light through the door to reveal steep concrete steps heading downwards ninety degrees to the right. They turned to the right again after some two meters and disappeared. "There are some stairs heading downwards," he said.

"Salome, do you want to go first?"

"Er... yes, no, er... this is crazy. See where the steps go and report back."

Phillip pointed his phone ahead of him and turned his video onto record. He trod carefully testing each step before descending further into the depths. The first five steps were made of timber taking him down from the housing to ground level where they changed to earth.

The stairwell was a meter wide and about two meters high. It had been hewn out of the sandy soil. He spotted faint indentations where the tools had cut into the surface. There were stone columns on both sides supporting the stairwell roof but the steps themselves had no protective coverings and seemed hardly used. Yet the air smelled fresh and there was no dust or cobwebs.

At the first turn, he directed his flashlight down and found another meter of steps. He continued and this time there was another meter of steps but with a flat passage at the bottom leading straight ahead. To the left-hand side of the passage was the other side of the solid timber entrance door they had seen with the camera. The timber appeared to be relatively new. Just beyond the door, the passage ended. He descended the last step, tested the passage floor, and moved into it. The space was just tall enough for him to stand upright. He spotted two long sturdy timber beams lying on the floor against the wall opposite the door but failed to understand their significance.

Phillip pulled and pushed the door handle above a keyhole on the left-hand side, but nothing budged. He inserted the remaining steel key into the keyhole and turned it. Again, it moved smoothly and silently. A distinctive click informed him that it was unlocked. He pushed but nothing happened, then pulled, and the door opened outwards with only the slightest of squeaks.

He wedged it against the end passage wall with one of the timber beams then shone his flashlight into the crypt and entered cautiously, listening carefully for any unexplained noises or smells. As he edged forward flicking his light from side to side, the contents of the crypt revealed themselves more clearly than on the small camera screen.

The walls and arched ceiling were clad with narrow terracotta bricks in the Mudejar style. The floor was divided by a central path of terracotta tiles which at first glance appeared to cover the length of the crypt. To each side of the path were two rows of large coffin-shaped slabs.

He stepped on one. It rocked slightly, so did the next. So, not cemented down, he thought; perhaps they're tombs. He bent to try and shift one, but it was much too heavy.

Phillip took a good look around and found himself in a bay between the door and the first stone arch. The bay was around three meters high, twelve meters wide and eight meters long. The dim light from the camera could be seen two bays ahead, but in this one, there were five lines of glass display cabinets with their tops at about waist height arranged precisely at ninety degrees to the arch. Each cabinet was three meters long by half a meter wide with a glass top of about sixty centimeters deep clipped together by chrome corners.

He walked along each aisle as if shopping in a supermarket admiring the sparkling contents; there were twenty in each, all labeled with the name

'Hoarders', along with descriptions that he guessed were the date of manufacture and originating location. Common to all was the superb quality of the pieces, mostly from Spain's finest cathedrals and dated thirteenth or fourteenth century.

The cabinet glass was spotless, suggesting that it was cleaned regularly and lovingly. The bottom section of the cabinet contained four drawers. He opened one slightly and found three dozen or so more artifacts laid on their sides wrapped in sackcloth, with a handwritten tag tied around the sack top keeping it closed. On it was written the date of manufacture and the place of origin. He opened one and found a beautiful gold statue of the baby Jesús.

"Mmm," he mumbled out loud, "No Hoarders written on any of these tags."

He shone his light on the side walls.

Two rows of three niches some forty centimeters high, twenty deep and twenty wide, had been recessed into each wall and lined with more slim terracotta bricks. Each contained one gold or silver artifact, some with inset jewels such as rubies, sapphires, and emeralds. Phillip moved to inspect the center niche more closely. It was at chest height with a small lamp mounted in front of the contents with its front shielded to reflect the light onto the artifact. Between each niche were large, metal art-deco styled lamps all on the same horizontal level about two meters off the ground. He tested his weight on one. It was extremely robust.

He picked up a chalice. It weighed heavy in his hand as he turned it around and upside down. There were hallmarks in the base, but he didn't understand them. The label said 'Cadiz, 1498', but didn't mention Hoarders. He took a photograph and saved it to his gallery noticing there was no phone signal. He replaced the chalice, turned, and took more photos of each wall. All in all, there were twenty-four niches in this first bay, each containing an artifact.

In the next bay, there were no cabinets just a plain concrete tomb about one meter high and two meters long. Phillip walked around it, shining his light on each surface. The top was covered in a mosaic of blue, green white and black colored ceramic tiles. Arabic writing was carved into sandstone plaques decorating each side and both ends. He filmed the bay and moved into the next. The light from the drain camera reflected on the dusty display case containing as Amanda had indicated; more chalices, each with a label.

He read a couple of them.

'Hoarders - Toledo. 1463.'

'Hoarders - Burgos. 1390.'

"They must be worth a fortune," he said out loud.

He looked up at the sidewall and gasped. There was one large niche containing a metal display case with a glass top. Its contents were the three golden ships of Columbus. He took a closer look, turned the label tied to La Pinta and read, 'Las Claras. 1497'. No mention of Hoarders.

"Is all the Las Claras treasure here?" he said, his voice echoing slightly. His mind wondering about the implications of this for Salome and her disgraced grandfather.

He turned around and directed his phone's light toward the throne.

It was enormous. As if tailormade for a giant and produced from excellent quality timber that he failed to recognize. Three steps led up to a two-meter square platform where a chair with ornate legs, exotically carved arms and back were mounted in the center. Hard against the wall, between the rear of the chair and the base of the platform was an exquisitely carved panel of a countryside scene with rolling hills, olive groves, and grazing goats. It was exquisite craftsmanship.

Phillip bent over, grabbed the side of the platform, and tried to move it. It gave a little but not much. He climbed up the steps, the timber creaked eerily as he moved toward the chair and sat down. He surveyed the scene and understood immediately what he was seeing. This was a private collection and the throne was there for the collector to appreciate his or her personal hoard. But whose was it, Sonia's? No, he thought, this is a masculine domain. It must be her father or her grandfather. Perhaps it all started with Max and has grown since. Clearly, someone is looking after it, but how did they get it all down here and there must be a light switch somewhere. He stood up, mind spinning and went to survey the final two bays. Bay four was identical to bay two. Bay five was the same as bay one but without a door. He went back up to rejoin the others.

Salome was beside herself with excitement. Amanda too, even Barbara appeared keen to hear what he had to say.

"Tell me," said Salome.

"It's too fantastic," said Phillip showing them the video. "But before we rush down there, I need to reassure everyone that the crypt has been built like a tank and I didn't see a trace of any rats."

"Rats?" said Barbara. "You sure?"

"Positive, not a trace of droppings anywhere."

"Well, just in case you're wrong, I'm not going

down there unarmed," said Barbara going to retrieve the hammer and chisel from the treasury. When she returned, she said, "I'm also a little bit claustrophobic but as long as it's not too narrow and there is some light, I'll be OK."

"The camera light is most effective," said Phillip. "But take your phone or is there a flashlight in your car?"

"No, my phone will have to do."

"Then are we ready?"

Nervous nods all round, each holding phones in hand with lights blazing. They gazed expectantly at Phillip, who led the way down the staircase, along the passage, and through the door that he'd left ajar. He went in; the ladies followed and gathered closely around him. He could smell their excitement tinged with a hint of fear. They looked around anxiously pointing their phone flashlights at everything, taking it all in.

"Any comments?" said Phillip.

"What is it," said Salome.

"A museum?" said Barbara clinging onto Phillip's arm.

"I think it's a collector's den," said Phillip. "And someone takes excellent care of everything. Feel free to wander about and let me know if you recognize anything resembling a light switch. Amanda, there is some Arabic script on the two tombs. See if you can translate any of it."

Slowly, everyone began to relax.

"I can't see any rats," said Barbara letting go of Phillip and venturing off on her own, chisel and hammer in one hand, phone in the other.

Phillip climbed back up and took a seat on the

throne. He placed his arms on the armrests and surveyed all that he could see. He fumbled around the arms trying to find a light switch but there was nothing.

Amanda returned from inspecting the tombs. "It's an ancient script so I can't recognize most of it," she said. "But I think the tomb in the second bay is the last Arab Mayor of Vélez, and I think that it's his wife in the fourth bay. If so, there's likely to be other graves but so far I haven't seen any sign of them."

"I think you'll find that you're standing on top of them," said Phillip.

Amanda rocked back and forth, looked up at him and said, "You're right. This must be an Arab graveyard. The archeologists would wet their pants to play with this lot. More relevant for us though is, are all the contents of Las Claras Treasury here? I'll start looking. She took the inventory out of her bag. She and Salome began walking up and down each aisle looking at the artifacts on display and comparing them with Abraham's sketches.

"These artifacts are in excellent condition," said Amanda looking at an exquisite cross. "And they all seem to be from Spanish Cathedrals. However, so far, other than the three ships and some items in the wall niches, I haven't seen anything from the Las Claras Treasury."

"I suspect they are in the drawers," said Phillip.

"Why do you think that?" said Salome.

"All the items in the display cases are marked 'Hoarders', whereas the only visible Las Claras pieces are not, along with all the items that I've seen so far in the drawers. Try a closer inspection of the stuff in the drawers and wall niches," said Phillip. "I'll think you'll find everything from the Las Claras inventory."

"What is the significance of 'Hoarders' written on some items and not on others?" said Salome.

"Hoarders implies collectors," said Phillip. "If this is a collection, items so marked are probably for sale or exchange, the others remain here for the enjoyment of the owner."

"This can't be a collection made by just one person," said Amanda. "There are too many pieces."

"Perhaps Max kick-started it with the Las Claras treasury," said Salome. "Then added to it over the years"

"When did Max die?" said Phillip.

"1972," said Salome.

"When was your grandfather reputed to have stolen the convent treasury?" said Phillip.

"1937," said Salome.

"So that's at least thirty-five years of collecting," said Phillip.

"How many items do you estimate are here?" said Salome.

"In excess of a thousand," said Phillip.

"Divided by thirty-five," said Salome. "That's almost twenty-nine items a year, or nearly one a fortnight? That's an incredible number for one man."

"Maybe Max stole fewer and his son carried on?" said Amanda.

"We can only speculate," said Phillip, "But what I am certain about, is that the entrance door was built about the same time as the Virgin and her housing upstairs. However, the wiring for the wall lamps and niche lighting is much newer and have you noticed how spotless everything is. So, my questions are, who is looking after the collection, are they still adding to it, and what is this Hoarders thing?"

"Perhaps it's a sale and exchange platform," said Amanda. "Where other collectors and artifact thieves can do anonymous business?"

"And maybe this is the showroom?" said Phillip.

A loud boom echoed eerily around the crypt, followed shortly after by the sound of a thump and several seconds later another. Everyone froze and pointed their lights in the direction of the noise.

"The door," shouted Phillip. "Someone's shut the fucking door."

Phillip sprinted over and threw himself against it.

"Come, everyone, help me," he said.

They all ran toward Phillip, placed their phones on the nearest display case and heaved as hard as they could against the door. Muscles were burning, sinews straining as the slow realization of their predicament became understood by each.

Phillip remembered the two beams lying on the floor in the passage. They must have been wedged between the door and the far passage wall. Nothing would shift them.

"Let us out," he shouted banging on the door in frustration.

The others joined in screaming and thumping the door, but they heard nothing beyond the thick timber. They quietened. All they could hear was each other breathing heavily.

Then the camera light went out.

Other than the ghostly glow of their phone lights illuminating the chalices in the display case, it was pitch black.

26

For a moment, there was absolute silence in the crypt as they collected their phones and pointed them around the first bay, too shocked to say a word.

Barbara screamed.

A feral piercing screech that echoed around the confined space terrifying everyone. "What's that in the corner?" said Barbara sobbing. They all pointed their phones in the direction she was indicating, but there was nothing there.

"Barbara, everyone," said Phillip. "Shall we try and remain calm. There is no need to allow your imagination to run riot. The crypt is the same as it was before the door was shut and the light went out. And just to remind you, we saw nothing to concern us."

"That may be," said Salome struggling not to cry. "Until some asshole entombed us down here with all these dead people?"

"There's only one door," said Barbara wailing. "And that is as solid as a rock. We're going to die in this hell-hole."

"We don't know," said Phillip. "Who shut us in here, why, or if it is an attempt to starve us to death. It could be that they reveal themselves to us and negotiate something. Until we are better informed, I suggest we don't waste any time speculating on disaster and concentrate on finding a way out of here. Does anyone have a phone signal? Mine doesn't."

They all checked their devices.

Phillip despaired when he saw them shaking their heads. Their only chance of communication with the outside world shot to pieces. Now, how the hell were they going to escape? Try and stay chilled, he told himself.

"We left the cold bag in the church," he said. "Did anyone bring water or a snack?"

"I have a small bottle," said Salome fishing it out of her bag.

"And I have a cereal bar," said Barbara holding it up.

"Just leave them on the display case for now," said Phillip. "We'll share them later."

"They won't keep us alive for long," said Barbara.

"You'd be surprised at how little humans need to survive on," said Phillip. "Although it varies from person-to-person. Even without water, we can last at least three to four days."

"You, maybe," said Barbara, sobbing. "But three to four hours down here will kill me."

"Nonsense," said Phillip stroking her shoulder. "You'll be fine and I'm sure that we'll be out in an hour or two. However, we should prepare for a long stay. I suggest we turn off all the phones bar mine to save battery. I'll turn mine off when the battery is at ten percent. Then we can turn on yours, Amanda. Etc."

"But what if my Mum calls?" said Barbara sobbing again. "She might need her incontinence pad changing."

The others tried to repress a giggle.

"Sorry, but she'll have to…er," said Phillip. "Well, I'm sure she'll be OK. Did any of you say where they were going?"

"No, we agreed to keep this secret," said Salome. "What about you Barbara?"

"I just told my sister that I was going to work in Vélez and if I was late, she was to call me."

"What time would you call late?" said Phillip.

"Mum's bedtime is around eleven. My sister usually pops in to say goodnight. She only lives in the next street. If I'm not there, she'll call me and just put Mum to bed."

"So that means nobody will know we're missing until the earliest at eleven tonight," said Phillip checking the time on his phone. "That's a tad more than twelve hours away meaning that nobody will start looking for us until tomorrow."

"What do you mean?" said Barbara shaking.

"The police usually wait twenty-four hours in missing person's cases before initiating searches," said Phillip. "As we are mature adults with no history of any mental problems, they will be reticent to start anything for at least forty-eight hours. Therefore, we should resolve ourselves to being here for at least two days, maybe three with practically no food and water. I suggest that we don't drink anything until tonight when we will share out half of what we have then try to sleep. We should take out the sackcloth wrappings from the drawers and use them as floor coverings and blankets.

Handbags can be used as pillows."

"Where did you learn all this survival stuff?" said Salome.

"British Intelligence Corps, but it was a long time ago since I've had to use it."

"What about, you know, er, the toilet?" said Barbara. "You're not expecting us to save it for later consumption?"

"Ew, disgusting," said Amanda.

"Hopefully, we'll be long gone prior to considering more drastic survival methods but your toilet, er... issue, is a fair point," said Phillip. "I suggest that we live at this end by the door and traipse to the far end to attend to business. Also, I think we should all move slowly from now on. Try to conserve as much energy as we can while we try and find a way out of here. Our goal should be to survive as long as we can, pray that Barbara's sister raises the alarm, and the police take her seriously."

"How do you propose to find a way out," said Salome.

"Barbara, would you mind taking the hammer and chisel and start chipping away at the wall surrounding the door frame. The timber might be newish, but the brickwork is over seven hundred years old and should crumble easily, after that it's relatively soft sandstone. If that proves too hard, then attack the timber. If we can chip through to the hinges on the external side and loosen them, we should be able to open the door."

Barbara turned her phone light back on, fished the tools out of her bag and turned toward the door. She was still upset and frightened but at least with something purposeful to take her mind off the negativity pulsing around her head.

"Salome," said Phillip. "The sketch you found under the memorial stone. Didn't it indicate an exit to the north around where the throne is?"

"If you mean the squiggly blue lines," said Salome. "Then yes."

"Shall we go and take a look," said Phillip. "Perhaps there is an alternative way out of here behind it."

They turned and headed for the throne.

Tentative hammering could soon be heard as Barbara attacked the brickwork. It gradually became more aggressive as she improved her technique. The occasional curse echoed around the crypt as she missed the chisel and connected with her thumb. Successive misses soon calmed her initial enthusiasm and the irregular banging evolved to a rhythmical tapping.

Amanda and Salome swarmed all over the throne, pulling and pushing on all its components. Phillip left them to it, turned his light on and went to inspect the far end of the crypt, looking for a change in the brickwork pattern that might denote a blocked up old entrance. He found nothing so went to see how Barbara was progressing.

"Anything?" he inquired as he passed Amanda and Salome crawling underneath the throne.

"No," came a muffled reply from one of them.

He found Barbara slumped by the door, perspiration running down her brow, stabbing at her phone, tears streaming down her face. Phillip inspected her work. There were a few holes in the brickwork, but she'd hardly made any progress.

"Sorry," she said holding up her right hand which was bleeding slightly between thumb and forefinger. "Blister burst."

Phillip picked up the chisel and continued where

Barbara had left off. After half an hour, his hand too was blistered but he persevered. He was making some progress, but the brickwork was proving more resilient than he'd anticipated. He switched to the timber around where he estimated the upper hinge to be and began anew. An hour later, the rock-hard timber had yielded hardly at all and the chisel was completely blunt. He stopped tapping and appraised his handiwork.

"That'll take weeks," said Amanda touching his arm.

"You're right, but I can't just do nothing."

"When was the equipment due back at the hire store?"

"Tomorrow, why?"

"Didn't you have to tell them where you would be using it?"

"Smart, why didn't I think of that? Yes, I had to pay a cash deposit and give them the site address."

"So, if you don't return everything, they may report you to the police."

"They may indeed. I wonder?"

"What?"

"The camera cable. Is it still there?"

"Let's go see."

They ran back to the throne. Phillip shone his light above the display case, then up at the ceiling.

"Fuck," he said.

"No cable," she said.

"Double fuck," said Phillip.

"And that means," she said.

"The rental contract was on the floor by the drill. If our jailor is smart, they'll have returned the equipment and probably collected my cash deposit."

"Another avenue closed then?" said Amanda as they returned to the others by the door.

"Perhaps."

"Tell you what. Let's swap," said Amanda. "We've prodded and tugged every possible component of the throne and found nothing."

"Good idea," said Phillip. "Barbara?" who was still sitting on the floor stabbing frustrated at her phone. "Fancy a go at the throne for a change?"

She stopped what she was doing. Phillip gave her a hand up and they walked slowly back to the center bay. He gently massaged his blistered hand feeling dejected at their lack of progress. His battery was down to thirty percent. He stood before the throne pointing his dying beam at it. He knew the girls had been thorough, so he ignored the structure and paid more attention to the brickwork surrounding the back panel of the throne.

He tried to put himself in the mindset of the architect of the collector's den. His gray cells wandered randomly considering all he had observed so far.

"Before we start," he said to Barbara. "Let's try and think this through. The crypt itself is ancient but the wall niches, lighting, display cabinets, artifacts, and this throne are newcomers. What do you think?"

"The door was made around the same time as the Virgin and housing," said Barbara. "Early 1920's I would estimate but the throne was made during the Civil War," "You can tell by the material used and the style of joints."

"Impressive," said Phillip.

"My father was a carpenter. I used to spend hours at his workshop listening to his conversations with customers and watching him work. When I'd finished school, I worked for him as an apprentice furniture maker until cheap Chinese imports put us out of business about ten years ago. That's when I started driving."

She climbed up and took a close inspection of the chair. "See, she said. "The chair has no nails or screws. During the war, all metals were used to make weapons or bullets. Carpenters had to revert to using dowels and glue."

"How do you know it's not an antique?"

"The timber is olive wood," said Barbara. "Which is all there was around here at that time. Olive is a beautiful looking timber but is terrible and time consuming to work. It seasons badly, is full of defects, can break your cutting edges and give off toxic sawdust. Having said that, because of its associations with Bethlehem, it is treasured by the religious community and is used in churches for small one-off projects."

"Then this could have been made by Max Augustin?"

"The style and quality of workmanship are as good as I saw upstairs in the church, and he built most of that didn't he?"

"So, I believe. Can you tell if it was built in situ, or made elsewhere and brought here?"

"It was definitely built in a workshop and brought in here in one piece."

"How do you know that?"

"To glue and dowel these legs and arms to the seat and back panel needed massive heavy metal clamps, and fresh air to blow the adhesive fumes away. There wasn't any air-conditioning in those days."

"Therefore, Max could have made it in his workshop and brought it here."

"Yes, but not down those stairs," said Barbara. "It's way too big, particularly this back panel."

"What about the display cases?"

"I think they maybe less than ten years old," said Barbara. "And were brought here in pieces and assembled in situ. The safety glass is beveled and pinned together by modern corner junctions that don't interrupt the viewers' enjoyment of the contents."

"Ten years," said Phillip. "Which would clearly implicate Sonia's involvement in setting all this up which means that three generations of her family have known about and exploited this crypt for illegal activities. But to keep it secret they couldn't use the church entrance. Too many nosy neighbors and it's also too narrow for large items. In which case, there must be a tunnel that connects the crypt to the workshop, and it can only be behind this throne. So, our only remaining question is how to move the damned thing?"

"Bearing in mind how the Virgin moved upstairs," said Barbara. "Why don't we just push it and see what happens?"

"You take one side," said Phillip. "I'll take the other."

They took their positions. One hand on the armchair, the other on the back panel.

"On the count of three," said Phillip. "One, Two, Three."

They heaved.

27

"Why isn't he answering his damn phone?" said Prado to el jefe. They were sitting in Prado's office reviewing the latest development in the Crown case.

"Is Phillip usually so elusive?" said el jefe.

"Never, always responds. Even if he's in a meeting, he'll text me and call me back at his first opportunity."

"Try Amanda, perhaps she knows where he is."

Prado called Amanda. He let it ring until her voice mail kicked in, left a message, and ended the call. He then sent them both texts asking to contact him urgently.

"Did either of them say where they were going?" said el jefe.

"He mentioned doing something to help a friend of theirs but omitted to tell me where or what."

"None of our business I suppose," said el jefe. "What did we do for translating before we worked with Phillip and Amanda?"

"With cases involving foreigners, not much."

"Point taken," said el jefe. "That's why we appointed you."

"One person for all these cases and this Crown one seems to be escalating into something potentially massive."

"All our resources are available to you as and when needed," said el jefe. "Perhaps I can help. What's the problem?"

"Until about five minutes ago, everything was fine. I was about to leave for Marbella to interview the sister of Marquez and her husband. Then I received a call to say that there's been a response to our article in Sur in English appealing for former staff at Marbella International College to come forward."

"Excellent why don't we go and meet whoever it is?"

"Do you think I'd be sitting here if it were that simple? It was the editor of the paper that called me. She had a call from Cudeca, the cancer charity in Benalmadena. One of their hospice patients is on her death bed and claims to be the former administrator of the College. She read the article and is desperate to tell us her story. I've spoken with the Hospice Director who informs me that she can't talk and her only means of communication is in handwritten notes. Problem is her handwriting is so bad, only native English speakers can make out what she is trying to tell them."

"Can't one of the nurses help?"

"Probably, but I'd prefer Phillip. His questioning techniques would be more effective."

"It doesn't sound if we have much time and we could be waiting hours for Phillip to contact us so I will come with you. I have a few urgent matters to attend to first. Shall we meet at the carpool in fifteen minutes?"

"Thanks, boss."

"My pleasure. Good to leave my desk and do some real policing for a change."

El jefe took went out the door, looking pleased with himself.

Prado spun around in his chair and stared out of the window in the direction of the neighbor's washing line and frowned. Today there was absolutely nothing delicate hanging there to distract him from his frustration. The offer from el jefe was helpful and his English was perfect, but he had about as many questioning skills as a gorilla.

"Where are Phillip and Amanda?" he said out loud then span around, picked up the Crown file and flicked through it aimlessly.

His phone rang.

"Hola Ana," he said to his forensics chief. "Anything to brighten my day?"

"Sorry Leon, no. The laboratory in Madrid has only been able to predict a facial likeness from one of the DNA samples on the film canister. The one made by Crown when he hid the canister up in the garage roof some two years ago. As for the remainder, all they could conclude is that they belonged to young persons between the approximate ages of ten and fourteen."

"Thanks, Ana, let's hope that will come in handy."

Prado picked up the Crown file and double-checked to see that the photos of Marquez and the class were there. He slipped the photos into his jacket pocket, placed his Panama hat at his preferred jaunty angle and headed out to meet el jefe.

***

The Cudeca Foundation was formed in the early 1990s by Costa de Sol English resident Joan Hunt. She lost her husband to cancer. The process of which revealed that there was little or no palliative care in Spain for cancer sufferers. To remedy this, she opened several charity shops along the coast to raise funds to build a free to use care center then ultimately a hospice with nine rooms and professional staff. It was opened in 2005.

Prado drove. It was the first time in decades that he'd been anywhere in a car with a senior officer. It made him feel inadequate and schoolboy-like. But in Phillip's absence he had no choice, they urgently needed whatever information this poor lady could reveal.

El jefe was talking on his phone as they headed west along the coastal motorway towards Benalmadena. Prado couldn't help but overhear his side of the conversation, but he may as well have been listening to Swahili. He understood the words, but the meaning was all gobbledygook and probably had something to do with police management or internal politics.

They turned off at the part of the motorway cut high up into the side of the limestone mountain where one of the many tourist attractions of Benalmadena, a cable car from the town passed over the road. It provided access to the top of the three thousand meters high Mount Calamorro, where there were falconry displays, hiking routes, and an open-air planetarium,

The junction sign also mentioned the Tivoli World amusement park. They headed down the hill, through a few residential streets and pulled up outside the Cudeca Hospice. The single-storey building surrounded by pleasant trees and gardens was situated just below the motorway with amazing views over the park, the busy tourist resort and sparkling blue Mediterranean.

The director, a dour-faced Spanish lady in her mid-fifties wearing a white coat led them to the room of Dorothy Newbold.

"Sadly, Dot, as she likes to be called, is near her end," said the Director. "She's ninety-one, has lived on her own in Marbella for over fifty years until about three months ago when she moved in here to recuperate from mouth cancer surgery. Sadly, it's spread all over, but her brain works fine, and her memory is amazing. It's just the rest of her that's fading fast."

"Thank you," said el jefe. "Is she in pain?"

"Only mildly," said the Director. "She's well medicated."

"We'll be as quick as we can."

Prado had to look twice. Who was this el jefe? Charming, polite, smooth even. Perhaps he'd misjudged him.

The director led them down a short corridor. Prado turned his nose up at the pervading smell of disinfectant as they passed several closed doors. He dreaded to think what was going on behind them. Hospitals were not his thing. She opened the next door on the right and led them in.

There were two beds in the room, Dorothy was in the one nearest the door propped up on pillows. She was tiny, extremely pale, wrinkled and dressed in a hospice gown. It's logo visible over her almost flat chest. A monitor was connected to her wrist and the end of a feeding tube hung out of one of her nostrils.

Prado thought she was dead already, but the steady heartbeat on the monitor confirmed that Dorothy was still ticking.

The Director approached the bed and gently picked up Dorothy's hand.

Dorothy opened her eyes and seemed relieved to see el jefe's uniform as he stood at the end of her bed.

"Dot," said the director. "This is Jefe Superior Gonzalez Ruiz and Inspector Prado. They are here to talk to you. They speak English."

Dorothy indicated her glasses, a pencil, and notepad on the bedside cabinet. The director passed them over. Dorothy put on her butterfly framed spectacles, scribbled her first note, and held it up. El jefe moved forward and looked at the note.

"I think it says photos," he said in Spanish. "Inspector, can you show Dorothy what we have?"

Prado removed the photos from his pocket. He held up the best photo of Marquez in front of Dorothy. She signaled that he should hold it nearer. He edged it forward until she nodded, then scribbled furiously, and held it up for el jefe.

"Headmaster Marquez, bastard," translated el jefe grinning at Dorothy.

With a large scar on her neck and facial skin stretched tightly over her jaw, it was a struggle for Dorothy to move her facial muscles. However, Prado's heart went out to her when he spotted her bloodshot eyes twinkling. She nodded that he should read the remainder of the note.

"He failed to pay me for the last six months of my work," said el jefe in Spanish before switching back to English. "Dot, what else can you tell us about him?"

Dorothy thought for a moment, continued writing

and turned the pad for el jefe.

"Unmarried, lived on own but had a strange relationship with sister. Taught art and photography. Suspected of abusing pupils but never caught. Had his hand in the till but was clever at covering up. Always having rows with Crown senior. When the school closed, he had cleaned out its bank accounts as well as doing a deal with golf course developer behind Crown's back."

"How much was in the accounts?" said el jefe.

Dorothy thought again and wrote down a number. She held it up. Prado whistled.

"Seven hundred thousand Euros," said Prado. "Plus, the four million from the developer."

"Did Marquez have any hobbies?" said el jefe.

Dorothy nodded, then wrote them down.

El jefe read them out for Prado. "Child pornography, betting on bullfights and collecting religious artifacts. There's one more but she can't remember. Show her the class photo please."

Prado extracted it and held it in front of Dorothy. She peered myopically at it and shook her head.

"The detail is too small for her," said the director. "I have a magnifying glass in reception, hold on, I'll fetch it."

The director left leaving Dorothy in the care of the two cops.

"Are you comfortable?" said el jefe. Dorothy nodded. "Anything I can do for you?" he said.

She scribbled, and her body shook with merriment as she held up her reply. "Water," read el jefe. "All this talking is thirsty work."

Prado saw some in a jug on the cabinet, poured her a glass and gave it to her. She took it with a trembling hand and sipped.

The director returned with a huge magnifying glass. Her otherwise dour expression softened to one of pleasant surprise when she saw Prado helping Dot with her water. "Thank you, Inspector," she said smiling now. "I think the two of you have made quite an impression on Dot. We're forever on the lookout for more volunteers. If you have the occasional spare moment, I'm sure we could find something for you to do."

"Thank you, director," said el jefe. "We'd be delighted. Can we call you when we are free?" She laughed and handed over the glass to Dot.

Prado held up the class photo and Dorothy peered at it through the lens and nodded. Prado waited with bated breath. Dorothy picked up the pencil and began writing.

"I can't recall all the names," she wrote. "But there is someone missing from the photo who will."

"Who?" said el jefe.

"The school psychologist; Diana Vega. She was fresh out of university but had an excellent memory. She only came one week in four but knew all the kids by name. I'll do my best here, but you really need to find her to get all the names."

28

"It's no good," said Phillip after several seconds of trying to heave the throne away from the wall. "It won't budge. Yet there just has to be a tunnel behind it."

"I'm sure you're right," said Barbara breathing heavily. "Perhaps it can only be opened and closed from the other side. It means that unless we can break through the other door, we're stuck here until someone comes to rescue us."

"Then let's all concentrate on the door we came in."

They went to join Salome and Amanda in the first bay and found them both in tears.

"What's wrong?" said Phillip putting his arm around Amanda.

"This," said Salome holding up a broken chisel and a hammer handle without a head.

"It's all my fault," said Salome shoulders shuddering. "I gave it an extra hard thump, the chisel snapped, and the hammerhead flew off. It's over there somewhere." She pointed toward the corner.

"I guess domestic quality tools aren't up to such a major task," said Phillip. "At least you didn't break a display cabinet. The last thing we need is broken glass under our feet in the pitch black." With that, his phone light went out, shortly followed by Amanda's.

They all looked at Barbara, her beam was fading fast. "Twenty percent remaining," she said.

Salome turned hers on. "Still at eighty percent," she said.

"That's about another hour's worth of light," said Phillip. "After that, we're in the dark. I propose that we spend that time gathering as many sacks from the drawers as we can and make ourselves as comfortable as possible. It's going to be a long two to three days."

Phillip was trying to stay positive for the ladies' benefit but inside he despaired. Nobody knew where they were, and it was only Barbara's sister with the possibility of raising the alarm. What if she didn't? He tried to banish the negative waves from his mind as they sat huddled around one of the display cabinet drawers.

"We're not making much progress," said Amanda. "At this rate, we'll be unpacking these drawers in the pitch black."

"But every piece is so beautiful," said Barbara passing a stunning golden cross to Salome for inspection.

"And something in my head is telling me to love and respect it, not just rip the sackcloth off and plonk it back where it came from," said Salome. "Also, we have to take the labels off the cloth and tie them to the piece. Otherwise, nobody will know where they came from."

"Why are we doing that?" said Phillip. "We need the sackcloth to keep warm and rest comfortably. Our survival is at stake here and we need all the cloth before we lose the light."

"Point taken," said Salome speeding up her unwrapping.

They worked faster but with one working light, they could open one drawer at a time before moving onto the next.

"How's the battery?" said Phillip after they'd moved into the fifth bay.

"Fifty-five percent," said Salome after glancing at the screen. "Do we have enough cloth yet?"

"Another half an hour should do it," said Phillip.

They worked as fast as they could. Not even bothering to replace items back in drawers. The cloth pile was growing but the light was fading.

"I don't know what most of these items are," said Phillip. "Anyone able to enlighten us?"

"What you're unwrapping there is a reliquary," said Barbara picking up the label from a small silver ornate and oval-shaped container. "The description says that it's a Gothic holy sepulcher made in Paris during the thirteenth century. It's from Catedral de Santa María de Vitoria-Gasteiz."

"What does a reliquary signify?" said Amanda.

"It's usually a container kept under the altar. It contains bones, skin, a remnant of clothing or something touched by a popular religious icon such as Jesús, one of his disciples or a local saint. A famous example is the remains of the apostle St. James, which are in a reliquary at the Cathedral in Santiago de Compostela in Galicia."

"I saw those in the crypt," said Phillip. "The bones

are divided into various compartments in a cedar box which is inside an embossed silver chest."

"You did the walk?" said Barbara, eyebrows raised in surprise. "Which one?"

"All the way from Saint-Jean-Pied-de-Port in France. Over 780 kilometers in thirty-four days."

"El Camino Frances," said Barbara. "Did you hug St. James's statue when you reached the cathedral? Most pilgrims do."

"No, the queue was too long," said Phillip. "And frankly, I was only there to have my certificate stamped proving that I'd completed the walk."

"But didn't you feel just a little bit religious after all that time walking with fellow Christians?"

"Actually, I found that most people I talked with were walking to discover themselves, not God," said Phillip. "But it was certainly a spiritual experience and helped me sort out my head which was truly fucked up at the time. Are you a practicing Catholic Barbara?"

"To a certain extent, yes. I take my Mum every Sunday. Despite her severe dementia, she has total recall of the hymns, prayers and worshipping routines and sings like a canary. It's almost creepy to watch her behaving normally inside the church, yet as soon as she's outside the church, she reverts back to her doolally state."

"This reliquary is from Huelva," said Amanda shaking it. "It appears to be empty."

"Most of them are nowadays," said Barbara. "The contents are too valuable to leave in an open church. However, some of the items here are bound to contain something precious."

"Does that mean worshippers have been paying homage to fresh air?" said Amanda.

"Yes, but they won't know that," said Barbara.

"What puzzles me," said Phillip as they were removing the sacking from a particularly stunning fifteenth-century reliquary from Zaragoza Cathedral. "Is why so many missing artifacts aren't public knowledge and subject to a police investigation?"

"Perhaps they are or were replaced by forgeries?" said Amanda.

"Or nobody noticed that they were stolen," said Salome.

"Precisely," said Amanda.

"Everyone in Vélez will tell you that Max Augustin was a genius with artifacts," said Barbara. "Perhaps it was him that made the forgeries and swapped them over when visiting his customers. He was so respected, that he could walk into any Cathedral in Spain unannounced and do whatever he liked."

"Then he brought the originals back here and added them to his collection," said Salome.

"And sat on his throne drinking them all in," said Phillip.

"I find it sad really," said Barbara. "That such a famous and well-respected gentleman resorted to gloating over his secret hoard six meters underground, as against enjoying his privileged position above it among the best of Vélez society. Perhaps he was funny in the head?"

"He fought in the trenches during the first world war," said Salome. "That was enough to drive anybody insane."

"I can vouch for that," said Phillip, "Two tours in Afghanistan nearly drove me mad."

"You didn't tell me that," said Amanda.

"I don't like to talk about it," said Phillip.

"Well this could be your last opportunity to talk about anything," said Amanda.

Phillip looked at her in the fading light. Reached out his hand and stroked her cheek. She looks like an angel, he thought.

"I guess we have nothing else to do and if it helps pass the time," said Phillip. "Are you all interested in this?"

"Yes," said all three.

"OK," said Phillip. "Not sure where to begin really."

"Just tell us what it was like," said Salome.

"Did you kill anyone?" said Amanda unwrapping another item and throwing the cloth onto the pile.

"My first tour was based at intelligence headquarters in Kabul. It was dangerous out on the street and I narrowly missed a few potentially fatal IDE's. Most of my time though was spent indoors on a computer in my office in one tent, in my bed in the next or at the canteen just around the corner."

"What were you doing?" said Salome.

"Monitoring enemy communications."

"But you don't speak Afghan or whatever they speak over there," said Amanda.

"They have two languages: *Dari* and *Pashto*. Dari is often referred to as Afghan Persian and no I don't speak either, but I had two translators who streamed everything at me in English. My job was to identify locations and movements of Taliban troops then feed them through to the Intelligence Committee, who passed on their conclusions to the front line."

"How long were you there?" said Salome.

"The first tour was eighteen months with a one month break back at the base near Bedford. That's in central England. The second tour was much shorter. I was in the front-line liaising with the Intelligence Committee and passing on information to the infantry. I had to join them in their direct attacks, and it was… it was." He paused as he remembered then bowed his head as the tears rolled down his cheeks. "Sorry," he said.

Amanda shuffled over to him on her backside and hugged him hard and whispered in his ear. "Sorry darling, I didn't mean to push you."

"No, it's OK," he said breathing deeply. "It might help us all put our current situation in perspective. We may well be doomed to die but at least it will be calmly and with dignity. There, you're just foreign scum to be eliminated at all costs by fanatics whose mental health is twisted so badly, they behave worse than animals. It's a question of kill or be killed. In order to protect yourself and colleagues, you do whatever is necessary and don't bat an eyelid. The hard bit is seeing your best mate blown to bits and scraping his brains off your uniform."

"Oh my God," said Barbara. "I had no idea."

"And so, you shouldn't," said Phillip. "The politicians and media filter that out and make brutal conflict sound like an ideological exercise. Whereas the reality of war is a barbarous business that usually achieves absolutely nothing but knowing that, we continue to do it. In many ways, I can relate to the emotional forces driving Max Augustin after the disgrace of the First World War and the unbalanced peace treaty afterward. It was bad enough for our boys but at least they had jobs and food to go back to. The German soldiers had it far worse; a terrible time on the Western Front followed by disease, starvation, and chaotic government. For Max to sit here in his throne in total silence and enjoy these calming artifacts must have helped him escape his nightmares of the trenches and the subsequent torment suffered by his fellow countrymen."

"Perhaps, that's what this is?" said Salome. "Max's heaven on Earth."

Salome's light flickered and went out.

29

El jefe drove the car toward Marbella to give his subordinate the opportunity to absorb Dorothy's list. She'd managed to remember two-thirds of them before tiredness overcame her. She fell asleep halfway through the last name.

The Crown twins were next to each other in the back row exactly where he and Phillip had placed them. Malcolm was standing behind Marquez. Patrick O'Reilly was also there but he was a lot smaller than Malcolm for his age and was sitting in the front row on the floor at the feet of an unknown Señora, whom Dorothy had recalled as the Spanish language teacher.

Prado looked at the other names, trying to guess at the identity of the other two with fingerprints on the film canister. If the ages had varied between ten and fourteen and Crown and O'Reilly were fourteen, it followed that the other two were younger.

He peered at the front row where the smaller children were concentrated. There was a pretty blond girl next to O'Reilly who looked about ten, but Dot had forgotten her name. In the same row, there were four other girls and seven boys all between ten and twelve. None of the names meant anything to Prado.

"Has Dot's testimony helped?" said el jefe.

"I'm happy she identified O'Reilly," said Prado taking his phone out of his pocket. "And it's good to know the names of some of the others in the photo but we really need to find the psychologist, Diana Vega. I'll tell the office so they can make a start."

Prado made his call.

"What are you expecting to find in Marbella?" said el jefe when he'd finished.

"Hopefully, to learn more about Marquez that might help point us to him."

"What do you think Dorothy was implying when she said they had a strange relationship?"

"Incestuous?" said Prado.

"That was my impression too. I understand the local officers visited the house to investigate a fake noise complaint. What was in their report?"

"The husband is in a wheelchair suffering from Muscular Sclerosis. The sister complained about the lack of police interest in the suspicious death of Pablo, her eldest brother. He died suddenly of a heart attack eighteen months ago. She was adamant that he had been murdered because he'd had a recent check over by his regular doctor who had declared him top fit for a man in his early seventies. However, the police physician was equally certain that he'd died of natural causes and declared there were no grounds for a postmortem. The body was cremated, and his ashes disposed of, so we have no way of reopening the case."

"How old is the sister?"

"She's fifty-nine. Her husband is sixty."

"So quite a lot younger than Marquez would be, right?"

"Correct, Sir."

"It might be a crazy idea, but could the husband be Marquez."

"According to the local officers, the husband is bald, tiny, withered and can only whisper in short bursts. Marquez was a big hairy man and eight years older than the husband. It seems unlikely."

"Then perhaps the sister pops out to meet Marquez from time-to-time. What I'm saying is that if Marquez and his sister were close as youngsters. It is possible that they are still in touch."

"Then let's ask her," said Prado. "We'll be there shortly."

Twenty minutes later they pulled into the driveway of a small detached townhouse on a tree-lined avenue in an urbanization on the outskirts of Marbella.

"How do you want to play this?" said Prado.

"Take no notice of me, Leon," said el jefe. "I've done my bit with Dorothy, now I want to see the maestro at work."

They climbed out and Prado rang the bell.

"Yes. I'm Teresa Marquez. Come in, Inspector, come in," said the medium height slender woman after they had presented their credentials. She bore a sad expression but had an incredibly pretty and youthful face for her age. Short dark hair framed her oval cheeks setting off her pert nose and light brown hazel eyes. She wore a pink print dress, black woolen tights and a thick black knitted cardigan wrapped around her shoulders. She slipped it off and hung it over a hook hanging on the wall with several other outer garments as she closed the door behind them. "It's colder than usual this evening. My husband Guillermo is in the lounge. Please go through. Can I fetch any refreshments for you both?"

"No, thank you Señora," said Prado looking around him.

They went through a glazed door to a room cozily furnished with flower print armchairs, a sofa, and a wooden coffee table. A fire crackled in the grate. The husband was sitting near it in his wheelchair covered by a blanket. He looked up as they entered and nodded. He watched them.

"He's extremely sensitive to the cold," said Teresa. "So, we have to keep the house extra warm. Feel free to remove your jackets."

"Thanks, but we won't stay long," said Prado as the two officers lowered themselves onto the comfortable sofa. "I'll come straight to the point. I have questions concerning your brother Rodriguez. We're aware that he disappeared back in the early eighties, with a substantial sum of money that he stole from his employer at the school where he worked. Señora Marquez, did you have any knowledge of your brother's crimes?"

"Not at the time."

"When did you discover what he had done?"

"My parents and I had a visit," said Teresa looking extremely uncomfortable.

"From the police?"

"No, from Señor Crown and some brute of an assistant."

"And what did Crown want?"

"He demanded that we send a message to Rodriguez."

"And what was the message?"

"Unless he returned the money, my family would be put through hell, as he put it."

"And did you pass on the message?"

"At the time, we had no way of contacting Rodriquez. We told Señor Crown that, but he refused to believe us."

"And?"

"He searched our house and garage but found nothing."

"Were you telling the truth when you told him that didn't have any contact details for Rodriguez?"

"Yes."

"What did Crown do when he found nothing?"

"He stormed out but promised that he would be closely monitoring everything we did."

"Do you think that he bugged your phone?"

"I hadn't thought about it."

"Do you mind if I check?" said Prado standing.

"Feel free, Inspector," said Teresa. "It's mounted on the wall by the coats in the hallway. It's not particularly fancy, I'm afraid."

Prado found the old push-button phone and unscrewed the earpiece. There was a tiny gadget stuck inside. He called Ana and requested a team to come and test the device. Maybe they could reverse trace it to where it was being monitored. He replaced the earpiece, returned to the lounge, and sat back down.

"How long have you lived in this house?" said Prado.

"Since we were married," said Teresa. "That was in 1988."

"Did Crown ever visit you here?"

"Yes, but only the once. It was just after we moved

in."

"What did he say?"

"He reminded us that wherever we moved to, he would be keeping an eye on us."

"It looks like he's been doing exactly that. Señora I'm sorry to inform you that your phone has been compromised."

"Do you mean someone's been listening in to our phone conversations?" said Teresa exchanging concerned glances with her husband.

"Depends on what type of device it is. Some listen to everything in the house as well. I've requested a communications expert to come and test it. They'll be here in an hour or so. Please don't call anyone until after they have departed. We'd prefer not to alarm whoever may be listening in so wish to leave the bug in place if you don't mind. We might be able to locate where the listening post is based. Will that be in order?"

"Of course, Inspector," said Teresa.

"Thank you Señora. Can you tell me something about Rodriguez?"

"Such as what?"

"What type of person was he, his interests, anything that might help us trace him?"

"You still want to find him, after all this time?"

"It might not surprise you to learn that the Crown family are still hunting for him. I'd hate to think what they may do to him. He'll be safer in our hands."

"Why are they still so persistent? Surely old man Crown must be dead by now?"

"Yes, he is," said Prado. "But you may not be aware of all your brother's crimes against the Crown family."

"What do you mean?"

"We have reason to believe that Rodriguez was

abusing children while he was at the school."

Teresa put her hand to her mouth. "Oh no," she mumbled.

"And we suspect that one of those children was Crown's son. He was a pupil of his."

Teresa buried her head in her hands.

"Señora, I apologize for adding yet more pain to our discussion, but now I have to address a more delicate matter," said Prado, then paused to gauge Teresa's expression. Her bottom lip was quivering. "We've received information that you and your brother were exceptionally close. Was that the case?"

Teresa blushed and looked down at the patterned rug underneath the coffee table.

"I'm ashamed to admit it Inspector but yes, it's true. We were," she said after nearly half a minute of chewing her bottom lip. "I blame myself for all that transpired subsequently. Those poor people lost their money because of me."

"Sorry, Señora but you've confused me," said Prado. "The evidence we've gathered so far indicates that your brother acted alone. Are you saying that you helped him defraud Señor Crown and the school's parents?"

"No," snapped Teresa. "Let me explain. Rodriguez was a difficult boy. A middle child who lived under the shadow of his elder brother Pablo, who in our parent's eyes could do no wrong. We were left on our own while Pablo was wheeled off to do whatever he wanted.

"As a teenager, Rodriguez wasn't good looking and suffered dreadfully from acne. He was obsessed with sex and was always pestering me to help him learn as no other girls wanted anything to do with him. I suppose I felt sorry for him and let him experiment with me."

Prado looked at the husband who sat with his eyes closed and head hanging down. "Señora, should we continue this conversation elsewhere?"

"That won't be necessary, Inspector. My husband and I have no secrets. As I was saying, after he returned from university, Rodriguez rented a small townhouse on Calle Toledo. We continued fooling around there until I was in my mid-twenties and met Guillermo. That was when I told Rodriguez that we must stop and that if he found that difficult, he should seek some therapy."

"He was furious and became violent. He came to my parent's house; they were out at the time; dragged me by my hair up to my room where he raped me."

"Why didn't you report him?"

"My parents persuaded me not to and demanded that Rodriguez seek therapy. He seemed to accept that I was no longer available to him, so we assumed that the therapy had worked. When Crown came around and told us about the stolen money, it was the first we'd heard of it. I immediately blamed myself."

"That was hardly your fault," said Prado.

"Maybe not, but if I'd let him continue our relationship, maybe he wouldn't have stolen the money or, as you now tell me, abused Crown's son."

"I strongly advise you not to think like that, Señora. There is only one person responsible for Rodriguez's actions and that is himself. Is there any way you can help us locate him?"

"I haven't had any face-to-face communications with him since he disappeared. However, when Guillermo became ill about two years ago, he lost his job and I had to quit mine to stay at home and look after him. I asked Pablo for some money as the bank had threatened us with eviction. He helped us out with a loan that enabled us to pay off the mortgage but told us to find Rodriguez to pay him back."

"And did you find him?"

"No, but he did contact us, repaid Pablo and sent us enough to tide us over until our pensions and sickness benefit came through."

"How much was that?"

"Altogether around forty thousand Euros."

"How did you contact him?"

"Many years after he disappeared, he sent me a postcard."

Prado exchanged expectant glances with el jefe.

"When did you receive it?"

"Five, maybe six years ago. I was relieved that he was still alive."

"After all he'd done to you?"

"He's my own flesh and blood, Inspector, and now he's the only one I have left."

"Do you have the postcard?"

"No, Rodriguez said to destroy it."

"From where was it sent?"

"Toulouse, in France."

"What did it say?"

"In the event of emergencies, we were to leave a message in the El Pais personal column saying, 'Graciosa is sinking'. He called me here at home two days after I'd placed the advert."

"How did he know your address and number?"

"We're in the telephone directory."

"Where did he call from?" said Prado.

"He wouldn't say and was only on the line for about twenty seconds."

"How did you receive the money?"

"Via Western Union, straight into our account."

"We'll need to see the bank receipt," said Prado. "Can you email it to us?"

"Sorry, Inspector," said Teresa. "We don't have a computer or a smartphone. I'll have to collect it from the bank and post it to you. Will that be all right?"

"Fine," said Prado. "Thank you for being so frank with us about what must be a difficult phase of your life."

"Life is full of hard times," said Teresa nodding toward her husband. "It was terrible not being able to have children, and now I have to play nurse to Guillermo. You mentioned my brother's interests."

"Only those that were important enough to stay with him through life."

"They're a strange mix, Inspector. Our parents brought us up as strict Catholics. We went to church regularly where he came to adore religious artifacts. He took his small collection of chalices and crosses with him when he disappeared. On the other hand, he loved bullfighting and traveled everywhere to watch his favorite toreros. That's what turned him on to photography which he studied at university. His other passion was paintings, particularly anything by Pablo Picasso. He visited the Picasso Museum in Barcelona at least twice a year and purchased hundreds of his prints. He pined for the day when he could afford to buy an original and was forever firing off letters to the Mayor of Málaga suggesting that they do something to celebrate the artist's birthplace."

Prado and el jefe exchanged glances at this revelation. Prado turned his eyes in the direction of the door. El jefe nodded.

"Before we go, Señora Marquez," said Prado struggling out of the low chair. "I have two more questions."

"How may I help, Inspector?" said Teresa returning his stern gaze.

"Does Rodriguez speak any other languages?"

"Fluent French and English," said Teresa.

"Finally, you told my local colleagues that your elder brother Pablo was probably murdered. Yet all the evidence points to that being impossible. What was it about his death that caused you to suspect foul play?"

"Have you not seen their report?"

"It's probably waiting for me on my desk. Would you mind running it by me one more time?"

"Oh, if I must. It's quite simple. The day after I received the payment from Rodriguez, Pablo told me that he was being followed by a tall smartly dressed man in his late thirties with long hair, he said that he looked like a gypsy. Then I couldn't contact him for a few days and went around to his apartment. Pablo wouldn't answer his door, so I asked the concierge to let me in. I found him dead in his armchair. The concierge told me that he'd returned home late the night before behaving as if he was drunk. Inspector, that was impossible. Pablo was allergic to alcohol. He hadn't touched a drop since that one time during his teens."

"Did the police inquire as to Pablo's whereabouts the night before you found him?"

"The police weren't interested. But I asked around."

"What did you discover?"

"One of his neighbor's spotted him the previous evening. He was in the bar around the corner from his apartment block talking with an attractive blond lady much younger than him. The café owner told me that he had drunk no alcohol as always but when Pablo had paid, his voice was slurring, and he seemed unsteady on his feet. I believe that she had spiked his coffee."

"I suppose that's possible. Was Pablo married?"

"No, he'd always lived at home and nursed our parents until they passed away. Then he'd downsized to an apartment."

"Was he gay?"

"I don't think so, but he was hard to read. He never showed interest in any type of relationship."

"Did you inform the police about him being followed or chatting with the blond?"

"No, his ashes had already been dispersed. What was the point?"

"Did you inherit from Pablo?"

"Everything. However, it wasn't much. He used to be wealthy but after the golf course went bust, he struggled to say solvent."

"I understand that both your brothers were fellow directors and shareholders of Greentrees; the golf course development company."

"What of it?"

"Surely, Pablo must have been aware of Rodriguez's plans to abscond with Crown's money?"

"Pablo and his other shareholders were astounded by what Rodriguez had done. They had no idea of his intentions. What made it even worse for them is that Crown and his bullies forced the company to repay some of what Rodriguez had stolen from him. It wasn't anywhere near the four million Euros, but it was a substantial chunk of the working capital they had needed to develop the course and build the properties. When the crash came in the late eighties it meant they were substantially more financially vulnerable than planned and consequently went bust."

"So, Rodriguez's actions even damaged his own brother?" said Prado.

"There was never any love lost between them. That finished it off totally."

"What did Pablo do after the golf course went bust?"

"He was a qualified accountant so after the bankruptcy was stripped of his license. He spent the next twenty years struggling to find any kind of work and as I said continued to live with my parents until they died."

"What was he living on prior to his death?"

"A small state pension and the remnants from selling our parents property."

"Did you also inherit something from your parents?"

"Under Spanish Law, I should have, but after Rodriguez disappeared, they made a special will leaving everything to Pablo."

"How did that make you feel?"

"Angry, but I was accustomed to that. My parents were glad when I, a mere girl in their eyes, married Guillermo. I was one less mouth to feed."

"Was anything stolen from Pablo's apartment?"

"Not that we could see."

"What happened to his files or computer?"

"After the police released his body for the funeral, we cleaned up his apartment and sold it with everything included. I gave his clothes to a charity shop but his personal effects I have upstairs. Would you like to see them?"

30

A ghostly silence loomed over the crypt. All four of them rooted to their respective spots and alone with their thoughts as they adjusted to an immediate future in absolute darkness. Phillip felt someone grab his arm and hang on tightly.

"Sorry," said Barbara trembling and struggling to speak. "I can't take this."

"Perhaps some food will help," said Amanda.

"And a drink," said Salome. "Where's the bottle?"

"On the display case by the door," said Phillip. "I suggest we transfer back to the first bay and set up house there by the door."

They all stood and held hands. Barbara gripped his tightly, her nails digging into his skin.

Phillip led groping his way toward the door, using the display cases to keep him on track. The others shuffled along behind him. He found the last glass cover, then waved his hand over the smooth surface until it bumped into their limited refreshments.

"Anybody wearing a watch?" he said.

"I have one," said Salome pressing the button on the side of her digital watch. It glowed green in the darkness. "It's coming up to four in the afternoon."

"We'll take a sip each and one small nibble of the bar, then try and rest," said Phillip. "We won't consume any more until tomorrow at the same time."

Barbara wailed. Her disarming cry bounced off the crypt walls as if the spirits of the long-buried Arabs were complaining in sympathy. Phillip put his arm around her shoulder to comfort her. She buried her head in his shoulder and trembled so violently, Phillip thought she was having an epileptic seizure. He picked up the energy bar with his free hand, bit the wrapper to open the top, spat out the plastic, took a tiny bite, passed it to Barbara and said, "Here. Take a bite."

He relished the sweetness of the raisins and crunchy oat flavor.

Barbara let go of him, grabbed the bar, ripped off the cover and stuffed it all in her mouth. She chewed it briefly then gulped it down.

"When you're done. Pass it on to the others," said Phillip concerned about the noises coming from Barbara.

Phillip reached out and connected with Barbara's hand. He grabbed the empty wrapper from it and realized what she'd done.

"Selfish bitch," he shouted pushing her away from him. "She's gobbled the fucking lot."

Barbara fell to the floor bawling.

"What is wrong with her?" said Amanda.

"I don't know," said Phillip. "Cracked under stress, perhaps."

"Here," said Salome touching his arm. "Take this."

She passed Phillip the half-liter water bottle. He shook it. There was still plenty inside. He took his ration, handed it back to Salome and said, "Whatever has happened to Barbara must be awful. I can't imagine what's going on in her head, however, she can no longer be trusted. I suggest you hold onto the bottle while she takes her sip. If she's uncontrollable now, just imagine how bad she'll be in twenty-four hours."

Salome bent down on her knees and groped her way up Barbara's legs until she arrived at her shoulders. She placed a hand underneath the distraught woman's head and heaved her up to a sitting position and presented the bottle to her mouth. "Come, Barbara. Take a sip."

Barbara grabbed the bottle and tried to wrench it from Salome, but Salome had anticipated that and said. "One sip Barbara, or none. Take your pick."

Barbara stopped sobbing. Phillip heard her take a sip and swallow. Salome yanked the drink away from her, replaced the top and put the bottle into her jacket pocket.

"We'll have to watch out for her," said Salome stroking Barbara's cheek.

"What now?" said Amanda sliding her arm around Phillip and resting her head on his chest. Phillip felt her shiver.

"We'll feel colder with less movement and no food inside us," said Phillip. "I suggest we collect all the sacking from the far end, bring it here and make up some bedding. Someone should stay with Barbara."

"I will," said Salome.

Phillip found Amanda's hand and they headed off to the far end of the crypt. They found the sacking easily enough. Phillip tripped over it which dragged Amanda down with him. They both landed softly on the pile of rough material. Phillip wrestled over to lie on his back. Amanda had landed face down on top of him.

"OK?" he whispered in her ear.

"With you, I'm always fine," she whispered squirming against him. "Listen, now that we're on our own, I need to say something to you."

"Go on my love."

"No matter what our fate is here, you are the best thing that ever happened to me. I feel blessed to love you and know that you love me. If I must die here, I won't mind, at least we'll be going together."

Phillip hugged her.

"That is so beautiful. Hopefully, it won't come to that," he said. "But I have no idea how we'll get out of here."

"Me neither," she said wiggling her hips against his. "So, this might just be our last opportunity to, you know, and it'll take my mind off food."

"Are you serious?" giggled Phillip kissing her neck. "We need to conserve all our energy if we're to make it out of here alive. Anyway, the others might hear."

Amanda kissed him.

"They might," she said coming up for air. "But they sure as hell won't be able to see."

"You are serious," he said.

"I sense that you're almost persuaded," she said caressing him. "Or are you just pleased to have me to yourself."

"I'm worried about Barbara," said Phillip. "She's unstable and could do anything. We shouldn't leave her alone too long with Salome."

"OK, let me put it this way," said Amanda reaching between them. "Assume that we gather all the sacking and make some bedding near the others. We're then likely to spend a day or two lying next to each other before someone finds us. What are we going to do? Talk about the weather or tease each other rotten. Couldn't you just for once forget about being Mr. Sensible and make love to me. Pretty please."

They clung desperately to each other and made love quietly but frantically. It didn't take long.

As they lay on the sackcloth in each other's arms and their breathing slowed to normal, Phillip turned to her, rubbed her nose with his and said. "Darling, that was just what the doctor ordered, and thank you for insisting. I was in danger of forgetting my priorities for a minute."

"Don't worry, my love. You stood no chance. Shall we grab the sacking and head back?"

They stumbled in the dark.

"How is she?" said Amanda as they approached the other two.

"Bit calmer now," said Salome. "Just like you two."

"Last chance saloon," said Amanda blushing while dropping a large pile of sackcloth next to her friend. "Here take these. We'll take turns at Barbara."

"Thanks, and talking about sharing," said Salome. "Didn't Phillip volunteer his services at the restaurant the other night?"

"Over my dead body," said Amanda.

"Steady there, ladies," said Phillip stifling a giggle. "Wrong place for graveyard humor. Shall we try and rest?"

They made up some bedding as best they could, but it was still way too early to sleep although Barbara was snoring quietly. The others sat on the cloth, covered their legs with more and leaned against the drawers of a display cabinet.

"I accept that we may not escape from here," said Salome. "However, for peace of mind, I'd prefer to know who shut us in here and why, any ideas?"

"History repeating itself?" said Phillip.

"Do you mean that this is what happened to my grandfather," said Salome. "He died in this hell-hole?"

"I can only guess at the truth," said Phillip. "But, logically, his remains are probably snuggled down in one of the tombstones jumbled up with its original occupant."

"Why do you think that?" said Amanda.

"Where else could he be?" said Phillip. "The Las Claras treasure disappeared with your grandfather in 1937. The police never found any trace of him, his corpse or the treasure."

"The Mother Superior said that the treasure was too heavy for one man to move on his own during a single night and suspected that my grandfather had an assistant," said Salome. "She was positive that it was still nearby."

"And we proved her right," said Phillip. "Here is the treasure, therefore, it's more than likely that your grandfather is still with it."

"Are you saying Max Augustin murdered my grandfather?" said Salome. "By locking him in this crypt and starving him to death. That seems an excessively cruel end to a favored worker."

"Who else could it have been? Max refurbished the church with Abraham's help. Perhaps they found the entrance to the crypt while they were digging out the foundation for the Virgin. She's extremely heavy and would need a solid base. Maybe the Moors had filled in the entrance with rubble to protect their tombs from

Christian abuse. Max and Abraham dug it out, incorporated it into the back of the statue and voila, one crypt that the nuns never knew existed."

"Let me try and understand the timeline on this," said Salome. "Max arrived in Vélez after the First World War. He married a local girl here in the convent during the early nineteen twenties. To thank the sisters for letting him use the place for his wedding, he built the Virgin, and her housing and maybe a few other items. This was when he and my grandfather discovered the entrance to the crypt that we used and was well before the nuns offered him his workshop."

"Correct," said Phillip. "So, at this point, there was no tunnel. When did Max build his workshop?"

"According to the deeds," said Salome. "The lease was signed in 1929."

"In those days, it would have taken him at least a couple of years to finish the workshop," said Phillip. "So, he wouldn't have started the tunnel until the early 1930s."

"The tunnel must be nearly one hundred meters long," said Salome. "It would have taken him years to build."

"Perhaps the Moors had already built it as an alternative exit," said Phillip. "And Max discovered it when he dug out the foundations to construct his workshop. All he had to do was expand it enough to provide easy access for large items, such as the throne."

"Therefore, by 1937," said Salome. "When my grandfather moved the treasure, the tunnel was finished, and the throne had been built to mask its entrance."

"Barbara used to be a carpenter before she began driving," said Phillip. "She estimates that the throne was made during the Civil War."

"So, it was only just in place when Abraham moved the treasure," said Salome.

"When he, and Max moved the treasure," said Phillip. "You've seen how much there is. It must have taken two persons at least."

"So why did Max then lock my grandfather into the crypt?" said Salome. "What had he done that sealed his fate?"

"It could be because Abraham saw that Max was using the crypt as a stash for stolen artifacts," said Phillip. "Or Max saw Abraham as a scapegoat to blame for the disappearance of the Las Claras treasure and grabbed the opportunity to add the convent's whole collection to his in one fell swoop."

"So Max was greedy?" said Salome.

"And ruthless," said Phillip.

"Sounds good to me," said Salome. "But who added the squiggly blue lines to the sketch under the memorial stone?"

"I think your parents did," said Phillip. "Felt tips weren't around during your grandfather's time but they were in the 1980s."

"But how did my parents know there might be a tunnel between the crypt and Max's workshop?"

"They may have reasoned it out as we did," said Phillip. "The throne was too large for the stairs we used so must have come in another way, via a tunnel. The only possible location for it was behind the throne."

"Sorry for being so picky," said Salome. "I'm just trying to understand what transpired. If my parents did add the blue lines. Who returned the sketch and the key back under the memorial stone and resealed it?"

"They did," said Phillip. "Having found their way

into the crypt, they wanted to leave a trail for you or someone to follow. Your grandfather deliberately bricked up all his clues into the toilet wall. Whereas your father gave you everything in a few envelopes along with a letter describing his plans, yet he deliberately left a puzzle still to be solved just in case his clues fell into the wrong hands."

"My parents are down here as well?"

"I think so," said Phillip.

"But by then Max was dead and Sonia must have been a baby," said Salome. "Who else could have locked them down here?"

"Max's son, Sonia's father," said Phillip.

"We don't even know his name?" said Amanda.

"Or anything about him?" said Salome.

"When, or if we manage to escape from here," said Phillip. "He should be our first line of inquiry."

"Followed closely by Sonia," said Salome. "She might be the front person, but her father could be pulling the strings in the background."

"What a scary family," said Amanda.

"Just the right frame of mind to try and sleep," said Phillip.

Salome checked her watch. The green light glowed. "Nine thirty," she said.

Phillip took the moment to check on everybody. Amanda had slipped down and was snuggled under the cloth, her head on her handbag. Salome was in the process of doing the same. But Barbara was lying on her back, wide awake and glaring wildly at him.

31

There hadn't been much in the spare bedroom of Teresa's house to represent over seventy years of a man's life. It was all taped into a small cardboard box half full of photos, a menu from a famous restaurant in Paris, a bible signed by the Bishop of Málaga and an ancient laptop with no cables. Prado had tried to fire it up, but the battery was completely dead, and Teresa had no idea what his password might have been. He'd given her a handwritten receipt for it. Perhaps forensics might be able to access it, but Prado wasn't worried too much about it. He didn't see Pablo effects as the key to this mystery and was only going through the motions to make sure that nothing was left open in the case.

"Thank you for your time," said Prado as they shook hands at the door. "Here's my card. If you kindly send the bank receipt for your brother's Western Union transfer to my office, I'd be most obliged. Sorry that I had to reopen some old wounds, but you've been most helpful. Let me know if anyone representing

Crown contacts you."

"I should thank you, Inspector," said Teresa. "You've opened my eyes to a side of Rodriguez that I hadn't considered. I'd never have dreamed that he had abused children but now I think about it maybe that was what he found attractive about me. I always looked much younger than my years."

"And if I may say, still do," said el jefe.

Teresa blushed and looked coyly downwards. She stood at the open door and watched as they reversed out and drove away.

"We were probably her first visitors' for weeks," said el jefe as they turned out of Teresa's avenue and on to the main road back down into Marbella. The streetlights glowing orange in what was now late evening.

"And she was most grateful for your compliment," said Prado. "Not sure what the #MeToo Movement would have made of it though."

"You thought it inappropriate," said el jefe frowning.

"I did, Sir. Especially, given the nature of her extremely personal interview."

"Then I consider myself reprimanded," said el jefe. "But she was damned attractive."

"I'm sure your wife would agree, sir."

"Yes Prado, you've made your point. So, Marquez posted a card from France. Do you think that signifies that he lives there?"

"We could send his photo to the Toulouse Police, see if a name comes up for a traffic offense or something but I'm relying more on the bank transfer. I can't see him traipsing through France with a briefcase full of cash to a Western Union office, so he must have transferred it from an account somewhere."

"And that might lead us straight to his door," said el jefe.

"Which hopefully will be before anyone else gets to him."

"What if he's had an operation to change his appearance?" said el jefe. "How will we know it's definitely him?"

Prado thought for a minute, his face as black as thunder remonstrating with himself for not thinking of that as a possibility. He turned on the hands-free and called forensics.

"Ana Galvez," came the reply.

"Prado, I'm with el jefe on the way back to the Comisaría. Is your technician on his way to the Marquez house?"

"He is. Forgotten something?"

"Yes, could he collect a DNA sample from Teresa Marquez?"

"Certainly, I'll call him. Anything else? Only I'm at home having supper with the family."

"Sorry to disturb, but I think we're on a hot trail to finding her brother. He sent a postcard from Toulouse to his sister about five years ago and we'll shortly receive a bank document confirming a transfer via Western Union from him to her about eighteen months ago."

"You want me to send his photo and her DNA sample to the French Police?"

"He may well have altered his appearance and of course he's nearly seventy now. Can we rustle up an aged version of his photo first? It will give them a better chance of finding him."

"We can but it will take a couple of days."

"Then do a hairy and a balding version and send everything off to France. One more thing about the device in Teresa's phone. I think it was placed there by Crown over thirty years ago. Is it still likely to be working?"

"The old analog devices were reliable and durable so it's more than probable. The biggest problem is its compatibility with digital lines and monitoring systems but our technician, Eduardo will know."

"Brilliant, call me when you learn something. The money transfer document will be with me in a few days, I'll bring it over as soon as it arrives."

"OK Leon, Good night."

"Thanks, Ana and once again, sorry to disturb you."

"Do you know, Leon?" said el jefe after Prado had ended the call with Ana. "I had a case like this years ago when I was a sergeant stationed in Sevilla. We used our equivalent of Marquez as bait to flush out the elusive mastermind. If we catch Marquez, we could do the same."

"Great idea, sir, but as you said. We have to find him first."

"Let's brainstorm that for a while and see where it takes us," said el jefe taking out his phone and tapping some text into Google maps. "Toulouse is about one hundred kilometers north of the Spanish border."

"That's too far to drive from Switzerland, Lichtenstein, and Monaco," said Prado. "Just to post a card to his sister."

"Why those countries?"

"After selling his boat in the Azores, Marquez would have had to transfer his money somewhere where it would be kept confidential and pay little tax. In those days, we didn't have the money laundering legislation in place as we do now, but he would still need an offshore location. Switzerland etc. were the obvious countries where they asked few questions when depositing money."

"Why not Gibraltar?" said el jefe.

"Too close to home and his previous life."

"Then where else is there?"

"Look on the map, sir. Head due south from Toulouse to the Spanish border. What do you see?"

El jefe was quiet while he swiped the map to expand the screen.

"Ye Gods, Leon," he said. "That must be it."

"That's right Sir, Andorra. A tiny Spanish speaking country most people have never heard of, high up in the Pyrenees with offshore status and fiercely protected bank accounts. It's also an extremely pleasant place to live, especially if you're into snow skiing and convenient for Toulouse or Barcelona airports. I would say that it's the perfect hiding place for our man."

"Catalán," said el jefe. "They speak Catalán, and I agree. Marquez, or at least his money must be there and thankfully, the Andorran Regime is considerably more obliging than our friends in Gibraltar. I'll call them tomorrow and set the ball in motion."

32

Phillip was dreaming of falling endlessly into a bottomless pit. Down and down he went, faster and faster. A fiery abyss burning brightly at the end. His skin tingled with the anticipation of a final roasting. He woke up to feel his shoulders being pinned to the floor by someone's knees and strong hands sliding around his neck then squeezing tightly. He grabbed the hands and tried to tear them away from his throat. Then the hands disappeared, and the weight was removed. He sat up and gulped air into his lungs, a hideous rasping sound coming from his throat.

"We've got her," said Salome panting.

"It's all his fault," screamed Barbara. "He lied through his teeth to lure us down here. He wants to kill us all can't you see that. Let me go, you bloody bitches. Ow. You're breaking my arm."

"What are we going to do with her," said Amanda, the words interspersed with grunts as she strained to hold Barbara tight.

"We'll have to tie her up," said Phillip massaging his neck. He grabbed some strips of his bedding, ripped them in half lengthways and stood up. He groped his way around the three ladies found that they held Barbara's arms behind her and bound hands tightly together.

"Better do her feet, while you're at it," said Salome. "She's so tightly wound it feels as if she's going to explode."

They stretched Barbara out face down on the bedding and held her legs while Phillip bound them securely. They then grabbed her arms and feet and placed her gently back on her own bedding.

"What's that noise?" said Amanda.

"And the smell?" said Salome.

"Oh my God, she's pissing her pants," said Amanda.

"She's cracked completely," said Phillip.

"Should we give her some water?" said Salome.

"Let's offer her a sip," said Phillip. "But we'll have to be careful, she's so desperate and could try anything that might cause the water to spill. I suggest that you two hold her arms and sit her up. I'll pour a few drops into her mouth. Salome, can you give me your watch for a moment? Then hopefully we can see what's happening to the water."

Salome unclipped her watch and handed it over to Phillip. He pushed the button on the side and the green glow illuminated the scene.

"Take her arms," said Phillip. "And sit her up."

Barbara seemed docile as they maneuvered her into a sitting position, her eyes were tightly closed.

Phillip held the watch near her face and said, "Barbara, I'm offering you a sip of water. Please open your mouth."

Barbara pursed her lips and shook her head.

Phillip gently squeezed her nose and after a stubborn thirty seconds, she reluctantly opened her mouth and gasped. Phillip let go of her nose, grabbed her chin, and poured some water into her mouth, spilling some on her chest. He then held her nose and mouth shut and waited for her to swallow. Eventually, she did. Phillip released his grip then said, "We can let her go now."

Barbara lay down, sobbing. Phillip turned out the light. Barbara screamed. Phillip turned the light on, and she stopped.

"Leave it on for a bit," said Salome. "It might help her sleep. What time is it anyway?"

"Almost six o'clock in the morning," said Phillip putting his arm around Amanda.

"And what about me," said Salome.

Phillip hugged the two girls to either side while they all watched over Barbara in an eerie green glow. "What a surreal situation," he said. "The only time in my life that I've been hugged by two beautiful women and all I can think about is a massive plate of greasy eggs and bacon."

33

Prado's phone rang as he shaved in his tiny apartment bathroom.

It was Ana.

"Can we meet at my Lab at nine?" she said. "By then I should know what's going on with the bug at the Marquez property."

"See you there," said Prado.

He took his usual breakfast at the café around the corner from the Comisaría and then headed up to Ana's Lab. As he walked through the door, he spotted her dressed in a white coat, in discussion with her senior technician, Eduardo who was yawning heavily.

He went over to join them.

"Buenos dias, Leon," she said.

"Hola Ana, Eduardo, *¿cómo va?*"

"Bien, gracias," said Ana. "Sorry, Leon. The analog device at the Marquez house is still working but is incompatible with her digital line."

"When did they convert to digital in Marbella?" said

Prado.

"Not sure exactly but at least fifteen years ago," said Eduardo.

"Would a local listening station still be able to pick up anything?"

"Yes, but it would have to be no more than five meters away," said Eduardo.

"Is that likely?" said Prado.

"No," said Eduardo. "I checked. No signal is being monitored from that device."

"Thanks, another door firmly shut. We'll have to hope the Western Union documentation points us in the right direction. I'll be in touch as soon as I have it."

"Would you like to see the aged images of Marquez?" said Ana.

"That was quick," said Prado.

"Eduardo's been working on them all night," said Ana picking up two prints from the desk and showing them to Prado.

Prado took them from her and compared the hairy with the thin on top. "Excellent," he said. "Good work Eduardo and thanks for the all-night sitting."

"It's the only time I'm allowed to play with the machine," said Eduardo. "The youngsters are on it all day."

"Can we send these off with Teresa's DNA to Toulouse now?" said Prado.

"Of course," said Ana. "I'll do it this morning."

"Great, I'll be in touch," said Prado and turned to leave.

He went up to his office, logged into the police database, printed out the latest updates on the Crown file and inserted them to the file on the corner of his desk. A quick glimpse of the Gibraltar report as he flicked through the thickening pile of paper reminded him of Phillip. He picked up his phone and checked his emails and messages. There was nothing from Phillip or Amanda. He called them both but there was still no reply from either. He shrugged and called his colleague in records.

"How may I help you Inspector?" said the clerk.

"I want you to check for any reports, information or crimes involving religious artifacts or Picasso paintings," said Prado.

"Over what time scale, Sir?" said the clerk.

"No more than thirty years, I would guess," said Prado. "If you do find anything, follow it back as far as it goes."

"Would that be local or national sir?"

"Again, follow where any trail leads you."

"Very well sir, I'll report to you later."

"Thank you," said Prado ending the call. I wonder, he thought and dialed Ana's number.

"That was fast," said Ana.

"What? Sorry, Ana, this is something completely different. I've lost two of my translators but don't want to keep calling them in case they are involved in private matters. If I give you their mobile numbers, could you kindly check their last known locations?"

"Strictly against protocol, Leon."

"Yes, I know but I need to consult them urgently about the Marquez case. I may have to travel to Andorra, and I'll want at least one of them with me."

"That sounds fine, I'll call you back shortly."

Prado slipped his jacket back on, walked the few steps along the corridor and knocked on el jefe's door.

"Come," said a faint voice from inside.

Prado entered, el jefe was on the phone and

indicated that he should take a seat.

"Andorra," he whispered with his hand covering the phone. "Hello, is that Deputy Director Reus?"

"Fine, thank you for taking my call. I'll be emailing you our file on Spanish national Rodriguez Marquez, now aged sixty-eight. We believe he may have settled in Andorra around thirty years ago with some four to five million Euros of stolen money that was probably transferred from a Portuguese Bank in the Azores. He is also suspected of several cases of child abuse at a school where he worked. He communicated with his sister Teresa Marquez by telephone some eighteen months ago and sent money via Western Union. Anyway, you'll read all the details in the file. Our Inspector Prado is handling the case and is prepared to travel up there to help with identification if necessary. Pardon?"

"Yes, it is possible that he has changed his name and appearance but we're sending you some aged photos and a DNA sample from his sister. Would your team have some free time to look into this, only this man is a link to a much larger case and could help us make significant progress in our investigations."

"You will? Thank you, Señor Reus. Look forward to your report."

Prado returned to his office to find a note on his desk from the records clerk that read, 'Found something interesting, please come down so we can go through together'. There was also another message asking him to call the missing persons section. He picked up his desk phone and dialed them.

"Prado here, you have something for me?" he said when a female officer answered the phone.

"Late last night we had a report called in from a

woman in La Trinidad," she said. "I wouldn't bother you normally, but el jefe told me that you may well be interested in this. The woman said that her sister Barbara didn't return home to her apartment on Calle Ecuador last night. Barbara is the registered caregiver for her mother and never, repeat never stays away from home."

"Why do I need to know?" said Prado.

"During the day Barbara runs a private hire service with her own vehicle. For the last week, she's been contracted to Salome Mendosa, the famous…"

"Yes, I know who she is," said Prado, the hairs on the back of his neck bristling. "Where was Barbara last seen?"

"She left at eight o'clock yesterday morning saying that she would be working in Vélez-Málaga and may be late."

"Did you try her mobile number?"

"It switched to voice mail. We ran a trace and its last position was inside the Las Claras Convent in Vélez-Málaga."

"Have you sent an officer to the scene?"

"Yes. He arrived just after ten and had to force entry through a side gate but found the convent doors open and her unlocked car in a side building. However, there was no sign of anything inside the church or convent buildings. He called her name with a megaphone but there was no reply. There was one thing though you should know."

"Tell me," said Prado.

"The church floor was covered with a message in red spray paint, saying, Salome, go home."

"Mmm… thank you," said Prado rubbing his earlobe furiously. His mind whirred like a clock as he mulled over this new information. Amanda and Phillip were helping Salome with her inheritance that somehow involved this Convent. Were they all there? He rang Ana.

"Any luck on those phone traces," he said when Ana answered.

"Freshly arrived on my desk, said Ana. "Last known contact with both phones was a Convent in Vélez-Málaga."

"Las Claras, right?"

"How did you know?"

"Missing persons told me that the last contact with their driver's phone was also in the church and her car is still there. Ana, I'm concerned. They have been out of contact for over twenty-four hours now, but a local officer is adamant that there is nobody in the convent. It's been abandoned for years."

"They're grown adults, Leon," said Ana. "They could be anywhere in Vélez."

"You're right," said Prado. "Then we'll leave it for now. If they haven't shown up by tomorrow, we'll send a search team out to check the convent.

Prado slammed down his desk phone, and headed down to the records office buried in the depths in the basement. Prado recognized the gray-haired sergeant sitting behind the records reception desk. They'd worked together in the field on many occasions before ill-health had forced the man to lighter duties.

"Hola, Emiliano, ¿cómo estás?" said Prado. "No wait, stay seated," he added as they shook hands.

"Thanks, Leon, legs aren't so good nowadays," said Emiliano. "Not sure how much longer they'll let me skive down here."

"Nonsense, we need your experience and insight,"

said Prado. "Today's youngsters think differently to us old soldiers and rely too much on technology. Now, what have you discovered among the dusty files of religious artifacts?"

"Nothing on Picasso paintings," said Emiliano. "However, artifacts are another story. I'll write it up later as there's a lot to cover but basically, Spain's finest and most expensive pieces started disappearing by the busload during the Civil War. At the time, the authorities put it down to soldiers looting whatever they came across so other than making a list of missing items, they didn't bother searching for the perpetrators. After the war, pieces continued to vanish, and a specialist squad was formed in Madrid to investigate. To cut a long story short, whoever was taking them proved too clever and nobody was ever caught.

"The thefts continued at a rate of a dozen or so a year until the 1960s when the police advised the church to check all their items for forgeries and start installing security systems. To their horror, they discovered another two hundred items had been replaced with almost perfect replicas. Whoever had made them was supremely talented, so they interviewed all the active and retired craftsmen capable of such quality and searched their premises. They found nothing."

"Do you have a list of the premises searched?" said Prado.

"I do," said Emiliano handing it over. "The thefts stopped just after the searches, so it was assumed the perpetrator was too nervous to continue."

"And there's been nothing since," said Prado.

"On the contrary," said Emiliano. "The thefts started again about eighteen months ago."

"Where?"

"In June last year," said Emiliano, "A valuable thirteenth-century gold chalice was stolen from the Castelló Cathedral in the Diocese of Segorbe-Castellón, that's in the Province of Valencia. Since then there have been four more robberies, all at different cathedrals spreading from San Sebastián in the north to Jerez de la Frontera in the south. This, despite the objects being protected by the latest cameras, steel bars, armored glass, sensors and the buildings patrolled by professional armed guards."

"What time were the items taken?"

"Between five and six in the morning."

"That seems late, they could be seen by early morning commuters. Any CCTV footage?"

"For each theft, there are two persons on film, but they are well disguised in balaclavas, gloves and padded overalls."

"To disguise their body shape?"

"It's impossible to tell what gender they are."

"What about external footage?"

"There's nothing reported. Apparently, they know the blind spots for each location and somehow seem to vanish into thin air."

"Security systems?"

"All competently disarmed. From start to finish none of the robberies took more than three minutes."

"How did they enter?"

"They had keys to everything, knew where the control panels were and the codes. They timed everything to avoid the patrols, even locked everything up and turned the alarm back on."

"So, the thefts weren't discovered until later," said Prado.

"Nothing was noticed until the change of shift when the new security guards check the inventory. Usually just after breakfast at ten-thirty in the morning."

"Do we have any suspects?"

"The usual culprits for these skill levels have all been interviewed. Some are in jail and the others have cast-iron alibis, but all are bitching about newcomers infringing their field of expertise and taking too many prized objects in a short period. They accuse them of undermining their market. Something they would never do."

"They always say that," said Prado.

"Not to the extent that they have volunteered their services to hunt them down."

"Wow, that is a rare offer. Have they come up with anything?"

"Nope but they reckon it has to be an inside job or someone who is well connected to Spanish Cathedrals."

"Interesting, OK Emiliano, write me up your report and make a file including copies of all the evidence, then deliver it to my office as soon as you can. Well done, excellent work."

34

"Do you think Barbara's asleep?" said Salome as the light from her watch grew ever dimmer. "Only she hasn't moved for half an hour."

"How's the time?" said Phillip removing his aching arms from around the two women.

"Getting on for ten," said Salome stretching.

"Try turning out the light," whispered Amanda.

Salome pushed the side button and returned them into total obscurity.

"Whew, no reaction. Perhaps we can rest now," said Amanda snuggling down next to Phillip.

Phillip closed his eyes as his mind flitted around like a butterfly. He reexamined everything they had tried to escape and attempted to think of new ideas, but nothing came into his head and it frustrated the hell out of him.

Then he heard it.

He wasn't quite sure what it was to start with. A voice maybe? Then it went quiet. Several minutes later he heard it again but this time it was much clearer. Someone was shouting for Barbara.

"Did you hear that?" he said.

"Sounded like someone calling Barbara," said Salome.

"Barbara, *donde estas*?" much louder this time.

"Someone's definitely calling her," said Amanda. Sitting up.

"They must be upstairs in the church," said Phillip jumping up and heading for the door. "Come everyone. Let's all bang on the door and shout."

"We're here," they screamed in unison again and again while simultaneously banging on the door with their hands and feet.

"Sssh," said Phillip after five minutes. "Maybe they heard and are trying to reply."

They put their ears against the door, straining to hear but the sound grew fainter and fainter until they no longer heard anything.

"Fuck," said Phillip. "They've gone."

"No," said Amanda. "It's good. It suggests that Barbara's sister has reported her missing and they've traced her mobile phone. That must have been the local police following instructions from Málaga. Missing persons will link her to Salome and eventually to us. Prado can't fail to hear about it. Now it's no longer a question as to whether we are found, just when."

They put their arms around each other and did a little jig.

"Ouch," giggled Salome as Phillip trod on her toe. "You can have free dancing lessons when we're out."

"Really," said Phillip. "I'd love to be able to dance the Sevillana without resembling a blundering elephant."

"I'm going to give you lessons," said Salome. "Not work bloody miracles. Come, let's see if news of our imminent rescue will help Barbara out of her fugue."

They turned and shuffled through the darkness towards their bedding. Salome sat down and gently stroked Barbara's arm. She was trembling and still wound as taut as a clock spring."

"Did you hear someone calling you from the church?" said Salome.

"I did," said Barbara. "But they've gone again."

"They'll be back. Your sister must have reported you missing. How are you feeling?"

"Why have you tied me up?"

"You don't remember?"

"No, and I smell disgusting."

"You had a funny turn, we had to restrain you for your own safety. Has anything like this happened to you before?"

"No."

"Shall we untie you?"

"Please, I need to go."

"Do you want me to help you through the dark?"

"No," she said. "I want to be alone."

Salome untied her and helped her to her feet.

Barbara was unsteady but after moving her limbs to boost her blood circulation, she was strong enough to stand on her own.

"You sure you don't need one of us with you?" said Phillip.

"I'm fine," snapped Barbara.

"Then call us if you need help," said Amanda. "Hang onto the display cases for some orientation."

They pointed Barbara in the direction of chamber

five and settled back down under the sacking.

They heard Barbara cursing as she banged into things. Then it went quiet for a while and they dozed.

They were woken by a loud clattering, followed by breaking glass and a horrific gurgling, choking sound. Then an erratic repetitive banging noise.

"She's trying to hang herself," said Phillip. "Sounds like the central bay. Probably from one of the wall lamps. Here, take my hand. When we get there, I'll take the right-hand light, you two take the left."

It seemed to take forever to cross the twenty-odd meters groping through the dark as the banging sounds grew more frantic. As they arrived in the central bay, it was obvious Barbara was using the left-hand lamp They shuffled over, and Salome grunted as she was kicked hard in the stomach by Barbara's flailing feet.

Phillip's feet crunched on broken glass as he threw his arms around Barbara's waist. He tried to lift and unhook her away from the light but without success. Barbara's gurgling continued. "Salome bend over," said Phillip. "Amanda, climb on her back and try to unhook the noose from the light. Hold on to me to stay upright."

Phillip felt Amanda's hands gripping onto his clothing.

"It's no good," said Amanda. "She's wrapped the sacking around the lamp."

"Climb back down, find a reasonably sized shard of glass, then cut her loose."

At hearing this. Barbara wriggled furiously.

Phillip struggled to hold the moving Barbara up high enough to relieve the pressure on the noose.

Amanda jumped down from Salome's back, carefully picked through the pieces of broken glass and selected one she thought was strong enough for the task. "Ouch," she said. As it cut her hand, but she persevered and clambered back up on top of Salome.

"Mind my back," screamed Salome as Amanda put her weight on her friend's spine and reached up to the lamp.

Amanda carved at the sacking with the glass, cutting her hand even more. Eventually, it parted, and Phillip was able to cradle a prostrate Barbara in his arms. He carried her away from the glass, sat her down on the throne's platform and untied the noose. The material felt wet and sticky as the distinctive coppery smell of human blood invaded his nostrils.

Barbara collapsed against him.

"She's barely alive," said Phillip testing the pulse on Barbara's wrist. "And not breathing."

He laid her down, putting his lips to hers and forced air rhythmically into her lungs. He then pumped her heart and continued switching between the two"

"I've cut my hand," said Amanda. "I think it's quite bad."

"Wrap sacking around it," said Phillip feeling Barbara's neck for any serious wounds. He recognized the indentation of the sacking but couldn't detect any blood, it must be Amanda's.

Barbara gasped and started breathing raggedly.

"Her pulse is stronger," said Phillip. "I think she's going to make it."

"What a relief," said Amanda. "The bleeding has slowed, but I've lost a lot of blood and am feeling faint."

"Best to keep warm my love," said Phillip. "Go back to the bedding and snuggle down, I'll be right with you." Phillip checked Barbara's breathing which was settling down into a regular pattern along with her pulse. "She's going to be a psychological wreck when she comes around. Salome, can you stay with her?"

"OK, but what do I say, when she does surface?"

"Hug her and reassure her that help is on its way and shouldn't be too long."

"I don't think I can hug anyone for a while," said Salome trying to stretch her back. "But I'll do my best to persuade her that our rescuers are on their way."

Phillip left to join Amanda. He found her lying down under the bedding shivering. He climbed in next to her, held her gently in his arms and waited for his body heat to do its business. Eventually, she slept.

35

"There's something nagging away at me," said el jefe, as Prado took a seat across from his desk. "Concerning CVS Holdings."

"In what respect?" said Prado.

"According to one of your earlier reports in the Ronda case; the Crown twins own a data center in India that provides web hosting and online booking to one of Spain's largest hotel groups."

"That's right," said Prado. "And when Phillip discovered that his laptop had been hacked. The malware that was monitoring his machine was traced back to a data center in Mumbai that was owned by CVS Holdings."

"Exactly," said el jefe. "So, are these two data centers one and the same?"

"That's what I'm presuming," said Prado. "Especially when you take into consideration that the funds earned from both Malcolm Crown's website and Patrick O'Reilly's were all transferred to the CVS

Holdings account in the Turks and Caicos Islands."

"It's all linked together," said el jefe.

"Precisely," said Prado.

"And somewhere among all that," said el jefe. "Is our elusive mastermind."

"I wonder if we can find out which hotel chain is buying its digital services from the data center?"

"What would that tell us," said el jefe

"Not sure, but it would be interesting to check out their shareholders and directors. One of them could be the missing piece in this ever more complex jigsaw."

"How do you suggest we proceed?"

"Phillip could ask his former army colleague for a digital analysis of the top five Spanish hotel groups. The providers of their online booking services should be easily identifiable. From there, it's just a question of checking out their ownership."

"I like it, Leon. I presume there will be a cost?"

"People have to make a living."

"OK, then instruct Phillip to ask his friend."

"At the moment that would prove a tad difficult."

"Why?"

"Phillip is out of contact, Amanda too."

"Perhaps they are working on their business?"

"They are working with Salome Mendosa."

"The Flamenco dancer, doing what?"

"Salome has inherited a convent in Vélez-Málaga. The last thing Phillip told me is that they were going to search this convent."

"When?"

"Tuesday."

"And now it's Wednesday."

"And I've heard nothing from them, and he won't return my calls."

"Have you traced his cell phone?"

"And Amanda's. Their last pings were both from the convent and there's something else that leads me to suspect that they might be in trouble."

"What?"

"Salome's driver has been reported missing since last night and her unlocked car is parked in the convent outbuilding."

"Then what are you waiting for? Go and tear the place apart."

"May I take Ana and her technician?"

"Of course, now go."

36

"Can I join you?" said Salome snuggling under the sacking on the other side of Phillip. "I'm freezing."

"What about Barbara?" said Phillip putting his spare arm around her and hugging her to him.

"Gently," she said. "My back is killing me. Barbara is sleeping soundly. I've covered her up and tied her hand to a throne leg just in case she wakes up. How's Amanda?"

"Still feeling a little dizzy," said Amanda yawning and stretching. "Do we know what time it is?"

"I've lost track," said Salome.

"It's around Wednesday lunchtime," said Phillip.

"Only thirty hours down here," said Amanda. "It seems so much longer."

"Prado will track us down," said Phillip.

"But when?" said Salome. "I'm running out of patience."

"Aren't we all," said Phillip. "Assuming we do get out of here. Do you still want to proceed with your project?"

"After this, I'm even more determined," said Salome.

"I'm unsure who locked us in here," said Phillip. "Or why they have left us to rot. I can only assume they want to dispose of us like your grandfather and parents. Now we know about their hoard, it makes us even more dangerous to them should Prado find us. They may even be considering finishing us off before he arrives."

"Sorry," said Salome. "Are you saying that they may attempt to kill us sooner rather than wait until we starve to death."

"It's possible, so we need to be prepared for it."

"How?" said Amanda.

"They won't want to risk damaging their stock, so won't use explosives. They could use gas, but that would delay them from entering and clearing out their stock. Their only quick and clean solution is to enter and shoot us. We need to think of a way to slow them down."

"We could block the entrances," said Amanda. "For example, we could stack the display cases in front of the door and throne. It would delay them at least."

"Shall we try?" said Phillip.

"I can't," said Salome. "My back is already killing me."

"Then we'll have a go," said Phillip.

They stood and moved to each end of the nearest case.

"On the count of three," said Phillip. "Lift and move toward the door."

The case didn't move. The combined weight of plate glass, metal fittings and drawers stuffed with statues made it much to heavy.

"Forget that idea, then," said Phillip settling back down under the sacking.

"A more cerebral defense is called for," said Salome.

"We bombard them with quiz questions?" said Phillip.

Amanda giggled.

"Perhaps we could hurl statues," said Salome.

"That would delay them," said Phillip. "But only a few are light enough to throw more than a few meters."

"I guess it also depends on how many they are," said Amanda. "I mean attackers not statues. If there is only one, we could divide their concentration."

"Good idea," said Phillip. "Let's think this through. We are bound to hear them coming, it will give us a few seconds to get into position."

"They will also turn the lights on."

"Then if you ladies hide behind the concrete tombs, I will draw fire from behind the display cases. They will waste a couple of bullets so will try and get nearer to me. You grab a candle stick each and while they are trying to shoot me, creep up behind them and whack them over the head. Then Salome you can use your self-defense skills to keep them pinned to the floor. Back permitting of course."

"It sounds absurd," said Salome. "But it could work. I'll need a massage first though. Amanda, could you?"

"It will have to be one handed," said Amanda. "Try, Phillip. I guarantee, you'll appreciate it."

"Mmm," said Salome a few minutes later as she was lying face down on the sacking, her shirt pulled up to her chest as Phillip kneeled over her and kneaded her spine. "I see what you mean. What was that we said about sharing?"

"If Phillip gets us out of here alive," said Amanda. "He can do whatever he wants."

"Thank you, ladies," said Phillip desperately thinking of a way to change the subject. "But don't worry, Prado will find us first. I meant to ask you, Salome. What prompted your self-defense lessons?"

Phillip felt Salome stiffen under his fingers.

There was total silence except for their breathing, and he could sense her pulse rate going through the roof.

"I fear I may have touched a raw nerve," said Phillip.

Amanda sniffed.

Closely followed by Salome.

"Does this concern both of you?"

"Yes," they whispered in unison.

"Up to telling me about it?"

"I've been meaning to," said Amanda.

"We both agreed to," said Salome. "Despite the potential damage it might do."

"It can't be that bad, surely?"

"It is," said Amanda.

"The worst," said Salome.

"It was during our first year at college," said Amanda.

"We were being stalked," said Salome.

"By a madman," said Amanda. "Phillip, darling. We killed him."

37

"Prado parked his car on the pavement behind a police forensics van jammed up against the wall of the Las Claras Convent blocking the wrought-iron gate that led to the main church entrance. He clambered out and banged on the side of the van but there was nobody inside. He heard drilling noises inside the church and walked past the van to the side gate which was taped off. A small crowd was gathering opposite. He flashed his credentials to a local officer standing by the gate.

"Any progress," said Prado.

"Dr. Galvez is talking with the town architect," said the young man. "They're in the church. Enter through the first door on the right and follow the drilling noises."

"Thank you, officer," said Prado.

"What shall I tell the press?" said the young man.

"The media are here already?"

"No, but, it's a small town, packed with nosy people. It's only a question of time."

"Tell them we're concerned about the safety of the church tower," said Prado looking up at the jaded walls of the old building. "We're conducting some tests and they are to keep well clear."

"That's ingenious, sir. I'd never have thought of that."

"You'll learn lad. The first door you said?"

"Yes, Sir."

Prado found his way in, walked around the cloisters and into the abandoned church. The red spray paint concerned him. The message repetition hinted at an unstable mind. He looked around, stunned at the church's beauty and how many of the original fittings remained. He'd assumed that it would have been stripped bare. He spotted Ana in the center of the tiled floor watching their young technician Fernandito; Eduardo's son, who was wearing blue overalls and feeding a long drill down a hole. Ana was chatting with an elegant bearded man in his early thirties wearing grey jeans and a thick black rain jacket. They were studying some large drawings spread out on a folding table.

"Ah, Leon," she said. "You made it. This is Lorenzo Zalando, the town architect."

"What's with the drilling?" said Prado shaking hands with the architect.

"Among all this decorative paintwork I found some sandy streaks. Someone had made a poor attempt at hiding their tracks."

"Why are you drilling?"

"I found a deep hole in the grouting. We're reaming it out so our camera cable will fit."

"What do you hope to find?" said Prado.

"We don't know," said Ana. "There's nothing on

the drawings. Maybe there's a crypt?"

"Hopefully, we're about to find out," said Lorenzo, eyes shining with excitement. "It could be the missing Arab burial plot that our historians have been banging on about for centuries."

"Forgive me for not sharing your enthusiasm," said Prado. "But currently, I'm more interested in locating our missing persons."

"Hang on until, we've finished drilling."

"Through," shouted Fernandito a few moments later. He switched to reverse, and they all watched expectantly as the bit and its extensions reappeared, sand spilling out onto the tiles. At last, the drill head was out. Fernandito placed it on the ground.

Ana grabbed the camera cable and started feeding it down the hole. Fernandito turned on the monitor and flicked a switch. The camera light came on and they could see the cable worming down the hole. Prado waited with bated breath. Was this a wild goose chase or was there a crypt below them and would Phillip and Amanda be there. He crossed his fingers and paced up and down, sporadically checking the monitor.

It seemed to take forever but eventually, it burst out into open air.

But they could see nothing but dust.

Fernandito gave the cable a shake and Prado almost danced with delight.

Phillip, Amanda, and Salome were waving at them.

"Does that thing have a microphone?" said Prado.

"Sorry," said Ana. "Wait, Phillip is signing something to us."

They watched as Phillip led them slowly through a series of gestures ending with; bring water, something to eat and a stretcher.

They all looked in the direction of the altar.

"If I understood Phillip correctly," said Prado dialing his office. "The entrance is at the back of the altar behind the Virgin."

They ran to the altar Prado speaking into his phone as he went. "Hello yes, this is Inspector Prado. I'm at Las Claras Convent in Vélez-Málaga and need an ambulance, drinking water and a variety of sandwiches enough for four people. Urgently please."

The youthful architect arrived at the Virgin first. He hurdled over the wall of the housing and groped around the back, eventually finding the lever, and pushing it in. He stood back in amazement as the Virgin whirred and slid slowly forward revealing a door behind it.

He tried it. It was locked and there was no key.

Fernandito stepped forward with a special tool from his shoulder, fumbled around with it for a few seconds. There was a click and he pushed the door; it opened. He led the way down, turning on a powerful flashlight as he went. The others followed.

"Wait," said Prado pausing at the door to the crypt. "Before anybody touches anything. It appears that somebody blocked them in here with these beams. There maybe prints. Therefore, everyone remains on the steps while Fernandito opens up. Then we'll have only one set to eliminate."

Fernandito heaved the beams out of the way and leaned them against the end wall. He then opened the lock, pulled it open and shone his flashlight inside.

The three of them were standing there grinning. Salome bent almost double from her back pain.

Prado stepped forward. "Is everyone OK?"

"No, Barbara needs urgent attention," said Phillip.

"She had a mental breakdown and tried to hang herself. Amanda has a serious cut on her hand and Salome's back is buggered. Otherwise, we're feeling wonderful, apart from a raging thirst and I'm so hungry I could even manage a spam sandwich."

"Ambulance and refreshments on the way," said Prado. "Sorry, Phillip, but they were out of spam. Lorenzo, if you could help the ladies upstairs, and ask the ambulance crew to attend to them when they arrive. Where's Barbara?"

"She's lying on the throne, in the middle bay," said Phillip.

"Ana, can you attend to her?" said Prado. "Phillip, are you up for showing us around? And tell me what the hell happened here?"

Phillip led Ana, Prado, and Fernandito to Barbara who appeared to be still sleeping. He showed them the broken display case that used to hold the three ships of Columbus. Glass was everywhere and crunched under their shoes. The three statues were scattered on the floor nearby.

"She stood on the case," said Phillip. "Hooked some sacking around her neck and the wall lamp, then jumped. Amanda sliced the cloth with some of the glass but cut her hand doing it which is where all the blood came from."

"What is in all these display cases?" said Prado. "And these things on the floor." He picked up a gold reliquary and read its attached tag." Good God, this must be worth a fortune."

Phillip explained his theories about Max Augustin and his successors.

"That fits," said Prado. "My records clerk has details of unresolved artifact robberies going back to the Civil War. I only heard about them this morning."

"I estimate that there must be over a thousand artifacts here," said Phillip. "Including all of the items stolen from the Las Claras Treasury in 1937, supposedly by Salome's grandfather. I think we'll find his remains and those of Salome's parents among the Arab tombs."

"This is turning out to be a detectives dream," said Prado. "So many cases resolved in one hit."

"I think there's more to come, Leon," said Phillip. "We've been racking our brains about who shut us in here and I think that there's a surefire way to find out."

"Tell me," said Prado.

"Behind this throne should be a tunnel leading to Max Augustin's workshop. The business is now run by his granddaughter Sonia. It must have been her, or her father, Max's son who shut us in here."

They were interrupted by the ambulance crew accompanied by a medic in a green overall arriving with a stretcher.

"Who needs the water and sandwiches?" said one of them, as the medic checked Barbara.

"Thanks," said Phillip, taking them from him, and helping himself to alternate nibbles and sips.

They watched as Barbara was loaded gently onto the stretcher.

"Will she be OK?" said Phillip.

"Physically, she should be," said the medic.

"Where will you take her?" said Prado.

"Emergencies in Vélez," said the medic. "After that, it's out of my hands."

"Thanks, I'll inform her sister," said Prado.

"What about the lady with the cut hand upstairs?" said Phillip.

"We're taking them both with us. They are both extremely dehydrated, the lady with the cut will need a tetanus jab. The other's back needs an X-ray and an anti-inflammatory."

"Vélez as well?"

"Yes."

"Thanks, tell them Phillip will come for them both as soon as he can."

"Right," said the medic.

They lifted Barbara and headed out the door.

The three men stood in front of the throne. Ana on the platform itself. Prado rubbed his earlobe. Fernandito scratched his balls with one hand and shone his flashlight at the throne with the other. Phillip continued nibbling and sipping.

"What makes you think that the throne is masking the entrance to a tunnel?" said Fernandito.

"We think the throne was made offsite and carried here in one piece," said Phillip. "However, it's too big to fit in the stairwell we all used."

Fernandito extracted a crowbar and hammer from his bag and advanced toward the back panel. He inserted it between the timber edging and wall then hammered it. The crowbar disappeared to the hilt with one hit.

"There's definitely a hole behind this panel," said Fernandito. "I'll need some heavier gear to shift the throne though."

"And we should call for back up," said Prado. "We need officers at this end of the tunnel and some at the workshop end. Phillip, you should go take care of your ladies. This is police business now."

"Leon," said Phillip. "Fuck off."

38

They adjourned upstairs to prepare for the raid on the Augustin Workshop. Ana drove off in Prado's car to collect her specialist on human remains; a local anthropologist who lived in a nearby village. Prado ordered two armed Guardia Civil officers from the local barracks to immediately block the entrance to Sonia's workshop. Nobody was to be allowed in or out.

Fernandito needed help with his equipment. Prado reluctantly accepted Phillip's offer to go with the young technician.

"Phillip," said Prado as he struggled to lift one of two heavy portable jacks out of the forensics van. "When he's done, stay out of the way. I've enough to worry about without your welfare."

"Of course, Leon," said Phillip turning to unload the other jack. "And thanks."

Prado nodded.

A young man with long hair and spectacles separated himself from the swelling crowd on the opposite pavement, came over to Prado, thrust a microphone under his nose and said. "I'm Kristoff from a local German Newspaper. Are you in charge?"

"How can I help?" said Prado with a sigh.

"Someone said the tower is about to fall down; is that right?"

"Any moment dear friend," said Prado. "Stay well back. Now excuse me, I have to work."

Prado withdrew back inside the Convent gate and continued to call his requests through to el jefe.

It took several trips for Phillip and Fernandito to carry everything below and set up the lighting. Phillip was shocked by the amount of blood that Amanda had lost as the bright light illuminated every niche and cranny of the crypt. He crossed his fingers that she was being well cared for.

"How do you propose to remove the throne?" said Phillip. There must be some substantial machinery on the other side to keep it in place."

"I don't think it's that complicated," said Fernandito. "It was made about the same time as the Virgin upstairs which is just a simple system of small wheels running on rails. The lever between her shoulders releases the locking mechanism and her weight rolls her down a shallow angle to a buffer. I suspect that this is something similar."

"How is the Virgin returned to her proper position?" said Phillip. "She looks extremely heavy."

"Just push her up," said Fernandito. "The slope is minimal, and her weight is spread evenly over the wheels. At the top, she'll reengage with the lock automatically. I'm banking on the throne being a similar system. While I raise one side of the platform with this crowbar, could you push the jack underneath?

Then we'll repeat that on the other side and simultaneously raise the platform. As it ascends it should disengage the locking mechanism in the tunnel and in theory, we should be able to pull the throne towards us on the jacks."

Five minutes later, they were ready.

"On the count of three," said Fernandito. "One, two and three. Heave."

It hardly took any effort at all.

The throne moved freely forward about two yards until it met some resistance.

"I was right," said Fernandito grinning at Phillip. "Just like the Virgin."

They went around to the back of the throne and there was the tunnel. Fernandito shone his flashlight into its depths. It was dead straight, and it was just possible to see a ramp going up at the far end.

The tunnel was two meters wide at its base, had an arched roof which at its highest point was over three meters high. The complete structure had been hewn out of a mix of rock and sandstone with no visible supports. Several cables were clipped tidily to the right-hand wall and every five meters a cable spurred upwards to a neon lamp mounted at the point of the arch.

"It must be possible to drive a small forklift truck through here," said Fernandito.

Mounted on the right wall near the entrance was a bank of switches. Fernandito clicked them all into the on position and both the crypt and tunnel lit up like a Christmas tree.

"There are the throne locks," said Fernandito pointing to each side.

They walked along the tunnel.

"Did the Arabs build this?" said Phillip. "Or is this more modern?"

"Difficult to say," said Fernandito. "We'll need a geologist to work that one out."

Ten meters into the tunnel was an opening that led into a bay around five meters square, again with an arched roof. To one side was a chair nestling under a desk with a laptop. Phillip pulled out the chair, sat down and pressed the on switch. It started booting up.

Against the opposite wall was a photographer's booth. Spotlights illuminated a purple backdrop and in the foreground was a circular plinth. A high-powered camera with a large telephoto lens stood in front of it on a tripod. Phillip switched on the spots.

"This is where they photograph the artifacts," said Phillip. "And the laptop must be where they load them to some sort of sales or auction site."

He sat down at the desk chair and waited for the home screen to appear. It went automatically to the Tor browser and a data entry page all written in English. "No password," said Phillip. "They must have been confident that we would never find our way in here."

Phillip scanned the page. It asked for details of the object for sale. Phillip filled in a fantasy entry and clicked go. It requested a photo, an estimated value, and a minimum sale price. Phillip entered a price and clicked browse. He found a golden chalice and went with that. The database paused for a few seconds then a pop-up box replied, 'Thank you for uploading your chalice onto the Hoarders auction site. The next sale will take place on Saturday, at ten hundred hours, Central European Time.' He then deleted his entry.

Phillip searched the remainder of the site and found

a list of transactions from previous auctions with the screen names of the purchasers and the sale price of each item. He whistled. The last auction had raised over four hundred thousand Euros. He checked as far back as the first sale which was dated sixteen months previously.

The banking section was password protected.

The delivery section was not.

Items had been delivered to luggage lockers at train stations all over Europe. Phillip noted that each delivery was always to the same locker number. He made screenshots of all the data and sent them to Prado's email address, but halfway through, the connection went dead. He checked the browser's history to see what was in the cache, but all trace of the site had been wiped and the Internet connection severed. Then the power was cut, so they went back to wait for Prado in the crypt.

The raid on the Augustin Workshop went exactly as planned. Two groups of officers hit both ends simultaneously. Prado led the group along the tunnel which had been illuminated with more police spotlights along its length. The ramp led gently up to a large metal door. Just as they arrived, it slid open.

When asked later, Prado was unsure who was more surprised, Sonia or himself. He'd been expecting his colleagues, but Sonia had locked the door to what was her secure workshop for restoring paintings and precious metal artifacts and was attempting to escape via the tunnel.

She was arrested and taken off to the cells at the Comisaría in Málaga leaving Ana and her team to analyze their findings.

39

Phillip found Salome and Amanda in the emergency waiting room at the hospital later that evening. They were exhausted and were both nodding in their respective chairs having been treated for their cuts and bruises.

Sonia's back would need further attention meanwhile, the anti-inflammatory meant she could walk upright, but gingerly. Amanda's right hand had been stitched and was lightly bandaged and in a sling.

Phillip wrapped an arm around them both and supported their weary limbs as he guided them to his car.

He brought them up to date with the raid and arrests, but they were too tired to take it all in. At the villa, he helped them indoors. The girls helped each other shower and they all went to bed and slept like logs.

First thing next morning, Phillip popped out to the bakery and they all gathered around the kitchen island for a hearty breakfast.

The elephant though was still firmly in the room.

Each waiting for someone else.

"Someone has to start," said Phillip. "And after our ordeal, this should be a breeze. Who was this stalker?"

"He seemed like a pleasant guy," said Amanda.

"He used to chat to Amanda while I was dancing at the juerga," said Salome.

"Nico something, was his name," said Amanda. "Dutch."

"He was studying Spanish literature, spoke several languages," said Salome. "Sometimes we spoke Spanish, others English."

"How did you pick up an American accent?" said Phillip.

"Mimicking Amanda," said Salome. "School taught me technical English, but it was from your wife to be, that I learned how to talk."

"Anyway, one night we were all a bit drunk," said Amanda. "We invited him back to our room for a nightcap. He assumed we wanted a threesome and when he started taking his clothes off, we threw him out. From then on, everywhere we were, so was he."

"He'd follow us to lectures," said Salome. "And be waiting outside when they were over. Everywhere we went he'd be there, staring; grinning lecherously."

"We asked him to stop being a creep," said Amanda. "But he ignored us. Each week he would get more daring and walk right next to us saying perverse things. Insisting that we were drooling for him. No matter what we said, he continued. After several weeks, we reported him to the college authorities, and he was reprimanded."

"He was furious," said Salome. "And started

emailing us photos of his erect penis."

"We took them to the police," said Amanda. "And he was arrested and deported."

"We assumed that would be the end of it," said Salome. "But it wasn't."

"He came back," said Amanda.

"He was waiting by the elevator at the campus car park," said Salome. "We were going up to Avila for the weekend."

"We each had overnight bags," said Amanda. "He pushed his way into the elevator with us, took his thing out and was ….," said Amanda. "Then he grabbed me and ripped my blouse off."

"He was obviously crazy," said Salome. "There was no point in reasoning with him."

"So, she swung her case at his head," said Amanda breathing heavily reliving the moment.

"He went down like a skittle," said Salome.

"There was a little blood coming out of his nose, but we presumed that he was just stunned," said Amanda. "We were terrified that he might regain consciousness and continue attacking us. So, we left him there, ran like crazy for the car and drove off to Avila, thinking that we'd report him when we returned on the Sunday night."

"When we got back," said Salome. "It was all over college social media."

"The headline read; Deported Student Found Dead in Campus Car Park," said Amanda.

"According to the reports, the police assumed that his head injury was incurred when he collapsed," said Salome.

"But we knew it was Salome's case that had killed him," said Amanda.

"We had no idea what to do," said Amanda. "Say nothing, or report what we did."

"Didn't the police interview you?" said Phillip.

"No," said Amanda. "We agreed that if they did, we would come clean. But they never came. After a while, we assumed that they were no longer interested and got on with our lives."

"Well, we tried anyway," said Salome. "Over time, it faded but I still have nightmares about it."

"Me too," said Amanda.

"Thanks for telling me," said Phillip. "It must have been hard, especially after what we've just endured."

"What are you going to do?" said Amanda.

"What would you like me to do?"

"We want to clear it up," said Salome.

"Even if it means going to prison?" said Phillip.

They both nodded.

"Do you want me to speak to Prado?"

They both nodded again.

Phillip picked up his phone.

40

Sonia and her husband were held in separate cells at the Comisaria under a charge of receiving stolen property. They had to wait for three days until forensics had completed their analysis of the crypt, tunnels, their home, and workshop before the police were ready to interview them. They were allowed no visitors and had declined the offer of a lawyer. The evidence against Sonia was overwhelming but there was a mountain of questions to which Prado and Phillip were keen to find answers.

Prado and Ana sat opposite Sonia in the same interview room where Crown and O'Reilly had been interrogated. Phillip watched and listened from a side room.

Prado pressed the recorder and informed Sonia of her rights which she acknowledged with a clear and audible voice. Phillip turned down the volume on the speaker and zoomed the camera onto her face.

She looked surprisingly calm and relaxed.

"Sonia Gudrun Augustin," said Prado. "Can you confirm that you were born September 1976, abiding at Cortijo de Aguacate, Trapiche, Vélez-Málaga and married to Anton Maya."

Wow. Thought Phillip. She looks incredible for her age.

"Yes," Sonia said with confidence.

"We have collected," said Prado. "More than enough evidence to put you away for fifteen years. However, we are also considering more charges that will ensure you remain in prison for the rest of your days. They are.

"Imprisonment of four adults against their will. We found your and your husband's prints on the crypt door and the two beams used to jam it shut. Attempted murder of the same four adults. Sale of substantial quantities of stolen property. Failing to report the presence of three recent skeletons discovered among the Arab tombstones. DNA tests have revealed their identities as Abraham Vargas, Jesús Vargas, and his wife Rosario Luengo.

"We also suspect that you and your husband were somehow involved in the murder of Pablo Marquez. You have been identified by the bar owner in Marbella as the last person to have had any contact with him before he was found dead by his sister the next day. Have you anything to say?"

Sonia returned Prado's stare and showed no reaction to these fresh charges.

"Failure to cooperate with us," said Prado extracting the class photo of Marbella International College and showing it to Sonia. "Means that all these charges will be brought against you. Do you recognize anyone in this picture?"

Sonia glanced down and while she said nothing, Phillip could see her struggling to stop the tears from flowing.

"Sonia," said Prado. "We know you attended this school. That's you on the front row isn't it?"

The tears were flowing but Sonia couldn't tear herself away from the photo.

"Just to prod your memory," said Prado. "We've brought someone to see you."

Prado nodded to Phillip who went out to join an officer standing next to a sour-faced Patrick O'Reilly, hands cuffed tightly behind him. "We can go in now," said Phillip opening the interview door.

The officer nudged O'Reilly who limped into the room after Phillip.

Sonia looked up.

Her and O'Reilly locked eyes.

Sonia jumped up, threw her arms around him, and sobbed her heart out.

Phillip watched as O'Reilly crumbled. Tears rolled down his cheek and he howled like a wolf; his body racked with pain as all those repressed memories flooded back into his consciousness. He staggered. The accompanying officer helped him to a chair. Sonia sat next to him, rested her head on his chest and held his arm. Both were shuddering.

Prado switched off the recorder and said between tight lips, "We're going to leave you two alone for a while, you obviously share some considerable pain and have a lot to catch up on. Coffee and sandwiches will be provided but afterward, we'll expect a full and frank confession from both of you about what the fuck this man," he picked up the largest photo of Marquez and threw it on the desk in front of them. "Has done to you?"

Prado nodded to the officer who uncuffed O'Reilly who immediately hugged Sonia. Ana was the last to file out and shut the door behind her. Her eyes were damp.

"Your instincts were right," said Prado turning to Phillip. "What made you think that these two were so close?"

"When you told me that Sonia's prints were one of the four sets on the film canister," said Phillip. "I assumed that she must have been at the same school as Crown and O'Reilly. I peered at the class photo with a large magnifying glass," said Phillip. "Where I could just make out that blond girl sitting next to him was rubbing O'Reilly's hand with her little finger and he's glancing at her in a sort of big brotherly way. I figured she had to be Sonia. Until now, O'Reilly has been as unmoving as a statue in his dealings with us. I just thought that bringing them together might cause exactly what we have just seen. How long shall we give them?"

Phillip sat in the side room occasionally sipping from a bottle of water and watched Sonia and O'Reilly. It took them a good ten minutes to stop crying but they continued holding each other's hands tightly as they looked at each other.

Phillip turned up the volume to maximum and when they did eventually speak it was in the faintest of whispers.

"Aside from this shit, how are you," said O'Reilly in English.

"As well as I could be," she said nodding at the photo of Marquez. "After what that bastard had done to us. Good to see you though."

"Likewise. Have the cops located him?" said

Patrick.

"I don't think so. Have we?" said Sonia.

"Not yet, so we shouldn't discuss it. They're bound to be listening."

"We're running out of time and options. How's…?"

"Getting worse by the day."

"Then we'll have to rely on our last chance."

"It's the strongest of all of them. Perhaps we should?" said Patrick nodding in the direction of the mirror. "Point them in the right direction."

"How?"

"I'll give them a clue. It will make them think that this meeting has softened me up."

"Patrick, it has," said Sonia bursting into tears.

They hugged again for several minutes then gazed into each other's eyes.

"I know," he croaked. "Do you know what really gets to me?"

"Sssh," said Sonia nodding toward the mirror. "I know. I'm the same. Come, let's dine at police expense. At least the sandwiches look half decent."

They moved the plate nearer then ate the food.

After they'd emptied their coffee cups they sat and hugged.

"Is Anton likely to?" said Patrick some minutes later.

"No," said Sonia. "Stupid idiot knows nothing."

Neither said another word.

"Were they referring to Crown's health?" said Prado after Phillip had translated.

"Must have been," said Phillip.

"Then we'll drag him off to the hospital and give him a full examination," said Prado taking his phone out of his pocket and calling the request through to el jefe.

Prado and Ana returned to the interview room. Phillip stayed in his seat and watched. When the door opened, Sonia and Patrick moved apart and sat up in their chairs facing the two officers.

"I hope," said Prado. "That you gleaned some comfort from your time together but that's it now. No matter how badly you were treated by Marquez, you can't take the law into your own hands and justice must be served. Why didn't you report him to the police while you were at school?"

They exchanged glances and Patrick nodded.

"We considered it," said Sonia in Spanish. "But he had too strong a hold over us."

"I appreciate that it's difficult for you to talk about, but can you at least give us some idea what Marquez was up to. The more serious his crimes, the more resources and determination we'll have to locate him and lock him up."

"To be frank, Inspector," said Patrick. "We only want you to find him as a last resort. Our goal is to hunt him down and to punish him personally and appropriately for what he did to us."

"There were four of you, right?" said Prado.

Sonia and Patrick exchanged glances. This time Sonia nodded, and Patrick said, "Yes."

"Is the fourth person in this class photo?" said Ana pointing to the image on the table.

Sonia and Patrick nodded in unison.

"But we're not going to say who it is," said Sonia. "They're our last chance of getting to Marquez before you do."

"Would that be male or female?" said Ana staring hard at them.

"I'll just say this," said Patrick. "There are only two kinds of women, goddesses, and doormats."

Despite further prodding from them Ana and Prado. They couldn't be drawn further.

Prado nodded to the mirror. A few seconds later, the door opened and in came two prison officers, one waving handcuffs at Patrick.

Patrick hugged Sonia, kissed her on the cheek and stood arms behind his back. He was re-cuffed and escorted out.

He paused at the door, stared hard at Prado, and said, "Good luck with your hunting."

He never looked back, and Sonia didn't say a word but somehow seemed more resolved to let fate deliver whatever was about to befall on her.

Prado looked at Sonia. He sensed renewed strength and pounced with his question. "Crown told us that Marquez was an evil monster. Would you agree?"

"Totally, Inspector."

Prado could see that she was unfazed.

"Listen, I'm not interested in the gory details," said Prado. "What I would like to know is why Marquez had such a hold over you that you felt unable to tell your parents or report him to the police?"

"Blackmail, Inspector," said Sonia. "Marquez discovered that most parents were leading members of the Costa del Crime, as it was then referred to by the media. He had researched each one and knew intimate details of their activities. For example, he knew that John Crown was a dodgy property developer and an expert in obtaining fraudulent mortgages. Somehow, he suspected that my grandfather had stolen religious artifacts and that Patrick's father was hiding from Irish Protestants. He took great glee in reminding us of that as he forced us to do unspeakable things to each other while we were naked in front of him. He filmed everything and threatened our parents with public exposure should we say anything to anyone. He's probably still looking at the damn movies relishing what he did to us. The man had no shame or sense of decency and deserves everything coming to him."

"What do you have in mind?" said Prado.

"That will remain our secret," said Sonia.

"We both have to find him first," said Prado.

"Have you made any progress, Inspector?"

"Until eighteen months ago, he was in Andorra living in plain sight under his own name but then after the death of his brother he vanished. If you did have anything to do with his brother's death, it only helped to force him further underground. Now he'll be extra cautious and much harder to track down. Can you tell me why his brother was killed?"

Sonia returned Prado's relentless gaze shook her head and said, "No comment."

Prado immediately recognized the point that they had reached. Now Sonia would be as stubborn as Crown and O'Reilly. They would learn nothing more from her. He switched the recorder back off, nodded to Ana and the mirror. He then charged Sonia with all the crimes on his list except the murder of Pablo Marquez where their evidence was too skimpy to stand up in court.

Two female officers entered, cuffed Sonia's hands behind her back and carted her off to the women's section of Alhaurin Prison to await her eventual trial.

41

They were a sorry duo awaiting the arrival of their Sunday lunch guests at Phillip's villa. Salome had to withdraw from her concert in Barcelona; her back still causing problems. Amanda's right arm still in a sling, stitches due out in two days' time. Phillip tried his best to cheer them up, but it was hard work.

Barbara was in a psychological clinic in Málaga paid for by Salome. Physically, she was fine, but the doctors were concerned about her mental recovery.

Amanda and Salome were seated at the beautifully laid dining table on Phillip's terrace looking gorgeous but helpless. Glenda was doing most of the work bringing the salads to the table and opening the wine.

Richard and Ingrid were the first to arrive, closely followed by Glenda's husband and three nieces. Barbecue smoke wafted around the terrace flavored by Rosemary from Phillip's garden and combined with the marinade from spicy chicken tikka dripping onto the glowing coals.

It was a beautiful December day with a light breeze and a clear blue sky.

Vicente arrived and left a large brown paper wrapped parcel in the kitchen threatening instant death to anyone that mentioned its presence to Salome. Then sat next to her making a fuss. She loved the attention.

Prado and his wife Inma were last but everyone forgave them. He was there to update them on the case. Cheek kisses and handshakes out of the way, drinks in hand and everyone was soon comfortably seated.

"I can't believe it's Christmas in just over a week," said Amanda. "I haven't done a thing."

"We have," said the nieces in unison. "Perhaps we can help you put up the tree?"

"That's a great idea," said Amanda. "Can you wait until after lunch?"

"OK," they said.

"Anyone interested in how the case is going?" said Prado.

"You bet," said the adults.

"Boring," said the children.

"The bad news is that the trail for Marquez has gone completely cold. The bank transfer to his sister Teresa proved that he'd sent the money from his account in Andorra to the Western Union Office in Toulouse. After that, he withdrew everything in cash, left Andorra by bus and hasn't used his passport since."

"Where could he have gone?" said Phillip.

"I really have no idea," said Prado. "Interpol is looking for him, but he may have changed his name and appearance so could be anywhere."

"The clue from O'Reilly," said Phillip. "What was it again?"

"There are only two kinds of women, goddesses, and doormats," said Prado. "But I have no idea what it means."

"Pablo Picasso said it," said Ingrid. "He's referring to his muses or women he loved and painted."

"Wow, thanks, Ingrid. How did you know that?"

"I studied art at university," said Ingrid. "And have read practically everything about Picasso. I adore all his work."

"Then when we have a moment," said Prado. "Would you mind brainstorming what Picasso may have alluded to when he said those words?"

"My pleasure, Leon," said Ingrid looking pleased with herself.

"Great thanks," said Prado. "Meanwhile, the good news is that Sonia is cooperating further to a limited extent. She still refuses to tell us how the bodies of Salome's grandfather and parents found their way into the tombs or anything significant about CVS, but some of the smaller outstanding issues she has admitted. For example, your hire equipment was returned to Granada by her husband. Needless to say, he pocketed the cash deposit. We've charged him with conspiracy to false imprisonment, but we've released him on bail. As Sonia said, he's not the sharpest knife in the drawer and just followed his wife's instructions."

"What about her father?" said Phillip. "Has she said anything about him?"

"His name was also Max," said Prado. "Sonia swears she has no idea where he is and has had no contact with him for over ten years. But I'm not convinced she's telling the truth.

"With regard to her computers. Sadly, they yielded no further information and the Hoarders website has vanished completely. She admits to being technically challenged so we suspect the main control for the website was not in her hands. Despite the efforts of our best technicians, its location remains a complete mystery.

"We confronted her with undeniable proof, and she eventually admitted, that the last five robberies were committed by two of her craftsmen on her behalf. They had worked in each of the cathedrals involved and had been so trusted that they were given security codes and keys. It enabled them to do their restoration work when it suited them, so they didn't disturb the usual rhythm of daily services. Their escape was ingenious. They parked street cleaner trolleys in the camera blind spots. After locking the cathedral, they hid the stolen items in the trolley and changed into Hi-Viz jackets of local cleaning staff. Then mingling with the other cleaners swept their way to where the Augustin vehicle was parked, stashed everything inside, and then went to work as normal for several days until their restoration project was done.

"Did you receive the screenshots I sent from the laptop in the tunnel?" said Phillip.

"Yes, two. The financials and the delivery list. We've traced payments for the sold items to an account in Hoarder's name at the bank in Turks and Caicos. Her balance there is over seven million and the bank has agreed to repatriate it. It also happens to be the same bank used by CVS Holdings proving she is also linked to them. Regretfully, the delivery list didn't lead us to any artifact purchasers and the left luggage lockers were all empty. However, all the stations involved have changed the locks. At least, we've closed down the distribution network but it's unlikely that we'll recover the items already sold or identify their purchasers."

"Will you return the other stolen items back to their cathedrals?" said Amanda.

"Eventually, yes," said Prado.

"What about the Las Claras Treasury items?" said Salome.

"We compared the recovered items with your grandfather's inventory and every piece was in the crypt either in the niches or display case drawers. The big question is what to do with them?"

"Surely, they belong to the sisters at the new Las Claras Convent," said Salome.

"They don't want them," said Prado. "They have no security system or place to display them and propose that you keep them."

"Me?" said Salome. "What am I going to do with them?"

"They mentioned," said Prado, "that the original treasury could be converted into a museum depicting the history of the old and new convent. You could open it to the public and local schoolchildren on special occasions."

"Great idea," said Salome.

"The sisters," said Prado. "Would, of course, be happy to receive a small donation in return for their generosity."

"My pleasure," said Salome beaming. "When may I collect the remains of my relatives? I'd like to give them a final send-off and inter their ashes in the cloisters garden before we start serious restoration work."

"Any time next week will be fine," said Prado. "Just call me when you're ready. Sorry for your loss."

"No don't be," said Salome. "Yes, it's sad but I

never knew them. I'm simply happy that the people of Vélez can relax knowing that the new owner of Las Claras is descended from fine and upstanding local citizens."

"Shall we say that I don't think you'll have any lack of cooperation in the building of your Flamenco University," said Prado.

"Any idea who was the sprayer with red paint?" said Salome.

"It won't be admitted," said Vicente. "But I've heard through the gypsy grapevine that Cristina was paid by Sonia to disrupt your project. It was probably one of her grandsons."

"And you have your first donor," said Inma. "My brother in law Juan, who heads up the Romero blood-free bullfighting dynasty, would like to provide bursaries for impoverished local artists to attend the university."

"Thank you Inma," said Salome. "That's amazing."

Phillip and his sister served lunch. Richard poured more wine.

The kids gobbled their food down and ran off to play in the garden. While the others chatted about Salome's forthcoming project.

Just after four, everyone started making their excuses to leave.

Vicente chose this moment to reveal his package from the kitchen. He brought it out, delicately unwrapped it and turned it around to Salome.

She gasped and tears came to her eye.

It was the restored photo of the double wedding.

She struggled to her feet, hobbled over to Vicente, hugged him, and then kissed him on the lips. Everyone applauded.

Prado and Inma lingered behind.

"I have some information about your stalker," Prado said when everyone had left.

They resumed their seats and looked at him nervously.

"The case was closed almost immediately," he said. "The Madrid police had CCTV footage of what they considered to be the whole event. First you should know that Nicolaas Visser was a serial stalker of any pretty girl with long dark hair. He was the subject of seven restraining orders and eighteen complaints and had been deported three times. According to the postmortem, he'd consumed a cocktail of drugs and alcohol which exacerbated his usual quiet demeanor. The terrible quality video shows the backs of two unknown girls entering the elevator on the ground floor. It was the only location where the campus car park had a camera. Then Visser barged in last minute. About twelve minutes later, the same camera spots him coming back out on his own staggering all over the place. He lurched toward the elevator wall banging his head heavily against it and collapsed onto the floor smashing his head yet again. He was found a few minutes later by the parking attendant and was dead on arrival at hospital from a severe heart attack. They did find his blood inside the elevator but assumed that it was from a slight nosebleed he had before exiting the lift. What it proves ladies, is that you did not kill him. Should you wish for the case to be reopened, the only possible charges against you would be assault and battery. In return you would plead self-defense against a violent sexual assault. He would also have been charged for not complying with restraining and deportation orders. Believe me when I say the courts are already overstretched. This case wouldn't even be considered. Even if it were, any judge would dismiss any charges against you. You are the victims here not the criminals. I'm afraid, therefore, that you've been tearing yourselves apart over this for no reason. Shall we let the matter drop?"

"Thank you, Inspector," said Salome. "That is a relief."

Amanda hugged Prado and Inma and they said their farewells.

Phillip stood at his gate with his arms around his two wounded soldiers as they watched Prado and Inma head in the direction of the main road.

"Any more surprises?" said Phillip.

"Not from me," said Amanda.

"Nor me," said Salome.

As the taillight disappeared around the corner another small car appeared heading toward them. They took no notice, turned, and headed indoors to begin the tidying up.

The car stopped outside Phillip's gate.

They all looked back to see who it was.

A svelte blond lady climbed out of the driver's seat and leaned on the gate.

"Hello Phillip," she said in English with a heavy accent.

It was Valentina.

The Author

Paul S Bradley, originally from London, England, has lived in Nerja, Spain since 1992 where he established a marketing agency to help Spanish businesses sharpen their communications to the rapidly growing number of foreign visitors. He's traveled extensively around the Iberian Peninsula, visiting most of the ancient cities and countless wine bodegas. In the early years, he published lifestyle and property magazines, guidebooks and travelogues in English, German and Spanish. More recently, groups of discerning Alumni of Americans and Canadians have enjoyed his tour director services. He's lectured about Living in Spain, bullfighting and has appeared on local radio and TV. The Andalusian Mystery Series draws on his own experiences as a voluntary translator in hospitals and police stations.

What did you think?

Reviews, good or bad fuel this independent author's continuous efforts to improve. If you enjoyed this book, please leave a comment with your favorite retailer.

www.paulbradley.eu

www.ingramcontent.com/pod-product-compliance
Lightning Source LLC
LaVergne TN
LVHW011927070526
838202LV00054B/4528